The Applecross Saga

Book One

The Wideawake Hat

Copyright © 2018 Amanda Giorgis

All rights reserved

To Terry,
my best friend through thick and thin.

Preface

The Mackenzie Basin, in the middle of New Zealand's South Island, is a unique and beautiful place. A high plateau surrounded by snow-capped mountains where the climate of this natural landscape is near desert. Brown grasslands slashed by braided rivers, more gravel than water, where unique flora and fauna survive despite the harsh conditions.

The area takes its name from James Mackenzie who, with his black and white collie dog Friday, famously rustled a thousand sheep and took them into the basin in the mid-1850s. Rather like Robin Hood, there is little doubt that James Mackenzie existed but the stories of his life vary greatly. Was he a freebooter and a rogue or was he taken advantage of by others?

In 2017 my ex-boss (and now good friend) Heather came to stay at our house in the basin. The story of James Mackenzie caught her imagination and we enjoyed finding places associated with his name including his memorial on the hills looking out across the flat lands. It is indeed an awesome place and this is where the seeds of this story were sown as we walked along the river past an abandoned homestead, which could once so easily have been James' home.

Here is my interpretation of James' story born from reports of the other sets of footprints found when he was arrested with the sheep in his care. You will need to read more to find out who may have made those footprints.

And what happened to James? It is told that he went to Australia, but nobody knows for certain. Perhaps this story provides the answer……

Prologue

Hinewai looked forward and back. Should she go on or should she go back? Where was the path? Matagouri, Taramea and thick tussocks of Haumata blocked the way. But looking back the path seemed to have melted into the undergrowth now. "Go forward, Hinewai," she whispered to herself, but loud enough to startle a small brown ground dwelling bird who squawked loudly as it ran past her feet, causing her to drop the carved spear balanced like a perfect extension to her fingers.

Picking up the spear and shrugging her shoulders to adjust the weight of the long, thin woven basket strapped over her breast, the young Maori girl stepped forward into a gap between two large spiky, scratchy plants which grew almost as tall as the girl herself. Matagouri needles raised red lines on her bare legs, but she was used to that. The patterns they made were like the designs pressed painfully into her father's face - they proudly told a story of her short life.

Hinewai - water maiden - her name given at birth had become her purpose in life. Did the name dictate the route she had taken? Would she have been here this day doing what she had to do if she'd been called Arihia or even Haeatatanga? She giggled at her sister's name which meant 'beam of light' and yet her sister never smiled, so how could that be her given name? As she raised her head to laugh out loud at the absurdity she stumbled into a tussock from which a cloud of tiny moths flew out.

Battling on across the vast plain she glanced back to the hill where smoke rose from the village fires. A faint smell of cooking reached her. "Mmm, I'm starving," she thought to herself and that spurred her on towards the sound of water. The bushes began to get further apart and the ground under her sandals less grass, more stone. Little lumps of round, polished grey pebbles pressed up through her soles, but she knew she must take those painful steps. Yesterday's rain would bring the water nearer to her and, with any luck, her mission would end in her contribution to dinner being baked over one of those cooking fires. It made her mouth water just to think of it.

Light reflected off the water as she stepped over the river bed stones. Heading upstream, she traced the journey of one of the braids of the river. Just like the long tresses of hair she combed each morning, the river's fingers followed their chosen path through the stones, joining, parting, bubbling, pooling. In one of these pools she could sense the depth - deep enough to hide an eel, perhaps. Crouching down she pulled her bait out of her woven kete; just a tiny piece of dried meat taken from the carcass of a water bird that had been their meal yesterday. Hinewai expertly attached the bait to her line and dangled it over the edge of the deepest part of the pool. Then she took up a pose of absolute stillness.

Her mind wandered as it always did while she waited patiently for the bait to be taken. She loved this place. Flat as one of her mother's flour breads, brown and, to some of her family, boring and unproductive, she knew this land held more treasures than you would think by just passing through it. Water gave you fish, eels, duck-like birds with succulent flesh and green leaves, which made good eating and could be used by the elders as salves to cuts and bruises, or medicines to cure a headache or a toothache. Grass gave you roots to eat, berries to pluck, birds to trap, and plants to be woven into clothes and baskets and beds to sleep on.

All around this flat land the hills stood guard in their enclosing circle. Each point or slope having a name and persona, the gaps between them allowing passage to other lands. At the end of the warm seasons Hinewai and her family pass through that gap over there to reach the places where the winds don't blow so hard and the cold rains and white frosts don't bite quite so much into your face and fingers and toes. But at this time of the year there is nowhere better in Hinewai's mind than this flat but abundant plain, crossed by its productive rivers.

Her mind wandering in the sun's warmth, Hinewai nearly missed the dark movement in the water and the sudden twitch of the bait in her fingers. Moving swiftly she turned, pulled the spear back enough to thrust into the depths and calmly pierced the flesh of a great, grey and slippery eel. For what seemed but a short while her strong shoulders wrestled with the writhing, muscular fish. She was small for her age, but adept at this process, so it wasn't long before the eel lay on the stones unmoving, his skin glistening with the water from which it had been taken. She whispered a short prayer to the water gods in thanks for a creature to eat and to appease the animal gods who had lost a kindred soul. Head first, the eel was dropped into her long basket. Such a big eel that his tail flopped out of the top, slapping Hinewai round the ear at every step as she started the journey back home.

Watching from a slight rise towards one of those circling hills, Hinewai's mother waited her return. As she slowed to a walk up hill, Hinewai waved to her mother. "Another eel for tea tonight, Whaea," she called, "and a big one."

Her mother surveyed the flat lands below and wondered at the abundance of this place which looked so barren, with nothing much to cause you to stop and spend time. What did Papatuanuku, the earth mother and maker of all things under the sky, have in mind for this unique flat plateau?

"One day, someone may find some use for this place," she thought to herself as she took Hinewai by the shoulder and they set off back to the village together to prepare their feast.

Chapter One

Arrivals

September 1848 - March 1850

Tears trickled slowly down Sophia's cheeks and dripped onto her blood-stained white pinafore. Looking down, it reminded her so much of the candy striped fabric her mother had used to make her favourite Sunday best dress. Oh how she had loved that dress until it had grown too tight and too short for her and been passed, with some alteration to the hem and bust, to her younger and shorter, stouter sister, Emily.

Thinking of the members of her family far away across the oceans just made the tears roll thicker and faster down her cheeks. Trying hard not to use the back of her salt-stained hands to wipe away the tears, Sophia blinked and chopped and blinked and sawed at the meat on the table in front of her.

It was so hard to stop thinking of the living beast that this carcass had been until earlier today. Ranging freely through the scrub, rootling into the soft earth to look for juicy plant roots and the odd earthworm, the young pig was unaware of the presence of a man behind him. And, out of nowhere came the pain of a sharp knife entering the neck, but not quite in the right place to mean instant death. The squealing noise of the small hog fighting for his life would live in Sophia's dreams for many years, while George plunged the knife in again and again, struggling each time to pull it out of the thick flesh to make another blow, all the time the beast writhing in agony and likely to trap George beneath its not inconsiderable weight if it fell his way.

After what seemed many hours to Sophia watching on, in a melee of blood and mud and sweat and slobber, the squealing ceased, a few noisy last gasps and George's heavy breathing was all that was left in the flattened circle of grass and short bushes. And now here was that body, stretched out in front of her on the wooden trestle table set up on the shaded side of the bullock cart, waiting for her to turn into the contents of their meat safe for the next few weeks. She really didn't know if she could actually do what she'd read about in her treasured copy of the Domestic Handbook. It all sounded so easy - 'Using a good, sharp knife, peel the skin away from the flesh keeping it in one piece if possible', or even more terrifying, 'Open the stomach cavity by at least 8 inches and remove all the internal organs one by one. Be sure to collect them with the blood in a large bucket for use later. In this way all parts of the animal can be of use'. How could there be any blood left in the beast? Most of it seemed to be draining into the ground in the clearing where George had happened upon the poor, unsuspecting creature.

But faced with the idea of being hungry again and rather tired of living on oats and the small, bony fish caught with great difficulty in the many rivers they seem to have crossed so far, Sophia took a deep breath and plunged on with the task in hand. Her precious stock of salt, stored in brown earthenware pots to keep it dry, provided a preserving rub which she placed by hand into the various cuts she had made and then rolled each joint in the remaining mixture until it was entirely covered. At least this evening they would have a fresh meat stew boiled in her cooking pot. Perhaps she could try those strange looking potato-like vegetables that she had been given by the native girls who lingered around them as they stepped ashore from the small boat which had transported them to land from the ship that had been their home for the last three months. All they wanted in return were some cheap beads and a silk handkerchief. Thanks to some last minute advice from the pastor's wife she had made sure she had a stock of such trinkets to hand that day. Coins were of little value, it seemed, in this strange land so far away from the butcher's block at home.

George appeared from the nearby bushes still looking rather pale and, having taken a plunge into a pool made by the river washing out a deep gouge in the shingle, he shook his head to dry his hair and buttoned up his slightly damp, white shirt, which hardly showed any signs of the recent struggle with the pig. He hoped Sophia had not heard the sounds of his violent retching. Killing a beast was a familiar thing to this farming son, but doing so with his bare hands and a knife less efficient than his father's slaughtering tools had made the job messy and unpleasant. He didn't have an issue with killing to eat - how else could they survive here? But if you are going to kill, then do so swiftly and efficiently. He knew he needed to do better next time. He just hoped the creature had not died a painful death in vain and every piece could be used in some way, even down to using the pigskin to make a cover to keep rain from their dry goods store. Not that rain had been a worry so far. In fact, he would like a downpour to freshen up this dusty ground. His throat and nose were full of it. Even his recent dip in the water had not washed it all away from his hair and between his toes.

Sophia's low spirits lifted when she saw her new husband. George was a handsome man with broad shoulders and long legs. If she was being really picky, Sophia would say his face was a bit too pinched, even more so now that the journey had taken its toll on any spare flesh he had carried. But what she needed was a strong man, capable of riding a horse, killing a pig and driving the bullocks in a straight line. Though this seemed to be something they really didn't want to do, despite George's strong shoulders handling the reins with a skill improved every day of their journey. They preferred, it seemed, to pick their own route through the thick undergrowth swinging the cart from side to side in an alarming way and making pots and pans rattle and crash behind the driver and his passenger. But they should know best, according to the stock seller in the market back in Port Chalmers, and often they had saved the whole cavalcade from driving into a deep ditch hidden by bushes with a last minute lurch to the left or right for no apparent reason.

This handsome man would be the perfect father to the child that she suspected was growing inside her. Sea sickness had turned into morning sickness somewhere off the coast of Australia. Rather than spending all day leaning over the ship's rail and wishing for a swift death from drowning to alleviate the misery of ongoing motion sickness, she had found that only at breakfast time did she feel the nausea rise and if a short walk around the deck was taken in time, the rest of the day could be spent feeling the movement of the ship without too much discomfort. Mrs McPherson, the pastor's wife, had warned her that her monthly course could be disrupted by the journey, but that it had ceased entirely could only mean one thing. But then Mrs McPherson had also said that her husband may not call upon her to perform her 'wifely duties', as she had put it in whispered tones, while at sea. This had not been the case as George had managed somehow to secure a private berth for them on board. She suspected that Captain Chivers had rather taken a fancy to her and was therefore happy to find the newlyweds a quieter corner of the overcrowded stowage deck. Hanging an extra woollen blanket secured by clothes pegs across the bunk had helped to give more privacy too, though they had felt the need to keep noise to a minimum. Since their arrival on dry land she had found the lack of a gentle rolling movement had caused their love-making to become stilted and awkward. No doubt, as she grew fatter, George would not want to join her in bed anyway. A shame, she thought, as there was much comfort in his presence in the dark, a strong man breathing gently beside her while the sounds around the tent scared her so much. Not the gentle hoot of an owl or the occasional call of a fox or deer - the rustling came from strange ground-dwelling birds who squawked and shrieked at night, and wild creatures who rustled by snorting and snuffling. "Oh, why did I remind myself of the pig?" she thought to herself, lifting her head suddenly and laughing out loud.

George saw his pretty young wife standing at the makeshift table with the sharpest knife they owned in her hands, blood dripping onto the ground and various joints of meat sitting amongst the skin, innards and general gore of the pig he had wrangled to a slow and painful death only a few hours before. Long strands of her beautiful blond hair had fallen from their tight grip behind her head and long red marks on her face showed where she had attempted to push them back with her bloodied fingers. Her pinafore would need a good wash to rid it of the red streaks. But no doubt she would know how to soak the blood from it in a bucket of cold water and, like magic, she would be wearing it again tomorrow freshly laundered and pressed with the heavy little iron, which she heated up over the stove and then spat on, to see if it was hot enough.

As he had done so many times in the last few months, he issued a silent prayer of thanks for the gift of finding this perfect woman to share his adventures. Beauty, brains and a rare ability to take anything in her stride. He could have asked for nothing more.

They had known each other for most of their lives, the farm boy, George, and the English girl, Sophia with that strange accent, meeting mainly on Sundays at the little stone chapel on the edge of the village. Both dressed in their best Sunday clothes and only able to share a smile across the path as their respective families chatted to the pastor about the sermon, or about harvest festival preparations, or the awful conditions of those who, over the years, had been removed from their homes to give absent landlords a bigger estate for their English friends to visit. Or more recently, the new young queen who had taken the throne of England and Scotland. When they were both young, a shy smile from Sophia always cheered George up, but as he grew into adolescence he would ignore her as much as he could and then back at home curse himself for doing so.

George's family were farmers, making a reasonable living and occasionally rich after the sale of a herd of good Angus beef stock. For a while they would eat well, and perhaps have a bolt of woollen corduroy cloth delivered for his mother to turn into new, but very itchy trousers for George, his father and his older brother, Hamish, and even maybe matching waistcoats with pockets far too small to hold all the things a young boy may want to collect about his person.

In times when the cattle failed to thrive, or the sale price fell, life became a little less comfortable and a diet of watery potato soup and home made oat bread was all that could be offered. Such is the farmer's way of life with its troughs and peaks. George attended the school next to the chapel for a while before his strong young body was needed on the farm. There he learned to read and write and, though he never entirely got to grips with numbers, he thrived on books of adventures and exploration. He would often be found pointing a grubby finger at all the pink bits of the map of the World.

"One day I will go there," he would say, pointing at British Guinea, India, Australia or New Zealand.

"And what will you do there if you can't add up?" would be the reply from the fearsome schoolmaster, Mr Potts.

"I'll make my fortune - you'll see," would be George's reply, earning him a clip round the ear as he escaped out into the schoolyard to meet his friends, Malcolm, Jack and Bertie.

"Thick as thieves, those boys." thought Mr Potts, "They'll all come to no good, I reckon!"

At the other end of the village from the McKay farmhouse there was a small, neat, single storey stone cottage with the perfect proportions of a central door and a small window on each side. Light often burned in the right hand window where Sophia Morling's family lived simply day-to-day and the kitchen range was hot and rag rugs kept the stone floor from feeling too cold to the stockinged feet in the bitter Highland winters. If you called to see them, not just the neighbourly calling round with a basket of apples or a few oatcakes on a plate, but called for something important, to discuss next week's carol service with the pastor, or to discuss Sophia's progress at Sunday School, a dim light may show in the left hand window behind heavy curtains. This is the drawing room, neat and tidy as can be and heavily furnished with a large, ugly plant taking pride of place in the middle of the table, exactly central to the embroidered lace doily upon which it sat. Sophia, her sister Emily and her noisy brothers were almost never allowed in that room unless perhaps an Aunt visited from far away Inverness for tea one Sunday afternoon when the children would be paraded in for a few moments to be told how much they had grown since last time. "Well," as Sophia often thought, "we would be unlikely to shrink as we grew older!" but she knew better than to say anything for fear of her Father's slipper, which would make contact with her bottom a few times for the cheek of it.

Mr Morling and his family had made the journey up to Scotland when Sophia was five years old. They moved from one of the large industrial towns of the English North. Mrs Morling, being of a delicate disposition would, he had hoped, find the air in Scotland better for her chest. And so it proved to be as, soon after arriving in the sleepy Scottish village, she had produced three strapping babies in quick succession, all of whom proved to be decidedly strong and healthy children. At a time when most mothers lost one or more babies at birth, or in their first year, Maria Morling defied all odds and her children grew well in the country air. Mr Morling didn't, it seemed to the neighbours, have much of a job or profession. It was a question often asked as to how the Morling family made ends meet. But meet they did, and quite well indeed. The truth of it was that Albert Morling's passion for music did indeed make him some money and, even better than that, he had been able to bring his work with him with the move further north. Though not trained at a musical academy, Albert had perfect pitch and could rattle off a new tune with ease when someone else had written the words. So a large envelope of closely written lyrics came by post boy each week and a return was made to that postie with last week's words set to a tune suitable for the music hall, arranged for a small orchestra or just a piano, or maybe a parlour quartet. Occasionally, Mr Morling would make the four or five day round trip to Inverness where his agent exchanged pleasantries and reasonably substantial amounts of cash. Back in the village, nobody knew of this regular income, but they did know that Albert Morling played the wheezing, clacketing organ in the chapel better than anyone had before. And for that they were grateful and made this family of incomers welcome despite their historical distrust of the English.

Sophia inherited much from her mother, but thankfully not her weak chest. The eldest of the four children, Sophia was healthy, vivacious and high-spirited from birth. She revelled in the countryside around her and chose to run rather than walk as much as she could except when adults told her to slow down. She too had attended the school at the same time as George, though they entered by different doors - Boys at one end, Girls and Infants at the other. But it was away from school that the children of the village mingled despite their social standing. Class didn't matter when you were measured by how fast you ran, how high you climbed, or how brave you were about jumping streams and snitching apples from the orchard. Sophia and George were up there at the front. A kind of mutual respect developed in time between them.

"Of course, she's only a girl," George would say to Bertie.

And Sophia and her friends would look at each other, raise their eyebrows and think, "Huh, boys, what do they know?"

At fourteen years of age Sophia's schooling came to an abrupt end when her mother's health became so poor that she couldn't keep up the standards of cleanliness and godliness that she would have wanted in their tiny home. So Sophia learned the skills of running a household and caring for her siblings. Being a resourceful young lady this was not a hard task and she soon learned to alter garments, prepare meals, launder tablecloths, clean stone steps and all those other duties usually done by those of more mature years. Little did she know then how it would stand her in good stead for the future.

Even after only a few months of marriage George knew he had made the best decision, though he also knew it had broken a corner of Sophia's heart to leave behind her parents and brothers and sister. In the beginning he had seen only a partnership. A good woman with the necessary skills to go into the unknown and carve a life on the frontier was all he had needed. On their wedding day it had been obvious to everyone present that they felt affection for each other, but his love for Sophia had blossomed during their long voyage and, in moments of great self-doubt, he had fallen deeply in love with Sophia as a person, not just as a fellow pioneer. Did she feel the same way? George sometimes saw the faraway look in her eyes and hoped that her home sickness would fade over time as she began to feel at home with him and maybe some babies would divert her attention into making a new family in due course.

But she never ceased to surprise him. What was she laughing about now? He hurried as much as he could through the long grass, up the bank to meet her across the blood stained table, her hysterical laughter somehow infectious. What a sight they would have looked if there had been anyone else to see them, laughing and holding onto each other over the remains of the pig. Their laughter babbling like the river as it ran towards the nearby sea.

Later, after a supper with the proportions of a feast had been taken and enjoyed by them both and the pots washed in the water nearby, Sophia and George snuggled down together under a mattress spread beneath the cart. They lay looking at the stars as they formed patterns not familiar to those from the Northern Hemisphere. For a second they gasped at a shooting star.

"Make a wish, my love," said George.

And the wish that Sophia made, but did not share in case it was broken, was to find a place where they could set up home and build a family.

"Maybe tomorrow," she thought as she fell asleep next to her beloved husband.

It was becoming their usual routine. Each morning as the bird song reached a crescendo around them and the sun rose with a red light against the mountains beyond, showing every crack and crevice in the early dawn light, George and Sophia began their day. First step for Sophia was to hang the cambric mattress out to air and, while George went to fetch water in a bucket, she washed with a damp cloth and donned her everyday dress over the corsets which were beginning to be tighter and tighter each day. The pinafore had been soaked and dried the previous evening and ironed flat with the heat of the dying fire before bedtime. It looked fresh and crisp and she was proud to tie it over her pale grey dress. Brushing her hair and tying every bit of it back with a grey ribbon, she did a quick check in the small metal-rimmed hand mirror which she had hung from the framework of the cart.

"I'll do," she said to herself. "Not bad."

George was back with a full bucket. He had splashed the river water on his face and he glowed with the cold of it. The icy water seemed to come straight from the snowy tops of the distant hills. He had brought some driftwood back, dragging it along the ground. It broke easily into dry pieces to set a fire under the hanging pot and it wasn't long before the water bubbled in the kettle and porridge warmed through. "We must find some milk today, my dear," he said to Sophia as she came around from the back of the bullock cart where he had left her to her modesty while she got herself dressed. Every morning he marvelled at her ability to look so fresh. No dressing table to do whatever it is ladies do while sitting in front of their mirror, just a tiny corner of reflective glass. But she looked stunning and ready as ever to tackle the next day of their new adventure.

His next task was to collect a little milk in the metal bucket. He was glad they had bought a milking cow in Hawksbury, even though she was slowing them down as she plodded along beside the bullock cart tethered with a light rope. The poor beast had little time to graze so her milk was flowing intermittently, but he knew it was a good source of healthy food for him and his wife. But then, with luck on their side, they should be finding a place where the cow could crop grass all day and they could start to make a home soon. He suspected he would need a base within a few months, so that the baby Sophia was trying so hard to hide would be born in a building rather than a cart.

So today was the day for turning inland. He had decided overnight, while Sophia slept silently beside him, a look of calm contentment on her lovely face. They needed a pasture near fresh water, with rising ground, so that the winter floods could drain away easily. They would find a sheltered valley perhaps, where he could build a cabin and let the cattle roam. They would need more cows and maybe calves would come along in the spring. And pigs and some chickens. And Sophia would like a dog. She missed her little terrier, Tam, so much. They had met a few travellers along the way who had dogs to work their small flocks of sheep. Perhaps he could ask if they had a spare pup. But then he would need fencing and then there's a need to register his plot. Could he leave Sophia for a while to ride on a borrowed pony back to Hawksbury or Dunedin to register their new domain? So many thoughts, so much to do. His head was spinning with all there was to do and now guessing it was more urgent, there was no time to lose.

Sleep just would not come to him as his thoughts went back over the last few months of what had seemed at times to be an endless journey into the unknown. Where could he say their journey had truly begun? Maybe he should start at the very beginning when a seed of an idea had been sown in his head. He had started stepping out with Sophia after they had danced at the Harvest Supper. They began to snatch whatever time they could together and, as both parents approved of the relationship, they could often be found in those long, dark winter evenings talking in the living room at the Morlings or in the farmhouse parlour. Of course, Mrs Morling and Mrs McKay would always be there in the background, finding an excuse to act as discrete chaperones. But often as not their whispered conversations were not entirely overheard.

Realising that their future would likely be together, their words turned often to what they would do, where they could go, and how they would live. George knew full well that the farm would be for Hamish. The eldest son would take the reins, of course. So what is there for the second son to do? He had often thought of joining up, but army life was tough, and with the present uncertainty in the World, was he prepared to take arms? Even maybe to kill another man?

As luck would have it, perhaps one could call it fate, old Reverend Pike had been called to meet his Redeemer just days after the Harvest Supper. Some said it was an over excess of apple pie that had brought on the fatal attack, and some said he had chosen his time badly as autumn was such a busy period in the church calendar. However, the elders of the chapel had dealt swiftly with the enforced interregnum and had been fortunate in signing up a younger man from Glasgow. Reverend Adams had arrived with his young wife and a babe in arms just in time to take up the Christmas responsibilities of carol singing and midnight service. He brought his family and some new fangled ideas, not welcomed by the whole congregation, but certainly popular with the younger flock.

One spring evening when the days were long enough to encourage people out after supper, he and Mrs Adams had held an event for the young people. They were of the opinion that young people should be 'managed' rather than just left to all sorts of ungodly behaviour down by the river, or behind the hay barn. So these young adults, ten or a dozen of them ranging from mid to late teenage, suddenly found themselves invited to spend time together. Food was offered, and cordials or cold tea, and it had fallen upon Mrs Adams to find a topic for each meeting. On one of these occasions, not being able to find a suitable speaker, she took it upon herself to pass on the things she had learned in Glasgow about the benefits of travelling to other parts of the Empire. She had even been part of a group of church wives who had worked with couples who wanted to leave the city for the chance of making a fortune overseas. In fact, she had become a little jealous of these cheerful, expectant young folk heading off on their voyages.

"If only Mr Adams had some adventure in him," she would muse.

So she had travelled to the Scottish countryside in the manner she would have expected to take had it been to Australia or India, and this spirit she intended to share with her audience.

Most of the group had found it hard to conceive of a land beyond the surrounding hills, let alone across the oceans, but she could see that George and Sophia had passed a secret look of hope and intrigue across the room. Telling everyone to come to her for more information at any time, she had not expected any follow up whatsoever, so it was a pleasant surprise when, a few days later, Sophia had come up to her quietly to ask about how long the journey may take, what people would wear and various other practical questions. It became a regular thing for them to chat about it in a nonchalant, non-committal sort of a way, and slowly Sophia had put meat on the bones of her and George's plans. At the same time, Reverend Adams became aware of George's presence almost every day, while he busied himself at the altar, or sat at his desk in the Manse. George too had many questions which the kind-hearted pastor attempted to answer, or promised to find out from people he knew back in Glasgow. In the end they had decided on New Zealand. India was for the military, and hot and disease-ridden according to Mrs Adams. Australia demanded hard work in mining, or quarrying, but New Zealand was for farmers. It all sounded like a land of opportunity for a farm boy, especially a second son with few prospects back home. He could make something of himself there, he was sure.

Still wide awake in his bed under the cart, George shifted gently to avoid waking his wife and thought about the biggest step they had taken, once they had decided on their grand adventure.

Of course, they needed to get married first. That had been easy, in the end. Both families were thrilled with the arrangement and the whole village had attended the simple ceremony held on a beautiful late Summer Day. Sophia looked radiant in a dress she had made herself of soft green fabric. The flowers made into a crown around her blonde hair made her look like a woodland elf. At that moment he was so happy to be marrying his beautiful bride and so excited by the journey and the promise of their future together. A wonderful day all round, but the families of both parties celebrated with just a tinge of sadness. They knew, because they had been told the day before, that the young couple planned to leave straight after the wedding night.

The marriage was consummated overnight in the small stone shepherd's cottage on the farm, which had been made comfortable and inviting by his mother. It was empty at this time of year as the shepherd was only required for lambing season, so it had needed airing and the blessing of a cheerful fire in the grate despite it being a warm evening. And so their long journey had begun. George preferred to leave out of his thoughts the sadness of saying goodbye to his family. So many tears, so many hugs. Realistically, he knew he may never see any of them again. He could see that Sophia was aware of that too, and he knew it was the hardest thing for her to bear.

Off they had gone, however, in the farm's best cart pulled by the bay mare, Tilly. Both items would be looked after by the Presbyterian Emigrant Organisation until Hamish next went for farm supplies.

The two chests strapped behind them, one for him and one for Sophia, seemed very small to form the basis of their new lives, but they had been assured by Mrs Adams that all the things they may need in New Zealand would be there for them on board the ship, collected and packed by the good ladies of the Emigrant Organisation.

Looking back George wondered how he and Sophia had got through those days. Everything was so alien to them both. Though they were used to the sea, being only a short walk to the coast where rollers crashed on the shore and the fresh air blew the cobwebs away, the sea in the port of Greenock was not the same at all. Stagnant, filthy and full of bobbing flotsam and jetsam, which had been discarded from the many, many ships tied up by huge ropes to bollards the size of a man. And the noise. One could hardly think straight with ship's whistles and bells, calling of sailors, sellers and even the street girls, who shouted out their trade at all hours. In a dizzy whirl of assault upon the senses, all the preparations were made swiftly. Kind ladies helped Sophia re-pack her chest with extra warm clothes, essential cooking supplies in dry containers, a blank journal for her to keep a diary, even a new brush and mirror had been donated by some kind lady of the local congregation. In his wooden chest, George now had, amongst other things, some new knives, some good rope, a few tools for fence building and a leather-bound bible in a strong card box to keep it safe. They had brought some savings in a leather bag. Their passage had been paid for by the church and a small bag of coins had been added at the last minute from last Sunday's collection plate. Enough to buy essentials on their arrival, they were told by the kind ladies who saw them off that day.

He remembered little of their setting out. The sea rolled once they hit the open water and his first few days were spent leaning over the side leaving what little he could eat to feed the seabirds following hopefully astern. "No wonder they grew so fat on the vomit of these new explorers to a foreign land," he thought. He barely felt well enough to tend to his new wife either. She too was overcome with sea-sickness which lasted for most of the three month voyage.

A shriek from a bird hiding in the long grass nearby woke Sophia with a start. The day had begun for them both with anticipation for George and some trepidation for Sophia.

As he sat down opposite Sophia for their warm tea and porridge he broached the subject. "Sophia, I think we need to head inland for our final destination today. You need a place to call your home and, if I'm right, you need a place to raise a family very soon." She blushed and, to George's amazement, tears fell silently into her porridge bowl, diluting the tiny spoon of honey she had given herself as a treat to sweeten the boring breakfast food.

"My dear, don't be sad, it is what we both want, isn't it?"

"I'm ... not ... sad," she gulped between sobs, "I'm just so scared and I need my mother. And ... you ... won't ... want me when I'm fat and ugly."

"Don't be silly, my love," he said as he came around the table and put a steadying hand on her shoulder. "I love you as you are and will love you all the more as the mother of my child. We will find help, there are other young wives who have travelled the same journey as us. You need a home and company of your own kind and we will find both, starting today."

So, they began by packing up the table and all the cooking equipment, picking off the prickles that had attached themselves to the bedding as it aired over a nearby bush, and storing the blankets in their usual spot. Then George began his usual struggle to attach the cattle to their pulling yokes while Sophia put the fire out with a little of the water before storing the rest in the cart for the journey. With everything in its place at last, they set off in a different direction, with Daisy the cow plodding alongside, putting the sound of the sea behind them.

With the sun also behind them Sophia felt drowsy in her seat beside George but fought to keep her eyes wide open to study this new land for signs of a place to stop this never ending journey. She felt like her life was one of constant motion and it would be good to stand still for a while. George's father had given them strict instructions for a good site for a farm. Water, shelter for the buildings from the wind, no chance of flood, and, most important in his view, an open place where you could see your enemies approaching. Sophia smiled to herself. She didn't think they would need to fend off the English marauders as Mr McKay's ancestors had done for centuries back in Scotland.

George had been casting an eye around for a place to cross the river. It had narrowed as they continued inland and slightly uphill. Looking across the streams, which seemed to mingle into one river in places, he saw a valley which looked greener and more sheltered than anything they had seen before.

"Let's cross here," he said to Sophia, who awoke from her daydreaming with a start. "Look," he continued, "that valley looks a bit like a Scottish glen."

Sophia saw a sharp v-shaped valley that seemed to turn away so that she couldn't see all the way to the top. But it certainly did look like some of the wooded valleys near her home, and perhaps even more like the rolling valleys she barely remembered from England.

Turning the cart into the water, they rolled and rocked across the shingle and flowing water. The cattle seemed to have a sense of where best to put their feet, but this involved lots of twists and turns, making Sophia feel quite sea-sick again.

Reaching dry land on the other side after nearly an hour of this tortuous journey, they pulled the cart to a slow halt to rest and take a drink.

The sound of horses' hooves made them both look up to see two horsemen approaching fast across the river they had just crossed. George jumped down and helped Sophia gently to the floor and they stood side by side to meet the fine, tall horses who snorted and threw their heads into the air as they were drawn to a stop. The two young riders dismounted.

"Good morning to you both, and where are you headed?" asked the older of the two men.

George, who wasn't keen to talk too openly, replied, "Inland for a good pasture. And you?"

"And you will find choice a-plenty for you and your pretty wife," said the man. "I'm Thomas Baylis, and this is my brother, Simon. We are seeking bigger things ourselves."

Something about these two men made George uncomfortable. Arrogant was the word that came to mind. And he could tell that Sophia was also unsure as she stood beside him. So his reply was polite, but did not encourage further discussion. "Well, we wish you good luck and safe travels in this land of opportunity," he said and began to turn away to draw some water out of the back of the cart to quench his wife's thirst.

"Ah, we will have good luck if we cross those hills," said the younger of the two men. "Beyond those hills, through the gap there," he pointed vaguely to a shallow dip between two hills, "they say there is a flat land of great plenty there, and we will make our fortune once we take it as our claim."

"Shh," said the first man, "these folk don't need to hear our dreams. They have their own. Good luck to you both and may you find your pasture. For now, good day and perhaps we will meet again one day. Come, Simon, time to move on." The young brothers swung themselves easily into their saddles and, with a cheery wave, they were gone in a cloud of dust, the horses' feet making light work of the dense undergrowth beneath them.

"Let us rest here a while," suggested George, guiding his young wife to sit on the steps leading up into the cart. "Here, drink some water while I go for a look round."

George left his wife sipping at the cold, fresh water in a battered tin mug and set out towards the sound of a stream babbling down through the valley to join the bigger river. He felt somewhat unsettled after their chance meeting with the two brothers. His expectations of a piece of land to call home were quite modest. Enough to live on was all he wanted. He didn't really understand the desire to take huge tracts of land for one's own benefit. He would like a plot big enough to see the edges and small enough to walk around the boundaries every day.

With these thoughts going round and round in his head, George realised he had been walking gently uphill into the valley along the bottom of which a stream wound its way through thickets of small trees and large, round, weather-worn rocks. The valley floor seemed greener than the land they had been crossing. Flat in places, but gently rolling back towards the coast. As he reached a small waterfall with just a trickle of water coming through at the moment, the view opened out. The wind, which had been quite strong at river level, seemed to have diminished in strength here, but the sun still streamed into the place. Bird calls came from the scrubland beyond, he saw a fish streak in the clear water of the gathering pool above the waterfall. There was evidence that someone had made a fire here, but not recently. Perhaps the native people passed this way on their journeys to fish or hunt and had found this a good place to stay along the way.

"Maybe this is it," he thought, "maybe this is our new home."

Sophia was feeling sick again and that brought on a bout of homesickness too. Nothing was familiar, nothing made her feel at home. The two men with big ideas had unsettled her. She just wanted a home with enough to live on and enough to feed a growing family. She missed her father, always humming a tune or singing a song. She really missed her mother despite her frailty, but who else could tell her how to bear this baby and bring it into the world? She even missed her brothers, Angus and Samuel who had always seemed hell bent on causing her to scold them, and her sister Emily, who would never have the courage to leave the village, let alone travel by ship for many months to a new country. And perhaps most of all she missed Tam, her wee terrier dog who followed her like a shadow wherever she went. Was he whining back at home, waiting at the door for his mistress to return? Poor Tam.....

Again the sight of George approaching pulled her out of her dreams. "Whatever is the matter?" she called as George came running towards her waving his arms to attract her attention. "What's wrong?"

"Nothing's wrong, my dear, just come with me," her husband called. "Come and see what I have found." And he led her, hand in hand into the valley. And she knew it too. This was a good place, a place where they could make a home together. A place where their child could be happy. A place where a dog could roam free.

"We have found it, haven't we?" whispered Sophia.

"Yes, I believe we have," replied George and he took her in his arms and, lifting her off her feet, they spun around to admire the view from what was to become their new front step.

Chapter Two

Putting down roots

March - June 1850

The days were as busy as anything they had ever known before and full of new experiences at every turn. Thankfully, the sun rose early and set late, leaving Sophia and George plenty of daylight to set up their new home. So much to do. On that first day, when they had both decided this place was to be their new home, they had slept once more under the bullock cart after a meal of cold pork and oatcakes, listening to the unfamiliar sounds around them. It seemed like the whole place was full of birds who one would expect to take to the sky when startled. But no, these birds seemed to be hidden in the dense undergrowth. However, that did not mean that they were quiet. Still rustling around, squawking and screeching long after dark. And after only a few hours of sleep, those same birds were off again with their dawn chorus. Difficult to spot as they seemed to have plumage of the same browns and greens as the grass and bush around them, nevertheless they made their presence felt.

Sophia was missing the familiar birds of her home. Thrushes and blackbirds and the colourful blue tits, and, of course, the robin who helped in the garden whenever anyone was out there hanging up the washing or digging the ground for potatoes. These odd creatures with their strange song were unsettling at night and annoying in the daylight. And where were the animals? There didn't seem to be any evidence of squirrels, foxes, badgers, nor even mice. "Perhaps the birds had eaten them all," she thought to herself as she tidied the breakfast dishes away neatly on a shelf George had made for her yesterday. What a strange land they had come to!

Daisy and the pulling cattle were enjoying their freedom and were sniffing and snorting as they took a morning bath in the brook. Steam rose above their leathery bodies and a plain looking bird hopped onto the back of one of the cattle to pick small insects from his back.

George had done a good job at fencing off an area for the cattle, allowing them access to the stream, but stopping them from wandering off along the river. He had cut down the small spike-laden trees above them at the top of the valley. The main trunks made good posts, the lesser branches could be split for panels in the fence woven in by Sophia and the rest piled up for firewood. Thank goodness that his chest of goods had included a good axe. It had come as a pleasant surprise to them both that a neat pile of gifts was waiting for them on the quay when they had climbed out of the small lighter which brought them ashore and onto dry land at last. The emigrant organisation had really meant it when they had told them that they would be fully supported on their journey. Tools of every kind, coils of rope, a keg of nails of varying sizes, several canvas sheets with ropes to tie them down or to make a shelter. And in another corner all the items needed for a basic kitchen including earthenware pots, enamel plates, various spoons and short knives. There was even a bolt of rough cloth and some sacking to make a mattress.

Each couple was met by a member of the local Presbyterian congregation and taken to collect their donated goods. What generosity they showed! Sophia had been on the verge of tears. Throughout the journey she had worried about the basic needs of existence - shelter, food and warmth, as well as the means to grow food and raise stock. She need not have had any concerns. Mrs Adams had assured them that the Emigrant Society was passionate about bringing young, God-fearing people to this land of heathens and was prepared to back that up in practical ways. But so much seemed to be ready for them, they were blessed indeed. Not that Sophia was terribly sure that God knew about this place across the oceans. She knew He lived in the old chapel back at home and that He could be seen amongst the trees and the hills and the sea around the village. But she had wondered many times since their idea to emigrate had hatched, "How does He know about New Zealand?" Well, she supposed that was why they needed people to come here.

To bring God with them to show the native people how good He was to them.

Bullock drays and cattle were made available to buy too. Several carts stood ready on the quayside and George chose a sturdy one with strong wheels as he knew they would be travelling over difficult terrain. With a farmer's eye for stock he swiftly chose what he considered the best of the beasts on offer. He hoped they could form the basis of his herd once their use as pulling beasts was done. Sophia was not too sure of these gentle giants, who stared back at her with laconic eyes, stamping an occasional hoof and emitting a nose full of steamy, sweet-smelling breath toward her. It took a sizeable chunk of their purse to acquire these beauties, but George was not about to skimp on such a necessity.

For several days wood cutting and fencing was all that he had done from daybreak to sunset. His shoulders were tired out and Sophia could see knots in his muscles before he put on his shirt each morning. It was her job to wind the thinnest rope they had been given between these strips, thereby forming a roll of fencing tied at the top and bottom. It was a bit like weaving. Over and under, over and under. George had started putting strong poles into the heavy ground to form a square. He had found a soft wooden mallet in his box of tools and this he used to pound the posts into the earth at about the length of a man lying down between each one. It was hard work in ground that seemed to be dry dust between many, many small stones. Each hole he made with his sharp-pointed shovel seemed to be full of these pebbles. In fact, once piled up beside the hole, it seemed to George that the stones formed a bigger heap than the size of the hole dug out. How could that be? Between each one he used some of his precious stock of metal nails to attach the woven strips that Sophia had made. Once an enclosure had been made for the cattle beasts, leaving a small gap as a gateway with just a rope across, he quickly moved on to creating a more permanent home for him and Sophia. This he saw as a pressing need - he wanted his son or daughter to be born in a house, not in a tent.

On their first day at this place he had fashioned a tent of sorts from branches and the canvas sheets they had been given. This gave them more space to live in and sleep, but the cooking fire remained outside. He had made some furniture for Sophia to store things and some simple seats and tables. The cart had, for now, become their pantry and storeroom, keeping goods off the ground which was sometimes damp in the dew of the morning. Any spare stones he pulled out while digging fence posts had been collected for the setting out of the footprint of the building he and Sophia would move into soon. He often found Sophia standing in this space, gently holding her growing belly and working out where cooking would happen, where beds could be laid and food eaten. She had lain short sticks on the ground inside to indicate where the door would be and a window should be formed, though these had been moved since the day of the big wind to provide more shelter from that direction.

The weather had so far been kind with nothing but an occasional spot of rain which dried on the ground almost as soon as it landed. In fact, George would have liked some rain to help him bind the mud and grass together for the cob mixture he needed for the house walls. But one afternoon a strong wind had come from nowhere, turning on like a person blowing out a candle. In a few seconds their belongings had taken flight. Above them a long, straight line of cloud had formed like nothing they had ever seen before, which they didn't know at the time, but soon came to understand, was a presage of the strong wind coming from beyond the hills. It hit with a vengeance, bending trees, folding the grass flat and whisking washing, buckets and anything else not held down wildly into the air.

Sophia chased her washing down the hill catching her white apron just before it went into the stream for an extra rinse. Gathering things up while the wind whipped her hair into strange shapes, she thought, "I must have a home soon, where these things can be stored safely, whatever the weather."

George divided his days into building their new home and finding food. Hunting for fish seemed to be more effective in the early morning, so this became his first task of each day. The salted ham was still giving them a good feed, although keeping the flies at bay was proving a task beyond Sophia's means. All she could do was cover as much food as she could with muslin cloth and, when that failed to stop the hordes of pesky black flies, she could be seen waving a handkerchief about wildly. A sight that amused George no end. But as the days began to shorten the insects seemed to be less of an issue and temperatures became bearable.

But fish made up most of their diet for now. He had fashioned a line with hooks made from some of the smallest metal nails. On a good day this device brought in three or four small fish. Sophia gutted his catch efficiently and cooked them to perfection over the small stone fireplace they had made on a flat and sheltered spot near the banks of the stream where any smoke would be blown away from their shelter. George had been quite anxious about fire. The ground was dry as dust and the grass crisp. A spark would cause devastation to their dreams, so the fireplace was made in a circle of stones with the vegetation removed a safe distance and a pail of water close by, just in case. Their stock of oatcakes was nearly spent, but flat bread using flour, salt and water helped each meal to fill their bellies. And their earthenware pots with butter and lard for cooking were doing well. Sophia had even drained the fat from the body of the pig and retained the stock in which it had been boiled. These pots stood with their feet in the cold stream under the shade of a small tree. They both yearned for fruit and vegetables. Used to apples and potatoes and cabbages and summer beans, they missed the variety of flavour and colour in their diet. Soon it would be time to dig a plot to plant the small seed potatoes they had carried across the ocean and to plant the beans which had travelled in a cloth bag in Sophia's travel chest. Although George was not sure how the winter would go - would the ground freeze, would there be endless rain, or would the season continue to give them sunshine most days?

Daisy was producing good milk at last. It hadn't been realistic for her to have milk in her udders while they were on the move, but it was beginning to flow regularly now. George had hopes that calves would come now that Daisy spent her days in the field with the pulling beasts. Sophia had tried to make some butter with the creamy top of the milk and it certainly helped to cheer up their bland diet. And, of course, Sophia needed fresh milk to supplement her diet. As everyone knew, it helped a baby to grow well.

So the building work continued while the sun beat down on their fair skins. George wore a wide brimmed hat and Sophia a straw bonnet with a ribbon to hold it in place under her chin. Nevertheless, her skin felt red and hot with the burning of the sun. George seemed to glow with brown health whereas she just seemed to burn until pieces of pink, dry skin fell from her arms. Shaking out the mattress each morning seemed to cause a shower like snowfall. And she had found that, as the day turned into evening, a million tiny flies took a fancy to a meal of her blood and she was left scratching and itching for days afterwards. It had taken her a day or two to remember a remedy that her mother had used when they first arrived in Scotland and the local mosquitoes had seen a chance for fresh English meat. She hunted out a tiny glass bottle of lavender water hidden in her embroidered vanity bag and found that dabbing just a tiny drop behind her ears was enough to see the ferocious predators away and give her some relief. In many ways Sophia was looking forward to colder weather when these pests would disappear for a while.

Laying stones, harvesting armfuls of long dry grass and mixing these with dry soil, which they then churned into a sticky mess with pails of water from the stream. All these were laborious and monotonous tasks which they found neither too hard, nor boring as their enthusiasm for creating their own home drove them along. A routine started to emerge. George fishing while Sophia tried valiantly to claim a few drops of milk from Daisy in a wooden bucket. Building work in the mornings, a short lunch break and an hour or two more of building before it was time to sit awhile and watch the pot bubble over the fire, talk over their dreams and then, as the stars appeared overhead, they took to their neatly made mattress at the rear of their shelter. They both felt a sense of urgency to complete this symbol of their permanence in this place and, as daylight seemed to diminish each day by a few minutes, they worked frantically to make use of as much of the day as was possible.

George now had the beginnings of a modest cottage in place. He had begun by laying a double layer of large, round stones, taken one by one from the river bed. Each one had to be carried singly, due to its weight, and lain next to one another to form the basic outline of two rectangles, one inside the other. The gap was filled with smaller stones to form the width of the walls, making a nice firm foundation layer up to window level. George had then made a wooden door frame and two small frames for windows. He had found a good source of strong wood when he took a walk downstream and happened on a fallen tree. It had once been a fine specimen, but had split from its roots some time ago, perhaps in one of those strong winds. The wood was now white and hard and George had found it easy to extract long, straight branches which he dragged back to the camp for storage. Only the jagged stump remained on the bank now. One day George planned to make good use of the rest of this fortunate find.

The frames he had made would be secured in place as he added the cob mixture. At the other end from the door he had made a chimney from more stones. As the roof would be made from wood and material gathered in the undergrowth around them, he was keen to build this entirely of stone to keep the roof safe from sparks.

He had been quite worried about mud. He needed a goodly amount to help make the simple cob walls. But water in the stream was low, and mostly babbled gently over pebbles and gravel. It became increasingly difficult to collect as much as he needed to make a sticky but pliable mixture, which he applied by the bucket load, tidying the edges by patting it flat with his hands. Despite this he had only one more layer all around to reach the top of the door frame, and then he would need gable ends with wooden slats set in to form a framework for the roof.

But one morning they awoke to the sound of drips on their canvas shelter, soon becoming a deafening torrent, and cold rain fell steadily for almost the whole day. Sophia huddled miserably under the canvas sheet while George checked the cattle were not pounding their pen to a sodden mess, that the river was not rising too close to their flat piece of land and that their dry foodstuff stayed dry. "Tomorrow the problem of mud will be solved," he thought to himself as he watched the stream rise to a raging torrent of brown water flowing swiftly by.

Sophia had taken a rest after a cold and rather damp lunch had been eaten. She tired easily in this later stage of her pregnancy, and with a warm blanket around her she had slept well despite the noise of the growing river and with only the occasional movement in her swollen belly causing her to stir. She awoke after an hour of slumber to a change in note. The river still pounded down the valley, but the rain had stopped. A watery sun had even made a brief appearance through the clouds and what wasn't dripping was now steaming in the heat.

Emerging from her bed like a butterfly unfolding from a cocoon, she stretched, yawned and set about putting things straight. A pair of shoes had got wet from being placed directly under a drip from the canvas shelter. She would dry them by the fire she would light soon. George had fashioned a cape from one of the canvas sheets which was soaked after his trips to keep an eye on things that morning. She had recently made herself a line to hang things up between two trees, and she rummaged in a basket to pull out some clothes pegs to pin the cape up to dry.

As she stretched up to reach the line a flash of unfamiliar colour caught her eye from the path which George had made to reach the trees to be cut down. Frozen in her stretched out state she couldn't believe what she thought she had seen. Was she still dreaming that a woman of about her age wearing a pale blue dress with a white pinafore over it was sliding down that path waving and calling out to her? Having spent many weeks now caring only what George saw of her she felt the need to press her own apron flat with her hands, tidy a collar and push back the loose bits of hair from her face. Another human being, could it be so?

"Hello," called this angel from heaven, "Hello, have you weathered the storm, my dear?"

"Err, hello," replied Sophia, wondering if she had lost the ability to speak while she slept. She stepped forward to meet a woman who was about her age, slightly more rounded but about the same height as her. This welcome guest was not so much beautiful as striking, with strong features that gave the impression that she would stand no nonsense. Her wavy brown hair appeared to be even less obedient than Sophia's. She put a hand up to push back the strands which had come loose from their ribbon. It looked like something she did often, almost unconsciously.

"I'm Nancy," she said and stuck out a hand to greet her new neighbour. "Well, technically I'm Nancy Cornfields Lawton, but the Cornfields thing is so confusing. I'm your neighbour, well, not quite next door as we are used to such things, but next door here. And are my two boys to have a playmate soon? My goodness, I must stop talking and take a breath. I'm so excited to see another soul, I can hardly stop myself from dancing." At which she took Sophia by the shoulders and they spun around like two small girls in the playground splashing each other with specks of mud from the wet ground. Sophia knew immediately that they would be the best of friends.

Coming to a halt she felt quite giddy from the twirling and from the sudden shift in her spirits. "I'm Sophia and my husband, George McKay, is somewhere around," she cast a glance around to find him, but to no avail. "But why haven't we seen you before? We've been here for a few months now."

"My twins are just two weeks old today, Benjamin and Edmund. So I haven't been away from my bed for a while and they are such demanding wee boys. Just as I feed one the other mews for more milk, though I'm still not sure I know which is which. It is all quite exhausting. But Edmund, that's my husband, passed by a while ago, but he chose not to disturb you. Today I just had to come and see if you had survived your first drenching, but I must go back soon or we will hear their wailing from here."

"Oh stay for some tea, please," pleaded Sophia, suddenly hungry for female company.

"Not today, my dear," said Nancy cheerfully, "but come and see me tomorrow and meet Mr Lawton and the terrible twins."

"Bring George too," she added as she turned and ran back up the hill.

"Where do we go?" called Sophia, wondering if perhaps Nancy was a mere apparition.

"Follow the stream up this path. You will see the house soon enough. Bye for now," and with that Nancy Cornfields Lawton was gone over the brow of the hill.

George was leaning on one of his new fence posts watching the cattle steam gently in the late and unexpected sunshine, flicking their tails at the annoying flies all around them. Life was good. Tomorrow he could complete the walls of his new house. It would be a hard day, he suspected, but worth it.

Suddenly he heard Sophia call out to him, "George, come quick, you'll never guess."

"Whatever is the matter, dear?" his concern for her wellbeing genuine. "Perhaps the baby is coming," he thought, but no, she didn't seem to be in pain and would hardly likely to be skipping towards him in so spritely a way had labour taken hold.

"We - have - neighbours," she was a bit breathless after all the excitement so the words came out each time she gasped for breath. "We have neighbours, just up the river and they have twin boys and Nancy is my age and they want us to go tomorrow and she's just lovely and I think we will be friends."

It took a while for all this information to sink into George's head. Relief helped to untie those knotted shoulder muscles and he realised how much he had been worried about Sophia giving birth without some female help. This Nancy person was just what she needed. His silent prayers to the God that he hoped had followed them here had come to something after all. "Tell me all about it while I get that fire going and you cook me some supper," he said, and off they went back to camp where much speculation was exchanged about their new-found friends.

Sophia slept badly with her head full of what-ifs and maybes. She was up before the sun had risen over the horizon and George woke to the crashing and banging of his wife looking through her chest of belongings. "What are you doing?" he muttered from underneath the blankets. The mornings were turning cooler and it was harder and harder to make a start to the day.

"I need a present for Nancy. I'm looking for some blue ribbon. What can we take for Mr Lawton?" her face all screwed up in a desire to make a good impression.

"Have you got some of your oatcakes we could take? You make the best ones ever, better than my own mother's," he said, feeling that flattery was one way to calm her down a bit.

"Oh yes, I'll tie them with the ribbon. They are good, aren't they?" and off she danced to get ready for this very important day.

George had hardly put his spoon down in his empty bowl than it was taken from him for washing and putting away. "Come on, let's tidy up quickly, check the cattle are safe and we can make a start," she said. George was a little reluctant to go and meet these folk. Apart from anything else he had planned to use that ready-made mud today. By tomorrow it would all be drying out again. And he had got used to life with just the two of them. But he knew Sophia needed company, and, better than that, a friend to help her with those womanly things that were such a mystery to him. So he would go cheerfully today and meet these kindred pioneers. They were both intrigued to find out their story and keen to tell their own.

As it turned out the four young people came together in a friendship that would last a lifetime. This day would be the first of many spent together and that path up the hill became a well-beaten track. Laughter followed Nancy wherever she went and though Edmund was of a sterner disposition, he and George had much in common.

They had set off up the path, Sophia quickly at first, but slowing as the weight of her belly held her back. George was surprised he hadn't seen something of their neighbour's place while cutting wood, but, as the swollen river took an unexpectedly tight turn they found themselves in a flat and green clearing with yellow cliffs behind. A truly hidden place, thought George, but ever the practical one, he thought to himself that the light would go early here and the land not drain as well as their spot downstream.

The Lawtons had, he observed, been here a while longer than he and Sophia and had made good use of their time. Next to a fine tall tree stood a neat cob cottage, smoke rising from the chimney at one end. For a moment he thought he had landed back in a Scottish farmyard. Chickens scratched around the door, Nancy was untethering a fat cow after nearly filling the milking pail and, to Sophia's obvious delight, a collie lay on her side while her four pups, no wait, five pups suckled furiously at her teats.

With a shriek of delight Nancy saw them coming and, losing some of her precious milk, she almost dropped the pail as she ran to meet them.

"You came!" she said as she grabbed Sophia again and whirled her round. "And this must be George? You are lucky to have such a handsome man. My Edmund is a plain soul, but with a good heart."

George had the decency to blush, though he managed to hide it under his hat until it became necessary to take it off for formal introductions. Edmund, having heard all the noise, appeared around the corner of the house and, with long strides, came over to shake their hands.

'Nancy had been right,' Sophia thought. 'He's no beauty but he's strong and tall and that's what counts here.'

Leaving the men to talk of farming matters, Sophia and Nancy went off arm in arm towards the house. Sophia remembered her gift and then became embarrassed at its modesty when Nancy pointed out a woven basket containing four brown eggs, a cake wrapped in a cheerful cloth and a small brown piece of sacking roughly sewn into a pillowcase. "I'll explain later," said Nancy mysteriously, and led Sophia into the makeshift nursery where two tiny babes lay next to each other in a cot fashioned from a travel chest, like two peas in a pod, their little curled up fists fighting with each other already.

It felt odd to Sophia to be in a building with a roof, all echo and darker than the sunlight she had grown accustomed to. And the babies suddenly made her quite emotional. She swayed slightly in her dizziness and Nancy caught her saying, "Come outside, my dear, and sit awhile."

The rest of the day flew by in a whirl of findings-out about each other. It seemed that the lack of company needed to be caught up on all in one day, so words tumbled from each of them in turn.

Over a lunch of potatoes freshly dug from the garden, salted ham and boiled onion they discovered that their journeys had been similar in so many ways. Nancy and Edmund had started their married life in Devon in the south west corner of England. Edmund, the second son of a sheep farmer on the moors and Nancy, the eldest daughter of the village parson. Like George, Edmund had to leave home to carve a living and Nancy had needed an escape from the drudgery of tending for her growing family. It seemed her mother produced sibling after sibling, Nancy couldn't quite remember all their names now, but escaping across the sea seemed like a fine way to avoid having to control her unruly brothers and sisters.

They had both been assisted passengers, though Nancy and Edmund were Church of England folk and had been helped by the Plymouth

Emigrant Society to sail from that famous port to Otago. They had arrived almost a year ago now.

Their route to this hidden valley had been similar too. Spending a day or two in the growing city of Dunedin while things got organised they then took the slow journey north over two great hills to the little community, which the pioneers were calling Hawksbury, the native name of this settlement being much too hard for British Empire mouths to say. The small community had grown from a few shacks and tents to a solid community of small wooden houses and a main street of well-stocked shops and stores. The wooden church had been there long enough to be in need of a fresh coat of paint. Edmund thought it would become a great town soon. Stocking up there with supplies and letting the cattle rest a while, they too had added a milking cow to their entourage and then headed north once more. Keeping to the coast wherever possible, they sometimes made good progress by travelling along on the firm sand of huge sweeping bays, where the waves rolled gently ashore beside them. On occasions they took a whole day to work their way inland around an estuary until they found the river mouth shallow enough for the cattle to pick their way across without too much lurching from side to side.

But once they reached a very wide river with fast flowing water too deep for the bullock dray to cross, they had both made the decision to head upstream, taking a course gently uphill and to the west. That river became easier to cross as it narrowed further, and though they had taken different crossing points, their journeys had both reached this same valley within one long day of travel from the coast.

Edmund had at first been keen to stay at George and Sophia's site. But one day the intrepid Nancy had gone exploring and found this perfect hidden platform. They had dragged everything they owned up the bank and set up a permanent base there. Nancy had acquired some fertile eggs while they rested in Hawksbury. It had been a precarious journey for them as the cart lurched from side to side, but they all hatched and her flock of chickens began to multiply. And their cattle, in a similar way to George's, had turned into the start of their herd. The grass here seemed greener so their milking cow was doing well. She had already had a calf who cavorted around the pasture being firmly put in place by her father on many occasions.

All this good fresh food had, as Nancy put it, made her productive too. So the twins had been conceived and duly arrived safely. She was used to the process of birth, having seen her mother through it many times, so it had all gone very smoothly despite Edmund's trepidation.

A month or so before the birth of the twins, Edmund had taken a trip back down the river and south along the coast to Hawksbury. On this journey he had, to his great surprise, come upon Sophia and George's little camp, but he had made an early start in darkness, so did not disturb them. He thanked God for the dry ground so that he left no footsteps to concern them, but thought to himself that he would call and meet their new neighbours on his return in a few days. He had given Nancy the excuse that he needed supplies and would like to see if any letters had arrived from Devon. They had agreed that post would be held for them at the general stores in Hawksbury, but he had no real expectations as his family were not good with their words. Perhaps Nancy's family would feel it their duty to write, but he guessed it would not be with love. True though it was that he needed to make the journey, his main reason for going on this arduous trip on foot was to seek advice on the risks of childbirth.

Once he had reached Hawksbury, arranged a bed for the night, drawn a blank at the stores as regards any envelopes addressed to him or Nancy, and collected his supplies in a sack, which now hung heavy over his shoulder, he sought out the vicar's wife who was tidying the small wooden church. Edmund was impressed that the community had come together to build such an impressive church. Perhaps one day other people would join them in his valley and they could worship together in such a building. Mrs Atkins was only too happy to show him around. Though it was an awkward topic for a young man to broach, he had set off home with not only a heavy sack, but a lot more knowledge which stood him in good stead on the day of her labour. Thinking at the time that Nancy had given him a wonderful healthy son and that was good, the second birth had come as a real surprise. But Nancy was capable and fit and had taken it all in her stride, apart from a frustrating period of recovery, which she found hard to cope with, as a girl who wanted to be up early and outside doing things until the sun set.

On the journey home he had happened upon a man raising a big stick to a poor, sickly looking collie dog. Cruelty to an innocent creature was not acceptable to a young Christian man, especially one whose lifetime had been spent raising animals on a farm. So in a moment of outrage he had wrested the stick away from the man as he raised it to beat the poor dog again. "Leave her alone," he shouted.

"Take the damnable cur," replied the shabby looking man, "She's in pup and I plan to drown the lot of them today."

Edmund pulled himself up to as tall as he could make himself and, waving the stick he had just acquired, he said, "Get out of here, you miserable man. You don't deserve a life here if you can't be good to animals." With that he chased him down the road with that same stick. The man sloped away secretly relieved to have the situation sorted out for him, albeit not in the way he had expected.

So there was Edmund, alone on the road with a poor looking dog and a long stick. He was not sure which would be of the most usefulness. Using the stick as a staff, he set off home wondering if the dog would follow. But looking round she seemed to have raised herself up and was padding along a few feet behind him. Although each time he turned towards her she cowed down in fear. In a moment of realisation, he put the stick down on the ground and she instantly came to him. She was a beauty, but in poor condition. Her deep brown eyes looked up at him with a look of thanks for being rescued. She was obviously a bright girl. Being a farm boy, he knew a pregnant animal when he saw one, and being certain that Nancy would relish the prospect of tending for puppies he left the stick on the side of the road, got to his feet and gave a gentle whistle. The dog walked along beside him all the way home.

The journey took longer than expected due to the slow pace of the dog so by the time he reached the valley it was dark. He scooped the tired dog into his arms and yet again crept past the neighbours sleeping peacefully in their shelter. Edmund thought to himself, "I'll help them put a roof on that house soon. They will need better shelter come winter."

Nancy, of course, had lavished the poor dog with affection, named her Meg and revelled in the appearance of four healthy pups and, finally, a small runt of a dog, who nevertheless showed spirit and survived the night despite being beaten to his mother's milk by his fatter, stronger siblings. All four firstborn pups had the usual black and white colouring, but the last born wee fellow had a third streak of rusty brown. He would never be a big dog, but he would certainly be handsome to the eye.

So this wonderful first day where four new friends had come together continued with food and drink and conversation and comparing notes. Finally, with the sun, as George had predicted, disappearing early behind the yellow cliffs, Sophia realised she was becoming very tired. "We should go home now," she said, "and you must come to see us very soon."

"Ah, but wait, I nearly forgot what that canvas pillow was for," Nancy jumped to her feet. "Come and choose a puppy."

"Oh, can I, please?" exclaimed Sophia, "Oh, that would be wonderful. I so miss my dog from home."

As it turned out, the puppy chose them. As George and Sophia stood over the box containing five balls of predominantly black and white fluff, the smallest boy with the brown streak crawled out from the pile and, on four unsteady paws, made his drunken way towards them. With one big yawn, Sophia was sold on him. "Can we have that one, please?" she asked, adding, "And I will call him Roy."

"Are you sure, my dear, he's the runt of the litter?" said the ever-practical Edmund.

"Oh yes, I'm sure, thank you," she said, picking the wee bundle up and giving him a cuddle which was rewarded with puppy yelps and a lick of her fingers. "Hello Roy," she said, and he replied in secret doggy words, "Hello human, I like you."

Agreeing that Sophia would come back as much as she could to see Roy until he no longer needed his mother's milk, and with much thanks for the basket of goods that George carried in a woven basket, it was a tired but happy couple that headed back down hill. There was many a backward wave and calls of, "See you soon," and "Thank you."

Once they had lost sight of each other, Sophia fell quiet, deep in thoughts of her own. She perhaps should not have indulged so much on all that lovely fresh food as her tummy was feeling quite uncomfortable. "Never mind," she thought, "I'll be fine after a good night's sleep."

It was pitch dark as George checked the cattle with a lantern swinging above his head to spread a little light into the paddock, and Sophia was already under the covers by the time he joined her in bed. It seemed barely a moment before George was snoring gently, but sleep seemed hard to come by for Sophia tonight. She lay as still as she could so as not to disturb George, but things just kept on rolling around in her head and her belly.

Sometime before dawn George awoke with a start to a low groan from his wife who lay doubled up in pain beside him. Poor Sophia had a look of sheer terror on her tear-stained face.

"Fetch Nancy," she cried through bouts of pain. "The baby....it's coming."

So for the second time in less than a day, George, abandoning all thoughts of finishing their house for another day, climbed the steep path to their neighbour's house to call upon their newfound friend to help bring his firstborn child into the world.

THE WIDEAWAKE HAT

Chapter Three

Growing Community

June - October 1850

Sophia found the rhythm of Freddie's sucking quite therapeutic. It gave her time to think, time to be spent in nothing but caring for her new son. Suck, suck, suck, the beat was like her father's metronome on top of the piano back in her home in Scotland.

She thought back over the past days and wondered how so much could have been packed into so little time with nothing other than a tiny human being to show for it. This thing seemed to take up every moment of her day and night, and even as he slept she would often just sit and watch him breathing gently in his makeshift cradle. Several days before the birth, when it was obvious to George that the baby would be here soon, he had made this cradle from a wooden crate, then mounted on wood cut into two semi-circles, allowing it to be rocked gently side-to-side. Sophia had cut one of her precious blankets into smaller squares and fashioned one square into a mattress which perfectly fitted the box. The other lay loosely on top.

It was probably just as well that she felt the need to watch over Freddie in his cradle as it gave her a reason to be still and quiet. Her body and soul needed time to heal too. It had not been an easy labour.

Some of the stages of Freddie's birth were lost to her in delirium, but she remembered George leaving to fetch Nancy. Torn between needing him to be there and needing him to fetch help, she had begged him to take her with him. Reasoning that this was just not practical, George had made her as comfortable as possible and then, reluctantly, abandoned her to her contractions as they came ever more frequently.

Time could not be measured while she lay down, or staggered helplessly around, or sunk to the ground in pain and fear. Nancy had come as quickly as it was possible for her to get there, followed later by Edmund carrying the twins, one under each arm. By the time he arrived Nancy snatched the twins from him, putting them into the cradle that had been prepared for the new arrival, and shooed him out of the shelter. "Go and help George finish the house," she had scolded, "he needs to be kept busy."

So it was that the gable ends of their new home were added to the sound of groans and cries which made George's heart ache for his wife's wellbeing. At every sound he wanted to run in to the shelter and take her in his arms and comfort her, but Edmund would not let him stop work. They had formed two triangles of cob into which, while the mud was still wet, they set straight poles of wood cut to length to reach both ends, about a foot apart from each other. The thickest of these was used as the ridge pole. Once the mud set, the poles formed a strong roof framework onto which grass, leaves and small branches could be laid in a form of rudimentary thatch. George had learned this design from the crofters cottages next to the sea in Scotland and knew it to be strong and capable of withstanding rain and wind.

Thankfully for Edmund, the gathering of this foliage took George out of earshot of their camp. Sophia's screams first became louder and then ominously quiet as exhaustion overtook her. But as they returned from their foraging with arms full of suitable material they were at first concerned that things were a little too quiet. George dropped all that he carried and set off at speed towards the camp. But just as he reached the stream the silence was broken by a sharp smack and a baby's hearty cry.

Nancy emerged briefly from under the canvas looking slightly dishevelled, but would not allow anyone else to enter for, what seemed to George, many hours. "You are going to need that house finished for your son," she hissed at George. In shock he turned back to his work, taking a while to realise that she had said, "son." He had a son!

Sophia did not remember much about the process of childbirth, but bits and pieces had come back into her mind over the last few days. She had been forced by Nancy to attempt to feed the wee boy. A painful and embarrassing experience at first, she, like most mothers, had found it came quite naturally in time. Where sleep had evaded her before the birth, it seemed to be all that she desired now. Sleep became the norm, and wakefulness just brief periods of activity in between.

She did remember George's first meeting with his son. Nancy had tidied everything up and wrapped the baby tightly in a cloth. She had even tidied Sophia's hair, although every single hair seemed to hurt as it was brushed. George had been summoned and, after initial concern for Sophia's health, Nancy handed him the tiny bundle. Tiny indeed in George's huge hands. But their eyes met and that father, son bond was there at once, never to be broken.

"We will call him Frederick George McKay," said Sophia in a weak and tearful voice. "Maybe Freddie while he's small."

"Hello, Freddie," whispered George, "Your mother is a clever person, isn't she?" If Freddie could have said yes, he would have replied, and George was certain that he did nod in affirmation. Edmund had been handed the twins to hold while the rightful owner of the cradle had taken up residence and Nancy had taken the opportunity to go quietly behind the cart and give her boys the feed for which they had been begging for a while now. Coming back under the canvas roof, Nancy had ordered, "Enough, get out and leave your new family to their sleep."

That had all been two weeks ago now. Today was the day that she and Freddie were moving into their new house. George and Edmund had completed the roof, fixed some sacking at the windows and formed a door, attached by leather hinges so that it swung to and fro unless the wooden latch was set against the frame.

They had been moving furniture and setting a fire this morning already and the winter sun was barely risen. George had been pleased to find a patch of bracken, similar to that which covered the hillsides in Scotland. He knew these fern-shaped leaves made a warm and sweet-smelling floor covering and had proudly covered the entire earth floor with a thick, fresh layer. Nancy had returned home with the twins several days ago, leaving Edmund to come and go each day to help George, but today she would be joining them to celebrate their house-warming.

Sophia was feeling strong enough to stand while they removed the bed and mattress and finally Freddie's little cradle was carried across with him in it. Nancy took her arm and guided her gently outside. She stood and surveyed her new home with a critical eye. "It will do," she said to George. "It will do."

All of a sudden, he whisked her into his arms and carried her laughing over the threshold. They whirled around so that she could see first the door, then the little windows, next the fireplace with wood burning bright, the bed set in a corner with Freddie's cot beside it and finally the table on which was a pot filled with twigs and grasses of browns and greens. Nancy's gift to 'warm the house'.

With her emotions still in turmoil from the birth, suddenly overcome by all that had happened, Sophia stood in her new home and sobbed and sobbed with huge gulps and tears pouring down her cheeks. Nancy had warned George that this day would be emotional for the new mother, so he simply took her by the shoulder and guided her gently to the bed. "Rest awhile. Freddie is asleep and all your organising here can wait a little longer," he whispered to his wife. He doubted she heard the last few words as she was almost immediately asleep, in their bed, in their home. He was immensely proud of himself.

Looking back George and Sophia always felt like their new life began properly that day. The act of creating a permanent home and filling it with their meagre possessions and furniture made from things found around them was really important to them. It felt to Sophia like the beginning of family life. Her health improved with a warm fire and good shelter and her spirit soared with, at last, the chance to build a routine of daily chores. She had always been busy with supporting her mother and her siblings and had felt frustrated at not having a proper home to run. So she relished the preparing and cooking of meals, the sweeping of floors, the making and mending of clothes and furnishings, and all the daily tasks that ensured the smooth running of their lives.

Much to George's surprise, with a lift in spirits, Sophia rediscovered her singing voice. Back home music had filled the house. Sophia's father was always humming a tune or sitting at his precious piano. Her mother would sing as she worked and Sophia now found she was doing the same. She sang quietly to Freddie to send him to sleep, hummed the same tunes to herself as she swept or sang out loud to Roy, who looked up at her with adoring puppy eyes as if he understood every word.

Roy had joined the family on the day they moved into the house having been carried down to them by Edmund and Nancy, along with the twins. He had found it all quite frightening. Where was he going and why were his mother and brothers not coming too? But he was a brave puppy and had taken everything in his stride, especially when he met his favourite human again. Sophia tickled him under the chin - he loved that. George had made a small shelter attached to the house for him to sleep in. He was growing so fast that the small sacking bed that Nancy had stitched for him was far too small now, but he still tried to curl up into a tiny ball on top of it because it smelt just right for a tiny, lonely pup.

Winter nights were very cold. Roy sometimes shivered in his kennel and missed the warmth of his mother, and George and Sophia shivered too until they were wrapped around each other under all the blankets they possessed. Freddie was wrapped up in his cradle, but even his little breaths turned to mist in the cold air. But the climate was so different from the dreary Scottish winters where the sun would not be seen between November and March. Cold though the nights could be, the sun would often give the benefit of a bright day and enough warmth for Freddie to be placed outdoors for an hour or two between feeds. Just occasionally they would all wake to the sound of heavy rain on the roof. As the day progressed raindrops would turn to huge wet snowflakes and every surface would be covered by a fresh white layer by the end of the day.

On days like that it seemed indulgent to spend an idle day indoors, but not much could be done without making a slushy mess everywhere anyway. Sophia would catch up on some sewing repairs and George would sit at the table cleaning his knives and tools. Freddie gurgled in his cot and practised grabbing things with his chubby fingers and Roy put his nose to the door to see if Sophia would let him in to sit near the fire for a while. The answer was always a stern "No, Roy," but there was no harm in trying again. One day she would give way, perhaps.

And winter seemed to pass quite quickly here. George made a note in his diary when he saw the first new bud on a tree by the river and the day the ice on the edges of the river melted for good. All these things he thought he should remember as he had no rules by which to plant seeds or dig soil, or all those things he had taken for granted back in Scotland.
By late September they all felt like spring had arrived and life was spent almost entirely outdoors. Bedding could be aired and flooring

replaced with fresh growth from the bracken by the river. George toiled for several days to dig a patch of ground for planting vegetables. Potatoes were dug in and beans planted once it seemed the danger of heavy frost had passed. Roy now spent all day at heel to his master. George taught him how to walk alongside and how to run ahead to flush out the odd duck. He wasn't quite big enough yet to catch fowl, but he knew he wanted to try his hand at it one day soon. He was a bit scared of the water, which was cold and sometimes covered his head. But he enjoyed a good shake afterwards with water flying from his nose first, right down to the tip of his tail.

It seemed that other people were emerging into the spring too. Not only did they see Nancy and Edmund and the twins every few days, but they now became aware of more people nearby. Smoke rose from several spots further down the river, or on the other side of the bigger river they had crossed to get there. Once or twice they caught sight of people crossing that river on horseback or with a cart. But it was an unusual day if these people came near to their spot by the river. One day, just as they had heard on their journey, the sound of two horses approaching fast made George look up from his gardening.

"You have made a home here, I see," called Thomas, the older of the two brothers they had met once before, "and doing well, by the look of things. Do you remember meeting me, Thomas Baylis and my brother, Simon?"

"Indeed," said George, feeling once more that he didn't quite trust these two young men. "Welcome, come and share a mug of tea," he pointed to the door of his house, "Come on in and see my wife again and meet my new son."

Thomas and Simon looped the reins of their horses onto the fence under a tree and followed George indoors.

"Sophia, do you remember meeting Thomas and Simon on our journey? They would like tea, if you can put the kettle on the stove, my dear," George ushered the men inside, both having to stoop to enter the room.

"Good day to you, ma'am, and thank you for your hospitality," said Thomas. "You have made a lovely home here."

"Welcome to you both. We are not so used to visitors, but pleased to see some nevertheless," said Sophia, sharing her husband's reticence with their guests.

Over a mug of tea and a plate of oatcakes George and Sophia heard news from Thomas of the growing number of people taking up residence in the area. It seemed they travelled widely and had got to know everyone. It came as a surprise to Sophia that they were actually part of a growing community of like-minded folk. It occurred to her that they should try to bring everyone together. It would be good for Freddie and the twins to have friends to play with as they grew up, and everyone occasionally yearns for company, especially when half way around the world from home.

Thomas was obviously the dominant brother. Simon hardly spoke, except for gruff thanks when handed his mug. Thomas told them about the couple who were building a small church across the big river. Would they be interested in attending services, he had asked them? Sophia thought that they very likely would, but she didn't feel she wanted to commit to anything in front of these two. "We will think about it, thank you," she said, "but with a new baby and so much to do, we can't promise." George nodded in approval.

"Well," said Thomas, getting up from the bench and nodding his thanks to Sophia, "Come Simon, we must leave these good folk to their chores and get going. We have sheep to sell. They are the future here. They can cope with the terrain and have ample in the way of food."

With a rattle of hooves they were gone and Sophia and George were left to consider all they had heard. "I would like to go to church again, George," said Sophia, "and it is nice to have neighbours. Freddie will have some friends, we may even need a school soon."

"Yes, I agree," said George. "Let's try to go on Sunday, we can carry Freddie that far."

Turning back to their chores, Sophia spent the afternoon thinking of church and who she might meet in the congregation. George's mind was full of new ideas. Sheep, perhaps. He quite liked sheep, he had done some shearing with those strange over-sized scissors which nicked the skin all too easily, and he liked the idea of having two crops from one beast in the form of wool and meat. But it was the horses that occupied his mind. Those two men could travel around the area so easily on horseback whereas he and Edmund had to walk and carry heavy sacks. He needed a horse!

The following day the conversation continued with Nancy and Edmund. They had been just as intrigued as Sophia and George to hear that they were part of a growing community. Nancy, who had grown up with church services as part of her everyday life, was keen to get back to regular church-going. It was agreed that they would all make the journey on the following Sunday. Nancy and Sophia, concerned that they had something to wear that could be considered 'Sunday best' went indoors to look through bonnets and ribbons and hems needing attention with a needle and thread.

Edmund and George's attention turned not to what to wear on Sunday, but how best to travel. "If only we had horses," said George, memories of the two visitors not far from the surface of his mind. Edmund, being a West Country boy, was used to horses being the preferred method of transport across the moors and valleys of his Devon home. George was more used to the short, rugged ponies used for hauling and carrying around the glens of his native Scotland, where horses were rarely ridden. More often they would pull a cart or carry items in panniers aside the saddle. George had never really mastered horsemanship, but was prepared to give it a try. Edmund, on the other hand, had been in the saddle from a very early age and relished the idea of sitting astride a horse again. They talked of what they could do, how far they could travel and how much help it would be. They even talked of the girls sitting aside them in the saddle and teaching the children to ride too. It all came down to approaching the Baylis boys. Edmund had met them too and didn't feel the same reticence that seemed to have affected Sophia and George. Edmund was keen to approach them and thought they would know where to purchase a couple of good horses.

On the following Sunday morning it was a positive cavalcade that approached the bare bones of what was obviously going to be a chapel once the building work was completed. Although there was to be a small tower at one end, a bell, rescued from a ship that had been wrecked near Port Chalmers, had been rigged up to swing on a wooden frame and two small boys were pushing and shoving it one side to the other until it chimed unevenly as a call to prayer.

George carried Freddie, Sophia and Nancy helped each other along, holding hems in the air to avoid too much mud and water attacking their best dresses and Edmund took up the rear carrying Ben and Little Ed, one under each arm in a most undignified way.

Progress had been slow and rests taken several times along the way to readjust babies in hand and to give Sophia a chance to catch her breath. But it was a happy group who was seen by the small congregation approaching the site of the chapel that morning. Women ran forward to relieve George and Edmund of their bundles and to coo over the babies wrapped up therein.

Introductions were made, although Sophia felt she would never remember all those names and was struggling to understand some of the accents. People had gathered, it seemed, from all over their home country. Welsh folk, with a lilting tone, other Scots both harsh and soft, indicating the east or west coasts of that country. Northern voices were familiar from her early years and the Devon or Cornwall burr she now understood having spent so much time with Nancy, though she couldn't quite tell which county was which.

All this time the bell was ringing in a persistent, if not tuneful way, making conversation difficult. But it changed now to a single tolling sound indicating it was time to enter the church. People who were used to this process streamed through the door, though it was not a door yet, just a gap in the walls. Benches had been set out in the manner of pews on the bare ground and an altar covered in a white cloth sat in the usual place at the front. There being no roof their songs and prayers reached the heavens all the sooner and the young man of the cloth took advantage of the open sky to use the heavens above as the theme for his sermon. As he said. "Heaven is all around us in our every day comings and goings. It is not just available on Sundays."

Sophia liked him immediately and sat transfixed at his words. Despite her Presbyterian upbringing she had always felt that God lived in the trees and the fields and the rivers and the stars as much as he did at church on Sundays. The hymns, sung so tunefully by the Welsh contingent, were familiar to them all and, though the words of the service were not quite what she and George had been used to reciting each week, they were uplifting and inspiring. They all felt better for being there and sharing the experience with other people.

As the service ended and the vicar swept out through the gap where a door would soon be placed, the congregation took turns to follow him and shake his hand. In the same way it happened in many places of worship around the world, people lingered and chatted and got to know each other in the churchyard, even though this yard was yet to be formally accepted as a place where people could be buried, or couples married, or children christened.

Sophia and Nancy were keen to corner the vicar and pick his brains over a date to have their babies christened. "What fun it would be to do all three at once," Nancy had said, in her usual matter-of-fact way. In the meantime Edmund had spotted the Baylis brothers standing to one side talking to a rough looking chap with a young dog at his side. This gentleman had obviously not attended the service and looked like he rarely thought of godly matters at all. He stood tall, his red hair and head well above those of Thomas and Simon. As the men approached this unlikely trio they overheard talk of sheep. So it seemed this huge man was a shepherd, hence the dog at his side.

"Thomas, Simon, we wanted to ask you something," said Edmund.

"What can we do for you, Edmund?" replied Thomas, "Oh, and hello George, how's that lovely wife of yours? Can we introduce you to James Mackenzie here? He's used to working with sheep and is looking for work."

James nodded and muttered a greeting, which George understood to be in Gaelic, but left Edmund looked slightly bemused. It was a language that George was used to hearing from older folk in his home village. He understood what people said, but found it hard to turn his mouth into the right shapes to make the awkward words. However, out of politeness he attempted a reply.

"Madainn mhath," he mouthed uncertainly. James, his head on one side, acknowledged the attempt at greeting him in his own tongue with a wide smile. Most people he had met on his travels were confused by his language and rudely continued in their own words or ignored him completely. There was something about this fellow Scot that made James think they had some future together.

Edmund, who had not entirely understood what had just passed, was keen to pursue the idea of purchasing horses. "Thomas, can you find a couple of decent horses for George and me? We have a little money, but we don't know who to approach for an honest deal."

It was Simon who answered, to Edmund's surprise. "I know a man who has a couple of nice geldings. Just right for you softies to try."

Edmund and George would have been offended by this if they hadn't been distracted by Simon issuing more words than they had ever heard him speak before.

"Cost you, though," said Thomas, picking up from his brother's words, "If you give me sixty pounds I'll choose a good pair and bring them to you."

George looked across at Edmund. They had put twenty pounds each on one side for a horse. "Would you take fifty?" asked Edmund before George could stop him. George was quickly counting up the coins in his precious leather pouch and wondering what they would have to miss out on if he spent that much.

"That seems fair," said Thomas, leaving George thinking they could have driven him down to their original budget. But too late now, Thomas and Edmund were shaking hands on the deal, and George followed suit reluctantly.

"We will be back before next Sunday with your new rides," said Thomas, "Ask your wife to put the kettle on again, maybe?"

It seemed to George that he was always to be irritated by these brothers. How dare Thomas give him the impression that he wanted to flirt with Sophia! But then, if they could get some decent horses, he supposed it was worth putting up with them both.

While the boys were negotiating their deal with the Baylis brothers, Nancy and Sophia had finished organising christening services. A date had been set, all they had to do was arrange godparents and perhaps do some sewing for christening robes. They chatted amiably as they walked across to their husbands.

"Who's that with George and Edmund and those bad Baylis boys?" asked Nancy. Sophia looked up to see the red-haired stranger standing tall and looking their way. Their eyes met over the heads of the other men and, without knowing quite why, Sophia shivered slightly.

A young, short-haired collie dog, more black than white, came over to meet them, but when Sophia put her hand out to greet the dog, the stranger called in a thick Scottish accent, "Dihaoine, Trobhad," and the dog obediently returned to her owner, sitting smartly at his left hand side.

Sophia and Nancy were introduced to James and given a chance to pat the collie who gave the impression that she didn't care a jot for such comforts. Sophia had learned a few words of Gaelic at school and she knew that the dog was called Friday and she thought he had used the command for "Come." She could understand James' words if she concentrated hard and she tried to reply as best she could. James, who appeared to be a serious fellow with a stern look, had a face that changed swiftly if he smiled. Sophia's attempts at saying "Good morning" in his mother tongue certainly made him smile.

"Ye can speak to me in English if ye wish," said James in his best English accent. Sophia laughed because Nancy was standing with her head on one side trying her hardest to understand a single word that James had spoken.

It was hard for everyone to tear themselves away from their newfound community, but in the end all three babies started crying at once and the new mothers knew it was time to take them home.

The vicar, his wife and several of the other members of the congregation waved from the churchyard until the party became mere specks on the far bank of the river. Reverend Job Nicol was pleased with himself. New members of his flock were always good, but new members who had offered to help complete the building of the church were even better.

The Baylis boys, pleased with the deal they had struck, rode off with a flurry leaving James and Friday alone to seek out a friendly face who would give them both a feed, and maybe a bed for the night.

True to their word, Thomas and Simon came riding up to George and Edmund one afternoon leading two bay geldings by a bridle and rope attached to each. As it happened, Sophia had taken Freddie and Roy up to see Nancy and the twins, so the men were alone. It fell to George to put the kettle on after all. He suspected the Baylis boys would have preferred a tot of something stronger, but knew better than to request it of god-fearing folk.

"We managed to buy them with saddles, so there's three pounds extra to pay," said the surly Simon. Edmund and George had no choice but to pay up and considered they had done quite well out of the deal after all. The horses looked good. Taller than George had hoped for and maybe a little bit scary.

"But we must be gone soon," said Thomas. "We have sheep to tend. We have picked up another hundred and fifty head from a man who was driving them south. Just as we did, he has travelled from Australia, but came ashore further north and then walked them down the length of this island. A different breed from those we brought over, but they are hardy stock and look in good shape. Would you care for a few each?"

George could see his savings dwindling at the hands of these two rogues, but there seemed no harm in adding to his stock. Edmund, as ever enthusiastic about any new venture, was already sealing a deal. They settled on twenty each for starters, at a guinea a head, with more if it worked well for them. Thomas thought some of the ewes were in lamb, so they may get a 'bonus package', as he called it.

The following morning the Baylis boys appeared again, this time on foot and driving forty sheep before them with the help of James Mackenzie and his dog Friday. When it became obvious that neither Edmund nor George had much idea about rounding up and separating twenty sheep each, it was James who whistled Friday into action and in no time at all Edmund's chosen score were ready to be driven on up the valley.

George, being very grateful for James' help, suggested that he stay for a meal. Sophia was more than happy to stretch their boiled fish and potatoes out to feed an extra person and Roy shared his bones and oatmeal happily with Friday. She smelt nice, like his mother. The canvas sheet of their old shelter was still in place and this was offered to James and Friday for a night's sleep afterwards. Conversation was somewhat stilted, although Sophia thought James understood more English than he gave away. It was, perhaps, just that he spent much of his time alone so had lost the art of talking out loud.

In the years to follow this day would be noted as the day that sheep came to the area. In time George's flock thrived and grew, Edmund's too did well with twin lambs being born a-plenty. So it was that the Lawtons and McKays became sheep farmers.

THE WIDEAWAKE HAT

Chapter Four

Life goes on

November 1850 - November 1852

The day of the christening was often seen by those early pioneers as the day they turned into a community rather than a collection of small families and individuals. To begin with it was just Benjamin Enoch and Edmund Noah Lawton and Frederick George McKay who would be accepted into God's family, but the Reverend Nicol had been out and about drumming up support for his growing flock and, by the time the day arrived, he had six infants and two adults ready to take holy water from the font upon their foreheads.

Of course, this involved so many family members and neighbours that the tiny wooden church, which had only acquired a roof in the last few days, was just not going to be big enough to fit them all in. So a makeshift font had been created from a cracked enamel bowl supported on a wooden tripod stand and the whole party assembled around it in the churchyard. Thankfully, the early summer sun shone brightly and the wind, which had been blustery for days, fell calm. Buds had burst into new leaf on the trees around the clearing and the banks of the stream were edged with white and yellow flowers. It was a pretty sight, made even more beautiful by the whole community being decked out in their Sunday best. There were even a couple of parasols nodding in the sunshine over delicate baby skins.

Aware that eight christenings would take a time of itself, Reverend Nicol had kept the words as short as could be rightfully achieved and had rattled through the adult ceremonies with ease. No handing round of babies or anticipated tears in these cases. So two young men, who had met good Christian girls on the journey around the world, were welcomed into the Church, albeit somewhat reluctantly. Neither of these two men had grown up in church-going homes, but they both believed it was good to do what they had been told by their new partners. And, as the girls had told them, they would not be happy marrying a heathen, so the wedding depended on this first step.

Then it came to the infants, the twins being the first on the agenda. George and Sophia were to be godparents, so Freddie was handed to Clara Nicol, the vicar's wife, who cooed and fussed over him while the boys were being made ready. As it was to be in the rest of their lives, Benjamin Enoch Lawton made all the noise, while his younger brother by ten minutes, Edmund Noah blinked as the water dripped into his eyes, but made not a sound. And then with much handing round of children, George and Sophia offered Frederick George to their new vicar and were duly thrilled when he cried loudly in surprise when the water hit his little face. This was surely a sign of the devil being called away. In a strange mixture of pagan and church ritual, a crying baby at a christening was taken to be a good sign of life to come.

Three more babies, all of whom had been born since their recent arrival in this land, were given up by their parents to be baptised and three more hearty yells issued forth. Such good luck these children were to have, if the legend held true.

The ladies of this small community had been planning the ensuing party for many days and had put together a feast fit for kings. Resources had been shared amongst them. Those with plenty of eggs had passed some around, those with fresh flour had given freely to others. Someone had been preparing a keg of beer which, though rather yeasty in taste, was enjoyed by all the men. "Wetting the babies' heads," they had said as they raised their mugs to each other.

As the day came to an end in the twilight songs were sung, fiddles played and dancing began. The mothers of those baptised today were keen to take their babies home so numbers dwindled to those hardened older folk who watched over the young people left to rouse away their time. Social events had been scarce in recent times for them all, something that had been missed from their home villages and advantage was taken of the opportunity to meet anew, or to renew recent meetings. It was said that at least three future marriages had their seeds set at that event.

It was a tired group who made their way across the river as stars began to rise above them. George had been hard at work changing the shafts of his cart to accommodate a single horse instead of two bullocks, and he was pleased that it seemed to make a comfortable ride for his family and friends. The new horse, which Sophia had named Star in honour of the white mark above his nose, was doing quite well considering training it to work as a pulling animal was only just beginning. So George sat at the reins with Sophia next to him, while Nancy balanced somewhat precariously behind them putting a hand out to steady the three cots which housed babies Ben, Little Ed and Freddie. Edmund trotted alongside on his new mount, Prince.

Sophia and Nancy exchanged an odd word, congratulating each other on the sewing of the christening gowns, mentioning the audacity of the younger people's dancing, recognising the good job the vicar had made of the service. All in all they were far too tired for much more than silence and the rocking to and fro as Star picked his way along the track which had now begun to form across the river. At the McKay's house Edmund dismounted and, after a tired good night to their friends, he and Nancy carried on up to their camp leading the horse and carrying a baby each. In the darkness Nancy wasn't sure if she carried Ben or Little Ed, but she didn't much care as long as they got home soon.

James Mackenzie had been watching the day's celebration from his favourite spot beneath a tree upon which yellow flowers had begun to appear. Insects swarmed to the nectar held inside each bloom and Friday irritably snapped at each one who dared to come near her face. James did not feel the need to join the party and was more than content to be a mere observer. He watched the service, hummed along to one of the hymns which had a familiar tune and then helped himself to a cold supper stored in his leather bag. Friday enjoyed the hard crusts of both cheese and bread and fell asleep next to her beloved master. James sat down next to her and propped himself against the tree. He was all set for a nap when two young girls, about fifteen or so, he suspected, came up to him and went to drag him down to join the dancing. "Nay, bonnie lasses, I doo na dance. Get on with yer," he said in his thick accent, scaring the girls into retreat, giggling about the mad stranger as they went back to join the revelry.

Solitude was no stranger to James Mackenzie. His whole life had been lived on the edge of the community, an observer rather than a participant in everyday life. His mother had given birth to him in a cold stone cottage aided only by an old woman who had taken pity on the poor, heavily pregnant girl begging for food that day at her door. She had offered the girl a hot supper and a bed for the night, little realising that she would have two guests by the morning. James' mother, Annie, ashamed at her present state which had been brought upon by the unwanted affections of the laird's son on the night before he left for India to rejoin his regiment, was only too glad to accept a stranger's shelter. In many ways luck had fallen her way that night as the owner of the house she had stumbled across was an able nurse and the birth of a strapping son was dealt with efficiently, if not with any great love.

Annie could neither read nor write so, when asked for details to enter on James' birth certificate she had muttered the surname of the supposed father as 'James McKenzie', but the English registrar had written, 'James Mackenzie (deceased)', out of kindness and to avoid the shame of illegitimacy. Her mark had been made by a cross without realising the subtle change of details.

Carrying her babe in arms, Annie had eventually been taken in as a housemaid at an estate on the Scottish borders where James grew up to be a strong, healthy child who spent his days exploring the world around him and learning as he went. More comfortable with adult company than children of his own age, his peers thought he was strange, even frightening and it was left to the estate manager to befriend this solitary boy. So James learned about husbandry, especially about sheep and the management of dogs. He grew to love dogs more than his fellow man and it became clear that he had a real talent for training the working collies who drove sheep from one farm to another, or from farm to market. Farmers were willing to pay for the services of a man who could take their large flocks of sheep from one place to another efficiently, and so James started to earn a good wage droving in and around the Scottish borders.

In the winter of 1843, when James was in his late teens, his mother, who had never been in good health, fell victim to the influenza epidemic which spread through the area like wildfire. Once he had put his mother in a grave at the local church and paid for an ornate headstone to be erected in due course, James had no reason to stay in the area. He took a commission to drive a large flock of sheep down the east coast of England into the flat lands of East Anglia. Having safely delivered his wards to Kings Lynn he found he could get work easily in this predominantly agricultural region. So many of the local agricultural labourers had seen the chance to make a fortune in the industrial cities making textiles, or milling grain. This left a shortage of people keen to work on the land. James could pick and choose his jobs and was well paid for his skills.

However, he soon became restless with the flat lands around him. He yearned for the hills of his youth and the fast flowing rivers where it took skill to catch a fish. He happened, one day, to be in the coastal port of Ipswich where the sailors who gathered in the taverns by the quay were full of tales of opportunity across the sea where rolling hills and big rivers made for good living and perhaps a chance to find gold in those rivers, or gemstones in the ground. A spark ignited in James' mind. Within a month he had travelled down the coast in a barge carrying bales of wool and bought himself a passage on a ship leaving the port of London and heading for Brisbane, Australia. On board were many like-minded young men who sought fame and fortune in this promised land. Most were of good character, like James, but a few were obvious rogues escaping their past by taking a trip half way around the globe. James had never lost his strong Scottish accent and, though he spoke English, he preferred to use his mother tongue of Gaelic. As a consequence he travelled on his own, in the main, with little interaction with his fellow pioneers. And that was just as he wanted it to be.

Arriving in the bustling port of Brisbane in June 1844 was an entirely new experience for James. A true frontier town. He found himself surrounded by all corners of humanity, all seeking a new life as an escape, or as a chance to make money. Or, in the case of many of his fellow travellers, a little bit of both! Most of them were set on heading straight for the goldfields but James, somewhat to his surprise, found himself amongst sheep again. A thriving industry in wool existed up in the hills and downs inland from Brisbane and James found work easily, bringing sheep in their hundreds from their hill station homes back to the port to be loaded on to ships for export to other coastal parts of Australia and to New Zealand. He had enough money to buy a good pair of dogs and soon held a reputation for his swift and efficient services as a drover. His leather purse filled fast with promissory notes for the bank of Brisbane and, as he lived frugally within his means, he became a reasonably wealthy man.

Having time to kill in Brisbane after one of his drives down from the hills, he headed for a quayside tavern to quench his thirst. In the gloomy interior he was surprised to hear his name called from across the room. "James Mackenzie, is that you?" asked the voice of a person he couldn't quite see, but who sounded familiar. The owner of the voice lifted the table candle to reveal Thomas Baylis, a fellow traveller from England. James could see his younger brother, Simon, at the table too.

"Join us, please, James," said Thomas, "We are discussing our next move." As James took his seat and ordered a beer Thomas saw his bulging leather pouch and wondered if James would be interested in joining them in their new venture. "We are thinking of heading to New Zealand where the climate is kinder and there's nothing that wriggles or bites, so they say," said Thomas. James smiled. He had had his fair share of snakes frightening the stock. He had even lost one of his precious dogs to a snake bite. So a land where they didn't exist sounded like a thing worth pursuing. He could take his young dog, Friday with him. She showed great promise and would love to be somewhere new.

So it came to be that James, Thomas and Simon boarded a ship leaving Moreton Bay for Bluff in November 1847 accompanied by their fellow adventurers, a thousand sheep, ten horses and a handful of dogs. The plan was that the sheep would be driven north with the use of horses and dogs. Along the way they would be sold in tens and twenties to the new pioneer families who had started to settle in the southern part of the island. Though Thomas had been determined to find ways to empty James' pouch of its coins, James had been frugal to the point of miserliness. Nevertheless, Thomas and Simon were glad to keep company with James, who had much more expertise in driving sheep through difficult terrain than either of the Baylis boys.

Expecting to find green swathes of grass and gentle hills like those back home, it had come as a shock to them all that they had to drive their flock through thick undergrowth and across wide rivers, which ran with deep trenches between slippery gravel banks. In many places it required trip after trip to bring a handful of sheep across a river each time, leaving half the dogs behind to keep the flock from splitting up. Progress had been painfully slow. And those who Thomas had hoped would be customers were reluctant to spend their limited resources on sheep that had lost weight and condition along their strenuous journey. The Baylis brothers began to be frustrated with a lack of income, all the while resenting James' apparently endless fortune. The brothers took off quite regularly to seek out other opportunities. James was never sorry to see them go. He was perfectly capable of doing the job alone and he suspected he would have more success in selling the stock without them. People seemed suspicious of those boys somehow. However, the brothers had a knack of making an appearance just as money was about to change hands, just to ensure they had their cut too.

By the time the three men reached the valley where George and Sophia had settled they had sold all their sheep. Friday had done well and was now the best working dog James had ever owned by far. Life was good for James and perhaps it was time for him to put down some roots. Looking back he had been on the move for a good part of his adult life. Time to settle down. He doubted that the Baylis boys would be around for long though. They had plans to explore territory inland where they believed there to be a chance for fame and fortune.

Sophia had written to her parents to tell them that they had a grandson. She tried hard to tell them a little bit about life, but it was hard to put it in terms they may understand. Things were so different from her childhood home. She mentioned the weather and some of the plants and trees and birds she had seen, but how much they could understand, she was not so sure. The envelope sealed with a red ribbon had been handed to Clara Nicol, who was to accompany her husband to Hawksbury on his regular meeting with the vicar there. Mrs Nicol deposited the letter at the Post Office and, some days later, it began its journey back to Scotland. News reached Mr and Mrs Morling in Scotland one autumn morning with the arrival of the post boy. It caused much excitement for the family and for Sophia's former neighbours.

The letter, apart from news of Freddie's safe arrival and some notes regarding flora and fauna, mentioned also the building of a church where the new community sang their hymns. Wanting to mark the arrival of his first grandson, Albert Morling hatched a plan. On his next trip to Inverness he put it into action.

Shortly after a Christmas celebrated in their new community with unaccompanied singing of carols, a horse and cart was heard approaching. Looking up from his preparation of next week's sermon Reverend Nicol could see that it was driven by the Hawksbury postmaster and the cart contained a large crate roped down at a precarious angle. Jumping down from his seat, the postmaster asked, "Can you direct me to the McKay household, please, Reverend?"

"I can indeed, but you will find it hard to deliver your parcel to their door as you will need to cross the river," replied Reverend Nicol, "I doubt your package will survive the journey."

"Can I leave it here then, sir? I need to get back to Hawksbury before dark," said the man.

A few other village folk had heard the commotion and had come out to see what had occurred. They now joined together to lift the heavy load onto the ground. In the middle of this hurly burly Sophia and Nancy appeared having set out together to deliver some fresh baked bread to the elderly Mrs Franks, who had taken a turn for the worse the day before.

"Sophia, this is for you, my dear," said the vicar, as the horse and cart trotted away leaving the package in the middle of the road.

"Whatever is it?" said Sophia as she and Nancy rushed across to read the words on the large label stuck to the outside of the packaging.

"To Mrs Sophia McKay, Hawksbury via Port Chalmers, New Zealand. To be shared with her local church as a blessing for our new grandson, Frederick," Nancy read it out loud.

It wasn't long before the wrappings were removed to reveal a wooden pedal organ. Carried carefully inside the church by four strong men and a gaggle of followers offering advice, it took no time at all to put it in place behind the wooden pulpit from which Reverend Nicol issued his sermons. It was a tight squeeze and the Reverend Nicol made a mental note that he may need to extend the building soon. Sophia was the only person able to play, so it was she who sat on the bench seat, though her feet could hardly reach the floor. She lifted the lid off the keys, stretched her feet out to pedal the foot paddles and began with a simple hymn tune. Music filled the small church and those people who had crowded in behind the organ were moved to silence. Wiping a tear from her eye, Clara Nicol declared it to be a miracle and a gift from God.

"Wasn't it a gift from your parents?" whispered Nancy to Sophia, and the pair fell into a fit of giggles which ended in tears of mirth as well as emotion.

The following Sunday service was the busiest Reverend Nicol had seen for a while. People came from near and far to hear the sound of the organ. Mr Morling had included several books of music, some more secular than others. So all the best singing hymns had been chosen in time for Sophia to try out beforehand, and she did a fine job at keeping to the music, though she was woefully out of practice.

From that day forward Sophia had a new routine to her week. On each Wednesday she would walk across the river carrying Freddie, meet up with Reverend Nicol to discuss music for the following Sunday service and then spend a happy hour rehearsing that music. People learned to listen out for music that morning and many a whistle or hum would be heard as they went about their Wednesday morning business.

Sophia's growing collie, Roy, often accompanied Sophia on the journey to organise her hymns each week. George got used to the idea that he had to manage his stock alone on that day of the week, and he was more than happy to let the young dog have a day off. Although Roy loved his mistress, it was not for that reason alone that he liked to join her. James had moved into a small bothy-sized cottage which he had built for himself on the edge of the village. It was a simple home unadorned by any ornament. But then James didn't spend much time at home, except perhaps to eat or sleep. Outside James' house, unless she was needed for work, Friday could usually be found laid out in the sun, or sniffing around the small garden, sometimes chewing a bone.

Roy liked Friday. In fact, he lusted after her. He was now a mature young dog and the urges he felt between his legs made him seek out female company. Friday, at the beginning, chased him away or bared her teeth at him. But she too was a young female dog and her desire to have pups overcame her initial reluctance. The two dogs could often be seen chasing each other, play fighting, or rolling around in the deep pool of water next to James' house. Sometimes their play turned into something more serious, so it was no surprise to James or Sophia that Friday was in pup.

The collie continued to visit Friday each week, but she became increasingly irritable as gestation took its course. He was confused by her behaviour and couldn't quite work out why she had changed so much. But one day he arrived ready to play as usual and found Friday lying on her side with five small pups suckling at her enlarged nipples. He was overcome with pride. "I did that," he thought to himself, "Aren't I clever?" Sophia laughed so much at his attempts to strut with pride that he took offence and headed off with his tail between his legs for a bath in the river on his own.

Sophia and Nancy were entranced with the puppies. They had written a list of names in advance. Seven names in case of seven pups, but in the end only five were required. Ruby and Saffy for the two girls, Silver, Gold and Blue for the boys. James was happy to indulge the two girls, but he made it clear that they would all need to earn their keep and that may involve them being sold to others. But they should choose a girl and a boy to keep. Not an easy decision for them to make as they were all, of course, just beautiful. But in the end they settled on the two pups who had inherited their father's third colouring. Ruby, the bigger and stronger of the girls, and Blue who seemed to have a superior presence not shared by his brothers.

So the puppies added to the growing numbers of people and animals in the village. People started referring to it as 'the village'. The tracks, which had, at first, been so hard to negotiate on foot, or with a cart, were being used so regularly that they now became dusty or muddy lanes, depending on the recent weather.

Old Mrs Franks had become the first mound in the churchyard and her widower moved in with their son and daughter-in-law. The house he left behind was now inhabited by the Baylis brothers, though word had it that Mr Franks had not received a brass farthing in rent so far. The Franks' family had started something of a village store where local folk could bring their produce and sell it directly to someone else or arrange a deal with Betsy Franks, who would take her small share and pass the rest back to the original owner. She and her new husband, Edgar, had met and fallen in love at the christening party. A wedding had been somewhat hastily arranged in time for Edgar's mother to attend, but it was obvious to all that the match had been made in heaven and the couple would do well for themselves. Edgar was a hard worker who fetched and carried whatever Betsy asked him to deal with. He fashioned a good strong cart with a large flat bed and was a regular traveller on the track to and from Hawksbury. The young ladies of the village benefitted from this regular service by catching a lift, though the ride was far from comfortable, or by receiving with great glee any magazine or newspaper that Edgar could acquire in the bigger village. The pictures of the latest fashions were endlessly discussed and often copied by clever seamstresses. Life in this small place was beginning to catch up with the rest of the World. Betsy kept meticulous records of each transaction and was an astute business woman with an eye for a fair price. The locals who supported her store were gaining income from her services and were happy to put it back into buying goods they could not grow or produce themselves.

Betsy's only regret was that she had not yet borne a child. Though she performed her duties as a wife on the regular basis demanded of her by Edgar, nothing seemed to come from these acts. "Perhaps I am just being impatient," she would say to herself as each month came and went without the prospect of pregnancy. In the meantime, she made do with the children of others, and she had taken a particular shine to Freddie, Ben and Little Ed. She had watched them move on from being carried everywhere, crawling at first so that their knees were thick with dust. She had seen them take their first teetering steps, often while grabbing at their mothers' skirts for balance.

The twins were slow in talking to others, although they seemed to have a few phrases they shared between themselves, so it was Freddie who spoke first. And it was Betsy who was first to recognise 'peez' and 'ankyou' from him, when prompted by his mother, after being given a sweet from the big glass jar full of stripy sweet delights.

It was Betsy who had the first idea about giving their community a name. It seemed to her, as she swept her front step to get rid of the dust yet again, that a place needed a name. If it was to grow into more than a collection of houses, it needed a name.

As each customer or seller came and went, she sowed the seed in their heads too. All of a sudden it became important to everyone to have a name. But what should they choose? Each person was keen to find a name that reminded them of home, but as there were folk from Scotland, Wales, East Anglia and the West Country, nobody could agree on a name that worked for all. No-one to this day can remember whose idea it was, but out of nowhere a name appeared that seemed to work for everyone. Reverend Nicol declared it an act of God that people should come to choose such a title for this place of fellowship, when in reality the arguments and counter-arguments had reached a point where most people were happy to accept whatever was chosen. In this way the small community on the southern bank of the river, spreading its fingers over the water and up into the narrow valley on the other side came to be called Marytown to match the dedication of St. Mary given to the small church at the heart of the place. As old Mr Franks put it, "There's a Mary in Scotland and in villages all over Wales and England, so nobody can be offended."

The McKays and the Lawtons had been doing well with their flocks of sheep. Their original flock of twenty sheep each, bought from the Baylis boys, had now grown to several hundred and there was pressure to spread out into new ground. George and Edmund were keen to explore around them, rather than uproot their young families and look for new land entirely. They both thought it would be possible to clear more ground around the village and beyond their valley homes. So they set out regularly on horseback to seek suitable land. George felt sure that, if he crossed the stream that ran past his and Edmund's homes, there would be land a-plenty. Although all he could see on the flat land across the water was covered in thick bushes and short, wind-blown trees, no doubt the sheep would clear their way through this and perhaps reach the higher ground beyond. As the ground rose the vegetation thinned and the slopes looked from a distance to be greener and more fertile.

Edmund had already found that, with a bit of rock clearing he could open up a wider track upstream from his home. Once he could get past that point there seemed to be a tract of land which looked promising. His plan was to burn the dense undergrowth to reveal grass which should thrive once it could see the sun. James had seen this method work well in his time on the flatter lands further south and was keen to help him out. One just had to be careful to control the burning and stop it tracking towards the house, so choosing a day when the wind was low, or at least blowing away from them, was key. It was a plan for spring as it was important to have access to water to dampen things down if necessary.

In the meantime, Edmund and James helped George with his plan. It meant creating a reliable track across the stream, which was achieved by moving some larger rocks on the water's edge and building a raised track with many loads of smaller stones. This job was best done in late Summer when the stream almost dried up entirely. Once they had made it easier to cross the stream George let his sheep go free on the other bank. James thought the sheep would keep close by as they would struggle to get through the shrubs and small trees. If the plan worked they would clear a small area by munching on the rich plants and slowly extend their range over time. There was, according to James, no need to fence them in. The natural rise of the land would limit their wandering and, with a couple of good dogs, George would be able to drive them back down when necessary.

During the winter months of June and July the sheep did exactly what James had predicted. George and Roy, with James and Friday, once her puppies had been weaned, only needed to cross the stream using their new track and the sheep were all nearby. They seemed happy to eat almost everything in their path and had already made significant progress in forming their own field. They looked well fed and content, though George suspected their fleeces would need some work to extract the twigs and leaves which lodged there when they brushed against the thicker undergrowth.

There was, however, a fundamental flaw in George's plan. Just as lambing season began the stream began to fill with water, despite there being very little rain of late. In fact the weather had been unseasonably warm. So where had all this water come from? It was Simon Baylis who worked it out. He and his brother had been further upstream than anyone else and knew that the hills beyond their valley were covered in snow for long periods of the year. The water, which churned with a milky consistency down past Edmund's house and then to George's place was, according to Simon, melted snow. It ran so fast that George and Sophia could hear rocks rolling along the riverbed at night. George became deeply concerned that his crossing would be washed away making it impossible to reach his ewes and lambs.

Once or twice he had taken to his horse and they had picked their way carefully through the rising water. The horse found it hard to get a good foothold on the slippery rocks and George was still not an assured rider and found the whole experience uncomfortable and frightening.

Towards the end of July the weather seemed to take a turn for the better and, presuming that all the snow that was going to melt had now done so, George could see the water level dropping. The days were lengthening slowly so George was able to cross the stream as soon as it was light and spend the day checking his pregnant ewes and seeking out new lambs. Roy happily splashed across the stream and shook from nose to tail on the far bank to remove the water from his coat. He loved scampering between the shrubs and finding sheep.

He knew which plants to avoid. The ones with the long spikes were the worst. It really hurt if he caught his paw on one of those low growing, spreading bushes. And there was a strappy grass-like plant with razor edges. He knew he had to avoid that, and he had the scars to prove it. George would follow him on horseback occasionally giving him a whistled instruction and by lunchtime Roy, George and the horse were panting and sweating and in need of a break.

But, on one particular day, George had found a bigger tree under which he and Roy could sit for their cold lunch. It was only when he sat down that George noticed the grey clouds gathering and the wind rising. By the time he had eaten his bread and cheese, saving the crusts for Roy, an odd drop of rain had started to fall. He shivered and said to his dog, "We'd better head for home, Roy, before the rain comes." Roy responded with a single bark before setting off in the wrong direction.

"Come back you stupid boy," called George, but to no avail. It was clear that Roy had picked up a scent. Pulling his oilskin coat around him and pushing his brimmed hat down firmly to avoid it flying away in the growing wind, George mounted his horse and followed the dog. His eyes stung with the rain which was now falling steadily. Star didn't like these conditions one bit. He tossed his head and shook it from side to side to get rid of the water which stopped him seeing where he was going. It was at the very last minute that George found Roy standing to attention indicating in the direction of a ewe who was obviously in distress. Jumping from his horse George could see a tail hanging down from the rear of the sheep as she stood panting with discomfort and the effort of a breech birth. "Bother," thought George. "This could take some time."

He set to with untying some ropes from his saddle and began the job of extracting each leg from the writhing ewe by attaching a rope and pulling as hard as he could. It was strenuous work for George and the ewe. Slowly, he was able to turn the lamb so that the top of his head could be seen. Although the poor ewe was exhausted she pushed and pushed. All of a sudden the awkward lamb slithered to the ground in a heap of blood and fluids. George rushed to clear his nose and mouth and rubbed the tiny body vigorously. Expecting that he may lose a lamb and a mother, it took several minutes before he heard a gasp and a plaintive bleating from the babe. Mother, who had lain exhausted and lifeless, rallied at the sound and turned around to begin the task of licking her new lamb. George stepped back and left them to it. He never ceased in his sense of wonder at new life starting and the bond between mother and child. It reminded him of Sophia and Freddie.

"Roy, we had better get home before dark, my boy," he had to shout over the storm, which seemed to have intensified in the last few minutes. He could hear thunder rumbling over the hills and the rain hit him like slaps in the face as it fell in sheets whipped sideways by the wind. He struggled to mount his horse, who by now was fair spooked by the weather. Darkness was only a half hour away and he cursed at not bringing a lantern, fully expecting to be home in daylight. They made slow progress. Even Roy had slowed to a crawl with muddy paws and sodden coat. He was a miserable dog and yearned for his warm, dry bed. But he wouldn't dream of leaving his master's side, of course.

As the sorry looking group approached the stream George heard the roaring of the water before he could see how fully it was running in the stream. Crossing was going to be difficult. He could just see a light in the house across the water, but the river had become a raging torrent. Should he find shelter on this bank? Or should he try to get home? George was tired and cold and hungry. He decided he needed to be home. He certainly didn't want Sophia to come looking for him in these conditions.

The crossing point that he had spent so much time building was nowhere to be seen. The lack of light made it hard to find a suitable place for his horse to enter the water. If he could find a safe step down the bank George thought they could wade through carefully. He called Roy to jump up on the saddle. Roy liked travelling this way normally, but he wasn't too sure about his slippery seat today. Nevertheless, he wasn't brave enough to swim across, so he would take up his seat, tummy across the saddle in front of his master.

George had been aware of lightning flashes behind him, followed a few seconds later by thunder, which seemed to rumble on for minutes at a time. Rain still fell and the wind blew in huge gusts. He thought he had found a good place. He clicked his teeth and pushed his heels in to make his ride step forward. Bravely the horse put his front feet down onto the slippery bank and prepared to take the next leap into the water. But just as he was about to jump a huge flash of lightning lit up the sky with a crackle, followed almost immediately by rolling thunder. It was just too much for the poor beast. He reared up with eyes rolling and nose snorting white flecks of saliva. With only his back legs for traction there was no way he could stay upright and he fell sideways into the raging torrent, tipping George and Roy in too.

What happened next could only be surmised by those who discovered George's body the following day, as neither Roy nor Star could recount the details. In something of a miracle, the horse had been washed down stream, legs thrashing beneath him. At a bend in the river he was thrown by the sheer force of the water against the huge branch of an overhanging tree that had broken off and lodged across the flow. By wriggling frantically Star eventually managed to put hooves to solid ground. With two enormous heaving motions he managed to work himself up onto the bank where he stood, chest heaving and water falling in sheets from his leathery sides.

In the meantime, Roy had spent far too long underwater but something within him made him fight for survival. He tried very hard to use his front legs to paddle, but it felt like a long time before his head broke the surface of the water and he was able to gulp mouthful after mouthful of clean air. This gave him extra strength to pull himself onto the bank in a muddy, wet heap. "Where's my master?" he said to himself. "I must find him."

He scampered up and down the bank seeking out his master, but in the dark it was so hard to see anything. His nose worked better than his eyes so it was the scent of George that drew him to a point on the bank where rocks, logs and debris had gathered, washed down by the torrent. Only one of George's arms was above water where he had attempted to grab hold of a huge tree trunk. His legs appeared to be trapped under the log keeping most of his body beneath the surface. He didn't appear to be moving so Roy decided that he must be having a sleep. He would be tired too. So Roy sat down and waited. It was now entirely dark, but thankfully the rain had eased a little. Roy was shivering with the cold and very, very hungry. Sometimes he slept a bit and once he took a short walk to relieve himself against a bush, but he was going to stay there until George woke up, even if it took all night.

THE WIDEAWAKE HAT

Chapter Five

Time to grieve

September - December 1852

The dust had begun to gather on the wooden organ in the tiny church. A spider's web stretched from the bench seat to the ivory stop labelled 'gravissima', an irony given the cause of the organ's lack of use. Two small boys ran into the church chasing each other and, through rays of sunshine, saw the dust collecting on the wooden seat. As Clara Nicol's youngest pupils in her recently opened village school, they had been learning to write their names on slate boards, so it was too much of a temptation for them both. 'Jack', one wrote carefully with his finger, then the taller boy inscribed, 'Frank'. His tongue followed the shape of the letters as he concentrated hard on spelling it correctly. Jack and Frank raced away out of the door leaving an echo of their laughter and a swirl of dust which sparkled in a ray of sun shining through the window.

Nobody in village of Marytown minded that they had been forced to sing their hymns without accompanying music for the last few months. They would all love to hear the sound of Sophia playing again, but they knew why she could not do so, and they nodded in acceptance to each other as they struggled to start a tune in time and key, or forgot how many verses there should be in each hymn.

The small group of people in the village had come together to deal with their first big crisis as a community. Of course, Nancy had been there first, comforting Sophia and helping out with all the practical things that Sophia's brain seemed incapable of understanding. Nancy had brushed her hair and chosen an outfit for the funeral, Nancy had tended to a distraught Freddie, Nancy had cooked food, which Sophia tried hard to eat despite it all tasting of nothing at all.

James and Edmund had helped to keep the farm going along with help from Roy, Friday and Meg's other grown up puppies, Roy's brothers and sisters. Even Ruby and Blue, who were barely 12 months old, were brought in to help guard the sheep, although they did a lot more playing than working, it had to be said.

Betsy Franks didn't mind at all that she got to be in charge of Freddie, Ben and Little Ed. The three boys were into everything and now they had found their feet they certainly used them as much as possible to wander far and wide. Betsy felt like a mother hen, constantly herding her brood back under her wings. But she was pleased to be able to be useful in this way.

Even the Baylis brothers had something they could do. It was they who set to with shovels to dig a hole not far from old Mrs Franks' grave. Six foot long and six foot deep. Though the two men rarely felt much emotion for a soul other than themselves, they had liked George and his family, so it was a sombre pair who toiled in silence in the hot spring sun to prepare George's final resting place.

Edgar Franks had fashioned George's coffin from the fine hard wood that he had been collecting to allow it to dry out. He had found some good straight pieces which made a fitting casket for his friend and, after Nancy and Clara Nicol had laid George out in his Sunday best, he was lifted gently by James and Edmund into place. Thankfully, they had been able to hide his horribly broken limbs from Sophia and his long hair lay discreetly over the gash which had probably knocked him unconscious and been the cause of his drowning. Sophia saw a peaceful man, as if asleep. Just like she had seen him every night since their marriage. Perhaps if she shook his shoulder, he would wake. She reached out, but Nancy quietly took her hand and squeezed it gently. No words needed to pass between them in their grief.

The next day the whole village gathered as the single bell was tolled slowly by old Mr Franks. Tears fell down his cheeks, partly for George but just as much for his dear, recently departed Isabella. At least she would have company in the churchyard now.

Reverend Nicol had to hold back the emotion himself to go through the sombre words of the burial service. He had liked George. He was a good, strong, dependable man and he had begun to build a prosperous family in this new land. What a waste of potential, and what a blow for Sophia! Job and Clara had talked late into the previous night about ways in which they could support Sophia and her poor wee son, Freddie. But just for now she must be allowed to grieve.

A single hymn was sung by the Welsh folk of the village. Spontaneously, they had broken into a favourite for them all. 'Amazing Grace', they sang in glorious harmony, 'How Sweet the Sound'.

Nancy wondered if she was the only person there who felt the irony in the line, 'Tis grace hath brought me safe thus far, and grace will lead me home'. Grace had obviously been missing on the night of the storm, then.

Sophia remembered little of the service and wandered through the day in oblivion. She walked, she talked, she even tried to sing a few words, but it was as if she was a machine doing each thing without conscious thought. Only later would she sob at the thought of her George being lowered into that deep, dark hole and covered up with soil and stones. Only in a few days time when she tried hard to explain to Freddie that his father would not be coming back did she really start to grieve properly. Then she would replay the whole dreadful night over in her mind. Again and again she would see the poor bedraggled horse standing in front of the house, reins broken and saddle slipping down the girth.

She had been worried about George all day. The crossing of the stream, especially on horseback, was something that concerned her greatly. George was not a good horseman, not like Edmund who seemed to find the horse an extension of his body and could manoeuvre swiftly through any terrain. Star put up with George being awkward in the saddle, but he could be a wilful animal, and she wondered if George could cope if the horse took fright.

As he left the house in first light, Sophia could see clouds building on the horizon. But George had said he would be home well before dark, so she went about her usual daily chores around the home without too many concerns. In the back of her mind she knew she would be pleased when she heard the jangle of Star's bridle, or Roy's happy bark signalling it was time to put food on the table for a tired husband. No such sound came though. Heavy rain began to fall while she and Freddie ate a cold luncheon. Later that afternoon the storm grew worse. One minute it was daytime, next it seemed to go ominously dark. She lit a lantern and, taking Freddie firmly by the hand, they both went out to the edge of the stream to see if they could see George approaching. There was nothing but darkness and perhaps the odd movement of small groups of sheep seeking shelter amongst the thick bushes.

The rain had become heavier still and Freddie was grizzling about being wet, so they both went back indoors to get dry. Sophia gave the pot a stir and hoped that George would be back before the lamb stew burned on the bottom. Time passed without a sound other than rain and wind and was that a distant rumble of thunder? In the end Freddie had his supper, with Sophia sharing just a few mouthfuls, and then he was put to bed. Boys of that age tend to wear themselves out all day, so he was fast asleep in moments clutching the ragged blanket that Aunty Nancy had made for him last Christmas.

She heard footsteps and rushed to the door. But it was James, a welcome sight of course, but not the one she was hoping for.

"Just called to see if you were all alright with this storm," said James as he stepped inside where he stood in a growing pool of water dripping from the oilskin cape he wore. "Is George home? I could'na see his horse."

Sophia explained to James that George had crossed the river for the day to check for newborn lambs. James, not wanting to alarm her, thought but did not say, "Well, he will be lucky to get back tonight then." Instead he said, "The river is quite high, but he should be fine on horseback and Roy can have a ride in the saddle. I'll take a lantern and go and wait by the crossing for him."

Standing alone beside the stream, which was now a raging torrent, James was filled with gloom. Lightning flashed and thunder followed almost on top. The water churned and debris was crashing downstream with the full force of water. As best as he could tell in the dark the crossing they had so carefully built had disappeared completely. "George is sensible enough to find shelter for the night," he thought to himself, "well, at least, let's hope so."

A particularly vicious flash of lightning, followed instantly by the roar of thunder, lit up the sky and James, now wet through entirely, turned reluctantly away from the river and back towards the warmth of Sophia's hearth. As he put his hand out to lift the latch and Sophia came to meet him with a look of expectation on her face, he heard the noise of an approaching horse behind him. Hoping it was George's he turned and swung the lantern round.

Indeed it was Star, but without his rider and looking somewhat the worse for wear. It was obvious that poor Star had been in the water and judging by the angle of the saddle and the broken reins, he had tipped his rider off somewhere along the line. It took a while to calm the poor creature, but James reassured him calmly while removing the horse's tack. Sophia found some dry sacking and they both rubbed his sides dry. This gentle act calmed the animal even more and slowly his snorting eased to a gentle breathe.

"Go indoors, my dear," ordered James, "I will try to cross this river and track them down. Din'na worry too much, lass."

Of course Sophia did worry indeed, for George and for James. And what had happened to Roy, who always came home first to see his mistress?

James too was now very worried. If George had fallen, was he hurt? He would be cold and wet, that was for sure. As the horse had approached from downstream, James headed that way, hoping to find a crossing point. He whistled to Roy, but there was no response, or at least he couldn't hear one against the howling wind. He began to worry for his own comfort. He was wet right down to his bones and shivering violently. His eyes were constantly streaming with water, and his hearing limited by having to push his hat down over his head to stop it blowing away. After an hour or so of no success he just had to turn back. He calculated it was only four hours until it would be light enough to see, so George would just have to wait. Sophia served a bowl of the overcooked stew to help warm James up. He was by that time so tired and hungry that it tasted like the best feast ever prepared. Neither he nor Sophia felt like sleep and Sophia was not keen to be alone. So rather than return to his bothy, James sat down at the small table across from Sophia. The odd whisper, so as not to wake Freddie, was all that they exchanged. They spent the remaining night in sombre silence.

James must have slept for a while because he came too with a start when the rain stopped. The wind had died down and there was a distant sound of birds chirruping with their dawn chorus. Freddie was already stirring and Sophia was preparing to get him up and dressed. Telling her to get breakfast ready for his return with George, he donned his damp coat and hat and set out to bring his friend home. A scene of utter chaos met him. Trees broken, debris strewn across the yard. The river still churned with dirty water and it took him several minutes to find a place where it would be possible to cross. Using his thick staff for balance, he slipped and slithered his way across wet rocks and took a final giant leap onto the far bank. Downstream he went again, but this time on the far bank. He fully expected Roy to come rushing up at any moment, but despite his whistling, no happy young dog appeared. However, after one whistle he thought he heard a distant bark.

"Why isn't that dog coming to his call?" he thought. His question was answered after the next bend in the river. There was Roy sitting to attention as if guarding his master. He knew he should have gone to James' whistle, but loyalty overcame obedience and here he was going to stay until George woke up.

It didn't take long for James to realise that George would be unlikely to wake up ever again. It did however take him a while to pull the poor battered body from the water. For a brief moment he rested with a hand out to comfort Roy, who was now ravenously hungry, shivering and frightened. The dog realised that something wasn't right, after all.

Knowing that it would be impossible for one man to carry George's body across the river, James left Roy to do one last bit of guarding beside his master and crossed the river by means of the branch that had saved the horse's life. He approached the village from another angle and raised the alarm. Reverend Nicol and his wife went straight to Sophia's house while Edgar Franks and James once more crossed the river with the necessary equipment to fashion a stretcher on which they carried George home. Roy trotted miserably alongside them all the way, hitching a ride on the makeshift bier over the water. His master felt cold, very cold.

Only much later that day, after Roy had been given some food and, much to his delight, a comfortable bed in front of the fire, did Nancy and Edmund hear the awful news. It was James who had taken the journey up the bank to tell them, and he knew it would hit them hard. The couple had immediately made arrangements to go to Sophia. Fortunately, by the time they arrived at their friends' house Betsy Franks was in full child-minding mode and Freddie, Ben and Little Ed were whisked away to be spoiled rotten for the rest of the day, and even overnight where they slept in a riotous pile of blankets on the Franks' large, red settee. They thought it was a great party, having no real understanding of the tragedy that had occurred.

In the days that followed the funeral things returned to normal around the village, but it was a much slower return for Sophia. The list of tasks seemed endless, each one a difficult chore. The hardest had been writing to George's parents in Scotland. The last letter sent overseas had been the joyous news of Freddie's arrival, but now the black edged envelope was delivered with trepidation by the post boy to the McKay's farmhouse. Nancy, who had some skill as an artist, had for the last year or so been practising her pencil drawing. She had drawn the puppies, the yard, her husband and, of course, the twins. As luck would have it she had drawn her friends' faces too. Sophia already wore a locket round her neck containing the tiniest image of George. It now became a very precious item, one which she held between her fingers many times a day. But the picture that had been drawn of the two of them sitting side by side on a bench outside their door, she carefully packaged up inside the letter and sent it to the McKays.

Sophia's tears had stained it on its dispatch and further tears dripped onto it when George's mother read the letter telling of her second son's demise. The drawing was framed and stood with the dignity of a black ribbon around it for months on the table in the drawing room. It was the only image they would ever have of their son.

Time, as they say, is a healer, though those who grieve find it the hardest thing when told that it is so. But time softened the blow. At first Sophia could not think of anything at all, but then her brain began to buzz with thoughts of the future without George. She would miss him as a soulmate, but in practical terms, what was she to do with herself and Freddie? In her darkest moments it seemed she had no choice but to pack her bags and return to her parents in Scotland. Perhaps Edmund would take over their animals and perhaps James could move into her house once he had found a wife.

In the end, the small community won the day. Discreetly, and without a need for reward, the people who shared the valley with Sophia supported her, cherished her and took on whatever they needed to do to encourage her to stay. They all knew that, should they be faced with similar disaster, it would be tempting to run for home, but they all loved and respected Sophia and wanted her to stay.

James and Edmund ran both farms over the long summer days. It meant double the workload, but they never complained. Betsy quietly took over some of the responsibility for Freddie's wellbeing. He put on weight, and who knew what damage it was doing to his teeth, but he enjoyed being spoilt with cakes and biscuits and sweets with his Aunty Betsy. When not spending time stuffing himself with sweet goodies, Freddie liked to be with James. Needing a father figure, though probably not aware of its lack, he had adopted James as his mentor and followed him everywhere. This was a new emotion for James. He had never really had a relationship with anyone, apart from his mother, perhaps. But he rather liked Freddie taking two small steps for every long stride of his own around the yard, even though it usually meant answering a hundred 'Why' or 'What if' questions. Fortunately Freddie didn't seem to notice if James made some of the answers up.

Betsy's reliable husband made sure repairs were done when necessary around the place. The storm had done a good deal of damage to Sophia's yard and things got tidied up quietly and efficiently. The crossing over the stream, which had been entirely washed away, was rebuilt and a wooden plank bridge was put in place, now made strong enough to withstand further storms and wide enough to be able to drive the sheep across. While rescuing logs and stones from downstream, Edgar had come across George's battered and sodden hat. He discreetly took it home where Betsy dried it out, mended the ripped material and put it safely away until such time as Freddie's head grew big enough to fit it.

It was harder to mend Sophia's soul. Clara Nicol did her best, spending hours just sitting in silence with Sophia. Sometimes sewing, sometimes reading, sometimes just plain sitting. Coaxing the odd anecdote of her short time together with George, Clara thought that reminiscing would be good for her. And so it proved to be. Sometimes Nancy joined them too. And who could be solemn in her presence? Her bubbly personality found it hard to be sombre, even though she had loved George as much as everyone else.

Over the weeks, then months, an occasional smile appeared on Sophia's face. Freddie needed his mother to carry on with life, and, though she found it hard, she willingly did all the things a mother needs to do to nurture a child of his age. Watching her son trying hard to keep up with James as he strode across the yard was something worth smiling about for sure. Sometimes there was regret for not having more than just a single son to remind her of George, but most of the time she was just happy when she saw something of him in Freddie. It was a great comfort to Sophia that over time he would grow to look very much like his father.

Her other great comfort was Roy. Somehow he seemed to make a connection to George, a bridge between his life and death. And Roy sensed a need to love Sophia back. He had winkled his way indoors and now slept in front of the fire each night, much to James' disgust. But his warmth comforted Sophia and his undying devotion was something she needed for now. If he wasn't inside in the warmth of the home, he could almost always be found lying in a sunny spot on, or near, his master's grave. There was still a smell of George in his doggy nose. "Perhaps one day he will come out of the hole they have put him in and whistle again for me to run," he thought to himself.

Toward the end of 1852, Freddie and all the children of the village were excited by the approaching Christmas festivities. Betsy Franks, not one to miss an opportunity to make some extra sales, had sourced some new stock to tempt the buyers including some of the new-fangled greetings cards which, somewhat incongruously, showed images of holly and snow and could be distributed as a gift to your new neighbours. It was hard to avoid the general feeling of excitement in Marytown and, despite the fact that summer days were hot and sunny, Christmas food would be, where possible, similar to the winter feasts of their homeland.

One morning Nancy arrived at Sophia's door to hear her gently humming a Christmas carol as she sat with her darning needles out to mend a tear in the knee of Freddie's breeches. She paused at the entrance thanking God for lifting her friend's spirits in this way.

Resting her hands on Sophia's shoulders, she asked gently, "Will you play this Christmas?"

"I think I could," replied Sophia after a moment's consideration. A corner had been turned. The friends embraced fondly and began the task of choosing appropriate carols for the Christmas Day service.

"The organ would need a duster taking to it," thought Clara Nicol, when she heard the good news.

Chapter Six

Broken bones

June 1853 - February 1854

By the nature of the geography of the place people rarely felt the need to pass by the McKay residence, unless they happened to be visiting the Lawtons. But in the months after George's death Sophia felt as though she lived in a very busy street indeed. Rarely a day went by when people did not call on her on some pretext of, 'just passing by'.

Of course, she knew this was just a way for the folk of Marytown to keep an eye on her. But she played the game, asking each one where they were going and would they like some refreshment along the way? She was grateful for their concern and pleased in a practical way to see people. Loneliness was the thing that hit her hardest. Freddie was with her constantly, but he could hardly be called a great conversationalist at the tender age of three. Her natural love of life and desire to share it with others had begun to return after that first Christmas, but she missed the companionship she had so cherished with George.

James, Nancy and Edmund were regular callers but, over time, began to realise they were not as much needed as they had been. Sophia told no-one of the tears she shed in the long dark evenings when she was truly alone. And even these began to ease in time. Sometimes she would worry about forgetting George. She had his tiny picture hanging round her neck but she was already beginning to lose the smell of him, the presence of him.

As time passed she learned to do some of the jobs around the farm. She was young and healthy and found that necessity was indeed the mother of invention. She could stand on an upturned barrel to reach things too high for her. She could push or roll things that George would have picked up and thrown over his shoulder with ease. And there was always James to come to her rescue, or Nancy and

Edmund to help out on the bigger issues concerning the stock, or planting crops or whatever was needed to run a small farm.

Freddie was as helpful as he could be for a small boy. If he wasn't sure how to help he would ask James' advice. "How do I catch a fish?" he would ask or, "How do I sharpen my knife?" James tried hard not to do the jobs for Freddie, but he was not a natural teacher and got impatient if Freddie failed at something to start with. "Och, give it here," he would say, rescuing whatever tool Freddie was trying to use. Freddie didn't mind at all. The job got done and he was quite happy if James did it for him.

Over time Sophia started to visit the village several times a week and her neighbours were pleased to see her out and about. A short trip to get some small provisions from Betsy Franks would take longer than expected as almost everyone paused to stoop down and talk to Freddie, or to chat with Sophia of this and that. Few people felt they should ask after Sophia's wellbeing directly, but they could sense her visits into the community to be a good sign of her strength returning. And Sundays were as they had always been. Morning service with Sophia playing the organ once again, followed by a good old catch up with community affairs. Nancy and Edmund, with the twins running ahead to jump over puddles, or run a noisy stick along the fence, would call in for Sophia and Freddie. In summer they could easily walk across the dry river bed on a track beaten into shape by many feet. But the autumn meant they took to using the horses. Only the very worst of the weather stopped them going. Sophia was understandably nervous of rivers running high.

James could not be persuaded to join them in church. He was happy to keep an eye on the stock of both farms. His God, if he claimed to have one, was of the hills and streams. His act of worship was to stand and admire a sunset, or to gaze into the starlit night and wonder at the scale of things.

Early one morning, in the spring of 1853, only months after George's death, Sophia was returning from collecting a creamy pail of milk from one of her precious cows when she saw a native woman walking by. Over the years since their arrival they had occasionally seen the native Maori people walking by, but had not had reason to talk to them. They seemed a quiet, shy people, not unfriendly, but not keen to interact with the pioneer folk. James had said they were used to passing this way in the spring on their way to the coast on the other side of the island where they collected precious stones. They would sometimes see them returning a few months later carrying woven sacks heavy with stones and the many carcasses of dead birds hung from poles carried by two people over their shoulders.

This morning the woman was alone and she paused when she realised that Sophia was looking at her. She was old and bent over with the aches and pains of age. She walked with a carved stick which, unbeknown to Sophia, told by its carvings the history of Atewhai's family as far back as could be remembered. She had left her husband back at their makeshift camp, downstream from Sophia's farm and had headed up river to seek an eel for the pot. Atewhai's mother, Hinewai, had taught her how to fish for the meaty eel and she practised her skills whenever they came to one of the rivers with braids in the spring. She and Hunu would follow the braids until they joined with each other and became a mere trickle in the hills beyond, though these days they would go only as far as they could manage. Perhaps this year, not very far at all. Hunu was getting sicker by the day and all the balms and mixtures she had tried had not made him any better.

Atewhai smiled toward Sophia and raised her stick in greeting. Sophia waved back cheerfully. Most of Sophia's neighbours were against any interaction with the native people, but Sophia and Nancy, along with some of the more enlightened woman in Marytown, felt they should share their corner of the earth with them.

"After all, mothers are mothers and children are children, wherever they come from," declared Nancy one day after church when the subject had been raised.

Sophia was just about to take a step towards the woman in order to speak to her when they heard the sharp crack of a branch splitting from a tree followed by an ear-splitting shriek from further up the valley. The sound was so filled with anguish that the two woman instinctively ran as fast as they could in the direction of the noise. They were met by Ben and Ed heading towards them, tears running down their cheeks. "We...were...climbing a tree and Freddie...fell," Ben took a breath between each word, "and his arm is all funny."

The two women, united in their concern, headed upstream. Sophia reached the young boy as he was trying to sit up, but finding it a hard task considering his obviously broken left arm. Shock had prevented him from crying so far, but he looked grey in the face with pain.

Blood oozed from a cut across his forehead, but Sophia could see that was just a scratch, it was the arm that concerned her most. "Gently, Freddie, sit up if you can, but keep that arm still," she said as she bent to help him up. She was glad to see that there were no bones protruding through her son's skin but her mind was already worrying about the long term effects. Freddie was far too young to be deformed.

Atewhai, not being able to move quite as fast, caught up with Sophia. Seeing the shape of Freddie's arm hanging at a strange angle, she knew immediately what to do. She turned this way and that to look for exactly the right tree. In a sheltered corner she found a small shrubby tree which, because it was springtime, was covered in yellow flowers. She knew that kowhai tree bark was a healer of broken bones, so she carefully peeled away a piece of it from the trunk, about the size of a small boy's arm from elbow to wrist.

Taking this to the water, she left it to soak thoroughly while she pulled a few good strong grass stems from their roots. Both these things she then took to the crouching mother and scared little boy. Freddie's eyes grew wide as the native woman came close and Sophia turned to see Atewhai reaching out with her homemade splint, a look of compassion on her face. Something about that look made Sophia step aside and let this strange old lady bend down and gently wrap it around Freddie's arm. With deft movements the whole thing was tied tight by straps of grass so quickly that Freddie hardly had time to realise what had happened. His arm hurt a lot, but the support around it eased the pain, and he was able to sit up at last.

"Let's get you home, young man," said Sophia as she scooped her son up, thanking God that he was still small enough for her to carry him. She turned to Atewhai to thank her, but the old lady was nowhere to be seen. It was as if she had just disappeared into the trees.

Freddie, although in pain, was quite enjoying the attention. He had been put to bed with his poorly arm resting gently on a pillow. He felt a bit sick but was being as brave as he could be. The twins had run home to get their mother so Nancy had arrived quickly and fussed over him too. Sophia explained how the splint had been applied and Nancy said she had seen the old woman on her way down the path. She seemed to be heading upstream, but they had merely nodded at each other as they passed.

James arrived too. He had seen broken bones before and knew that swift action to correct the deformity was important. He marvelled at the story of the Maori woman, although he had heard many stories on his travels of their ability to tend to wounds and injuries.

"You'll have a wee scar on that forehead," he said to Freddie, "but they say that the ladies like a mark of battles fought." Freddie put his good hand up to his head and found a finger tipped with his own blood.

Sophia patted the wound gently with a damp cloth. "Just a surface wound," she whispered. That's what her mother would have said when she or her sister or brothers had fallen over as children.

Shock set in overnight and Sophia woke to her son sobbing with the pain and barely conscious with delirium. But he settled once she lay beside him in his little box bed and carefully wrapped her arms around him. By morning he was tired, but Sophia stopped worrying too much when he demanded food.

She was preparing his favourite porridge when a faint swirl of cold air made her turn towards the door. Atewhai stood there holding out a small clay pot containing a green paste and a spoon made of bone. She said something that Sophia did not understand but it was obvious she wanted to go to Freddie. For reasons she couldn't discern, Sophia felt total trust in this woman she hardly knew and let her go to Freddie's bed. Atewhai hummed a soothing tune which calmed Freddie while she gently undid the bindings she had tied the day before and, using the spoon, spread the strange-smelling salve across the skin around the break. She then, firmly but carefully, re-attached the splint and gently placed Freddie's arm back on the blanket.

Freddie's arm tingled. It was a feeling he was to get used to as Atewhai visited every day to reapply the salve. Each day the tingling was followed by less pain. Young bones heal quickly, so it was not long before he could wiggle his fingers and not long before he asked to get up and play with his friends again. One morning Atewhai applied the salve, but not the splint. She made a fist with her own hand and Freddie realised he was supposed to do the same. It hurt and his fingers were stiff and didn't want to do what his head was telling them to do. But he tried hard and Atewhai nodded and smiled. He liked Atewhai, she was kind and gentle.

Sophia had prepared some oatcakes to give to Atewhai and she held them out to the woman as she went to leave. "Thank you," she said simply.

"He mahi pai noa iho," replied Atewhai and, "Tēnā rawa atu koe," as she took the basket of oatcakes.

Sophia realised that the last part of these words must be thanks, so she tried to make her mouth say, "Tēnā rawa atu koe," though it was hard to copy what the woman was saying.

Atewhai smiled widely and replied with a hesitant, "Thank you." Both woman laughed shyly at their attempts to communicate, but the ice had been broken.

Even though Freddie didn't need a nurse any more, Atewhai became a regular visitor to the McKay household. Sophia was shy of using another language, but Freddie had no such inhibitions and began to learn a few Maori words and phrases. Atewhai would often sing to him and Sophia tried to teach her a Scottish tune too. When words didn't seem to work there would be much hand waving and pointing and slowly, over several months, the women learned to speak to each other in a strange mixture of both languages. Freddie was very happy. He loved Atewhai and he was happy to see his mother happy too. Even Nancy began to join in. Atewhai had been a little reticent of Nancy's natural exuberance, but soon learned to laugh with her. It was a strange friendship between the three women, but it worked for them all. Sophia cooked broth for Hunu, and it seemed to make him feel better. Nancy provided fresh eggs and showed Atewhai how to cook them on a hot plate. And Atewhai showed the girls how to weave baskets and bowls from the reeds which grew by the river and how to pick certain leaves to help relieve stings or bruises or indigestion or headaches.

Rather surprisingly, Edmund was not in favour of the girls' new friend. He was suspicious of these native people and expected them to take advantage of the pioneers in some way.

"I don't trust them," he told James one day, "They are after our farms." James was not so sure. He couldn't see why an old couple would want to take on any more work than they had to. Atewhai just could not understand James. He spoke the same language as Sophia and Nancy, but with an accent which made his words seem thick and sticky to Atewhai's brain. She turned to Freddie for translation, which made them all laugh together. But somehow Freddie always knew what James had said. He was becoming fluent in all three dialects.

So daily life continued throughout the year. Summer came and went with Sophia and Nancy harvesting some of the new crops they had planted under Atewhai's instructions. Lambing had gone well and the elderly Maori couple came to love the delicate taste of tender lamb wrapped in leaves and cooked in their oven dug into the soil.

The leaves were turning a sumptuous yellow colour and seemed reluctant to leave the branches upon which they grew. It was unseasonably warm and the rains had been sufficient to make everything grow well this year. George had travelled half way around the world with five pots containing cedar trees seeded from the trees around his farm at home. They had only had time to plant one next to the house before his death and, in many ways, Sophia was glad that it was so. She still was not sure that this was her long term home, and she wanted to plant the trees where her family would see them for many generations to come. So three remained in their pots, the fourth she had planted with Freddie's help not far from George's grave. She hoped it would give shade and shelter to

George and the other members of the community who would join him in years to come. Both the trees that had been planted had thrived this summer and were now taller than Freddie, despite him growing too, like the tall grasses at the riverside, according to Atewhai.

One cold and frosty morning, towards the end of May, the post boy arrived at Betsy Franks with a satchel full of letters for the people of Marytown. Betsy, not wishing to be nosy, but keen to keep an eye on village affairs, flicked through the pile of envelopes. Two for the vicar, one probably from the mission people in London, one letter addressed in a spidery hand to the mother of Frank and Jack, perhaps from their grandmother back home. And, at the bottom of the heap, an envelope addressed to Mrs George McKay. Reading George's name made Betsy stop in her tracks. She still missed her good friend and felt sad for Sophia's fate as a widowed mother. As there were no customers about she thought she would walk over and visit Sophia, and, of course, have a cuddle from Freddie. She packed a few apples into her basket with the letter and set off across the dried up riverbed.

Sophia was hanging some washing on the line which stretched from the house to a nearby tree. She hummed a tune as she went about this everyday task and Betsy joined her in the chorus as she approached. Freddie ran across to hug his Aunty Betsy and to see if she had any sweet treats in her basket.

"Mama, there's a letter," he said, clutching the envelope from amongst the apples and waving it in the air. "Is it for us?" he asked Betsy who nodded. She had an ominous feeling that she was not the bearer of good news.

Sophia put her pegs down and took the envelope from Freddie. "It looks like my father's writing," she said, thinking that it was unusual for him to be the one to put pen to paper. Breaking the seal she opened the folded paper and began to read out loud, "Dear Sophia, I am sorry to tell you that your mother has succumbed at last to her continuing weaknesses…..", Sophia did not need to read any further. So her mother was gone too. It was hard to feel anything after the four years that had passed since last she had seen her parents, but grief strikes in many ways.

"Why don't you take those apples inside, my dear?" said Betsy to Freddie, handing him the basket, "And mind you don't eat them all." She then turned and took her good friend into her arms while Sophia sobbed and sobbed for the loss of her mother and her husband.

Had she read the remainder of the letter she would perhaps have not been so surprised when, a few weeks later, a horse and cart drew up outside the house and her brother, Samuel, and his new wife stepped down to greet her.

In truth, she would not have recognised him had it not been for his voice. He sounded just like his father as he jumped down from the cart and called, "Carrie, come and meet my big sister, Sophia." Angus had his mother's dark hair, so this had to be the fair-haired Samuel, the younger of her two brothers.

"Samuel?" she questioned. "What are you doing here? And who is this, Carrie, you say? Come on in, my dear, and take some refreshment, you must be exhausted. Come and meet my friend, Nancy and the boys."

Samuel was left alone in front of the house wondering, not for the first time, whether he had done the right thing. He had married his bride in something of a hurry in order for his mother to see him settled. She had died three days after the wedding. Father had not entirely approved of his marriage at the young age of nineteen, but he knew Carrie was the only one for him. And having travelled across the globe with her, he now knew he had made the right decision.

His father had quickly decided that there was nothing to keep him in Scotland once his wife was gone. His agent had spent years trying to encourage him back to Northern England where the music halls would offer him every opportunity, and that is what he had done in short order after the funeral. Samuel's sister, Emily, had been in service for a while and had no reason to come home now either. Samuel suspected she preferred the company of a handsome young footman. And Angus would take over the family house and continue to build up his blacksmith trade. So there was nothing for him at home.

Sophia's occasional letters home had, apart from George's death, painted a pretty picture of a land of opportunity. Carrie was a strong and resilient girl and relished the challenge Samuel had presented to her on their wedding night, so they had followed in the footsteps of his older sister. Father's letter would get there before them, so Sophia would have made arrangements for them to stay nearby. Or that was what he had expected. It seemed perhaps that she did not know they were coming at all.

Again the community rallied round making Samuel and Carrie welcome and finding them a place to stay for a while. The Baylis brothers had not been seen around the village for some time so the house they had been renting was available. It took a while to tidy it up and remove the empty bottles and unwashed clothing, but Betsy and Edgar were happy to help. In the meantime Samuel and Carrie slept on the same red settee that the boys had shared on the night after George's accident.

Sophia quickly recovered from the shock arrival and, having finally read the whole of her father's letter, now felt guilty that she had not prepared a welcome for them both. Carrie was a plain girl, so young, but cheerful and capable and keen to help out with chores around the place.

Samuel had worked for a while with his brother and had learned some skills as a blacksmith. The village needed his abilities with the growing number of horses being brought in and all kinds of metal objects needing to be fashioned or repaired. Finding a site for a forge was not easy though. Most of the flat land beside the main river was taken up by houses now and it was important for a forge to be near water. A temporary workshop was created alongside James' hut and Samuel started taking in business from his new friends and neighbours. But in his spare moments he wandered far and wide looking for the perfect spot to build a permanent home.

Sophia was as happy as she had been since George's death. Freddie was settled and contented and he had Ben and Little Ed as daily playmates. James, Edmund and Samuel were always there to help her if she needed them and Nancy and Betsy and now Carrie were constant companions. The four girls had much in common and never tired of each other's company.

So it was a rare day when she was alone for long, much to the annoyance of Thomas Baylis.

George's death had offered Thomas an opportunity that he was keen to exploit. Surely now Sophia would need a man. And a man like Thomas who, in his own opinion, was strong and handsome. He had always lusted after her, but George had got in the way, and now he was gone.

Even Thomas had a modicum of decency in him so he was willing to wait a short period to allow Sophia to mourn. But all through the summer, when not riding into the hills with his brother, he had watched from a distance for his chance. It had been hard to tear himself away to go towards the coast to meet up with one of the newest sheep farmers who had taken up residence on the flat plains nearer the sea. Simon had insisted that it was going to be a lucrative trip. He had met a young Maori man who had been taken on as a shepherd by the family that ran this sheep farm, and he had promised them that there was money to be made there.

On their return from an initial meeting down on the level lands to the east Thomas and Simon were alarmed to find that the house they had been living in had been taken over by Sophia's brother and wife. But Edgar had been firm with them both. They had paid no rent for the house for most of the time they had been there, so they had no right to claim it for their own. The Baylis boys had made themselves unpopular by taking advantage of the kindness of the Franks family so nobody else was willing to give them a home in the village. They had been forced to set up a temporary camp by the stream where they spent far too much time brooding over the unfairness of life in general. Simon was keen to move on, perhaps back to the level ground where some of the wealthiest farmers seemed to be setting themselves up. But Thomas would not think of leaving the village. He had Sophia to consider, after all.

Fate dealt him a fair hand one afternoon when he saw that Sophia was alone for a change. James and Friday had set out several days ago on an expedition to look for further land for the sheep, and Nancy and Edmund and the twins were in Hawksbury fetching supplies. Samuel and Carrie had, at the last minute, asked to go too. Now they had settled in there were things they needed which could only be found in Hawksbury and Samuel's work had provided them with a little spare money to spend. They would all be absent for some time. Edgar had agreed to keep an eye on the stock in between his other work. This was a time of year when sheep could look after themselves in the main. Lambing was over and it would be a month or two before shearing began in earnest.

Freddie was with Betsy Franks for the day. Sophia was relishing the quiet without Freddie getting under her feet. A rare day to get some serious housework done. She wanted to give the bedding a good airing, beat the dust from the rugs and generally settle the house down before the bad weather set in. As she went about her chores she hummed a tune to herself, pausing occasionally to listen to the late summer sounds of crickets and birds around her.

She was not at all pleased when she saw Thomas coming towards the house. "Where's that brother of his," she wondered to herself, "they are rarely apart?"

"Good day to you," said Thomas as he approached Sophia. She was holding a carpet beater made from woven branches and she looked ready enough to beat the man rather than her rugs. "I came to see if you needed help while the men are away."

"Good afternoon, Thomas, and thank you, but we are managing just fine for a day or two," replied Sophia. Sophia went to reach up to pull the largest of her rugs from the line on which it had been stretched to air. As she did so Thomas saw his chance.

"Here, let me help you with that," he offered. His arms being considerably longer than Sophia's he was able to reach above her and, just as she decided to pull away to leave him to the heavy job, he grasped her arms and swiftly turned her around to face him.

"What are you doing?" hissed Sophia. "The men will be back shortly."

"Oh, Sophia, I know you need me. I'm strong and healthy, and you must be missing the feel of a man," whispered Thomas, holding his face far too close to Sophia's flushed cheeks. She could smell beer on his breath and it made her retch.

He was strong and, though she tried hard, she could not release her arms from his grasp. Barely before she had time to realise what was happening she found herself being pushed through the door and towards the bed. The carpet beater had fallen to the ground and she wondered if she could reach it to beat her attacker around the head, but by this time he had pushed her backwards onto the bare mattress and he stood astride her.

She had no memory of doing so but James later told her that he could hear her screaming from Nancy and Edmund's house. Realising that something serious was happening he had run as fast as he could down the hill, stumbling over loose rocks and gaining balance by putting a hand out to small trees as he sped by. He had burst through the doorway and taken in immediately the scene inside. Grabbing Thomas by the scruff of his neck he dragged him away from the bed and turned him around to face the fist which struck his nose with considerable force. James had the big, strong hands of a Scottish warrior, while Thomas was wiry with a pointed, bony face. There was no doubt that James had broken Thomas' nose as blood poured freely from it. Thomas staggered backwards holding his shattered face and stumbling over the table. Pottery was sent crashing to the floor and the table tipped over under the force of the punch. With not a moment of sympathy, James again picked Thomas up by his collar and dragged him outside without ceremony. Thomas' breeches were down around his knees which didn't make it easy to take a dignified exit, and James had time to pick up the wooden pail of water and throw it over the man.

"That'll cool your ardour," said James between clenched teeth, "Now go on your way, and ne'er come here again, or you will have me to answer to." He raised the empty pail ready to beat Thomas around the ear again. James was a tall and broad shouldered man who towered over Thomas, who knew when he was beaten. He staggered off to his makeshift camp buttoning his trousers and shaking the blood from his face as he ran.

Next James turned towards the house. His instinct was to rush inside but, realising she may need some time to tidy herself up, he knocked gently on the door instead. "Sophia," he said gently. "Are you alright? Can I come in?"

"Please do come in," sobbed Sophia. James entered the house to see Sophia smoothing her dress down and then reaching up to tidy her hair. Furniture lay in disarray and the bed frame was broken in half. Not entirely sure how far things had been taken by Thomas he suddenly felt awkward in Sophia's presence. "Oh, if only Nancy were here," he thought to himself as he gingerly felt his knuckles where a bruise was beginning to appear.

"What can I do?" he asked as Sophia began picking things up from the floor.

"I don't know," replied Sophia. "I just don't know."

James righted the table, though he noted a leg would need mending, and as Sophia went to put the broken pottery down their hands touched. "Oh James," said Sophia, "please, would you hold me for a moment?"

She was shaking from sheer fright as he gently took her into his arms. It felt like being wrapped in a blanket, his arms were strong and his body comforting. Her sobbing slowed and she wriggled free from him, found a small handkerchief and wiped her eyes.

"I need a cup of tea," she said, trying hard to sound cheerful. "No harm done."

James wasn't sure if she meant that no harm had been done to the furniture or to herself. But those three words were a great relief for him. He certainly did not want to contemplate the consequences of an enforced liaison with that rogue.

Sophia found two mugs which had not been broken and as they sat over their hot drink she told him more of what had happened. It should have been embarrassing, but she felt fine sharing it with James. No harm had been done indeed, other than perhaps a dent in Sophia's pride, but who knew what may have happened if James had not been near enough to the house to hear her screams.

Sophia replaced the broken pottery at Betsy Franks' store under the pretext of having dropped the tray she was carrying by tripping over one of Freddie's toys. The furniture was put back in place and James mended both the bed frame and the table with fresh wood. Not a sign remained of the incident by the time Nancy and Edmund returned and no mention was made of it by Sophia nor James.

However, two things had changed that day. Thomas grew even more resentful of James. His broken nose added salt to his wounds as it set with a somewhat bizarre tilt to the right. Not only had he lost the prize of Sophia, but James had ruined his handsome features too. Nobody in the village questioned Thomas about his black eyes and bloody nose. It came as no surprise to anyone that he had been in a fight. Perhaps the only surprise was that it had not happened before. Simon, who had never really liked James, sympathised entirely with his brother and the two rogues spent many an hour brooding by their campfire while the need for revenge grew in their hearts.

And secondly, a relationship between Sophia and James began to grow. A very different relationship to the one she had enjoyed with George. Where George and Sophia had been equal partners in their pioneer adventure, Sophia now needed someone to comfort her, someone who could make the decisions for her. James was happy to fulfil this role. For the first time since his mother died he had a human being, rather than a dog, to love and cherish. Their friends,

Nancy and Edmund, were happy for them both and, though James was viewed by some as an outsider as he did not attend church or waste words in idle chatter, the community were glad for Sophia. In this land of pioneers a woman needed a man and a child needed a father.

The Wideawake Hat

Chapter Seven

Revenge

January - March 1855

The settlers between the sea and the hills were doing well for themselves. Sheep thrived in the rough ground and were efficient at clearing the undergrowth to allow themselves room to roam. In some areas controlled burning of the thickest bushes and grasses was an efficient tool. Although in the short term the ground was scorched and useless, the climate was such that new grass came through quickly and within a year sheep could be moved in. The land owners became rich on the sale of wool which would be sent back to England by ship to be turned into quality clothing, blankets and carpeting. The meat was eaten by the families of the area because, unlike pork or beef, it was hard to salt, cure or preserve lamb.

The biggest earners were the large tracts of land nearer to the coast where the grasslands could be established more easily and transporting wool in bales required less effort. The families who settled there grew rich, building substantial homes and employing large numbers of itinerate workers, including the native Maori men who were hard-working and reliable by nature.

One such sheep station was on the level ground beside the same river that supported the community of Marytown. But here, near the coast, it was wide and provided good irrigation to the fields along the banks. Two young Maori men worked with the sheep here. Taiko's family could normally be found roaming the high country seeking food and occasionally travelling over the mountains to search for the precious green stones from which tools and adornments were made. But Taiko liked the idea of having money to buy things for himself. Why should he walk for days to find nothing but a few birds, or a fish to eat when he could be fed by the farm owner's wife and buy items which he thought were luxuries from the stores in Hawksbury? He had a natural talent for working with animals and the sheep that his masters had brought across the seas were docile creatures who followed each other wherever he wanted them to go. He had persuaded his brother, Aperahama to approach the owner for a job and Mr Rhodes had agreed that he could assist Taiko on one condition. The Maori words were hard for European folk to pronounce, so a new name would be required for Taiko's brother. This was not the first time Mr Rhodes had felt the need to rename a worker. In fact, it was the seventeenth time, so Aperahama became Seventeen by name.

At the end of each summer a large mob of sheep would be selected for sale and separated from the main flock and, in early 1855, the Baylis brothers had come across Taiko and Seventeen as they worked with their boss, Mr Sidebottom, to cut this flock from the main group in readiness for their journey inland to be sold in tens and twenties to the communities which had sprung up further up the valley. Neither Taiko nor Seventeen could read, but they had been taught enough English words to get by and the ability to count their numbers and tally up sales along the route.

Mr Sidebottom was a firm man who stood no nonsense from his workers. He would have preferred to employ good English boys to do this job, but Maori labour was cheap and they had so far proved to be reliable men, if a little idle unless given direction at all times. He was a man of few words who preferred to use the whip rather than his tongue to admonish transgressions. Taiko and Seventeen were frightened of their immediate boss and did everything they could to avoid his wrath.

Thomas and Simon had enjoyed a successful journey to Lyttleton and had spent their Christmas celebrating in the way they knew best. Boxing day was required to sleep off their hangovers before they started back to Marytown. Thomas thought they had been away enough time now that any memories of his fight with James would have faded, just like the bruises on his face. And, with a boost to his ego, it seemed the slight disfigurement of his nose just made him more attractive to the street girls from whom he had taken his pleasure. One of these girls, he couldn't remember her name, had even run her finger down the broken line of his nose with a sigh of pure pleasure. In Thomas' vain opinion he was already a handsome man and perhaps James had inadvertently contributed to increasing his good looks.

Their money pouches were full after finding work moving sheep around the flat lands beyond this port. It seemed to them that sheep could be counted in hundreds of thousands. They streamed down the gangplanks of the ships from Australian ports and into the holding pens built on the outskirts of town before being sold to the pioneer station owners of the Canterbury Plains. As experienced handlers they were in demand and could pick and choose the most lucrative jobs without spending too much time in any one place.

It was as they crossed the wide river, before heading west towards their old home, that they had come across the native shepherd boys. Taiko and Seventeen were happy to talk to the brothers and told them all about the boss' plan to drive one thousand sheep up into the valleys for sale. They shared a campsite overnight and once Simon and Thomas had taken their leave from the campfire and hunkered down in their tent, it was Simon, being more a thinker than a man of action, who had come up with the idea of using the sheep as a means of exacting revenge upon James. The brothers had seen how the farmers further north had expanded their sheep numbers, which inevitably led to a need for more land and they knew that James and the other men from Marytown had already been looking further inland where it was said the grazing was good.

It was indeed true that James and Edmund had a desire to expand. With James' help, Sophia had kept the farm going since George's death and now her stock and that of Edmund and Nancy were in desperate need of more room. There was a danger that their land would become barren with the pounding of hooves and the endless munching of many mouths. Edmund and James had come up with a solution, but there was something that James needed to deal with first.

Sophia had found life hard since George's death. It was physically demanding and mentally confounding and, though she had mastered much of the background work with help from Edmund and Nancy, she could not have kept the farm going without James about the place each day. In many ways he had stepped into George's boots, the only difference being his tactful retreat each evening to his own small cottage across the stream. To begin with she had wondered whether she should give up and perhaps move Freddie and herself into a cottage in the village and take up dressmaking and mending. But for George's sake she carried on carrying, fetching, even digging and handling the stock. Slowly James had taken over those heavy tasks, stepping carefully so as not to impose on Sophia. It was hard not to be part of the family though. Freddie made sure that he was invited for a cold lunch and a hot supper every day, and Freddie followed James around each day helping out when he could, though he was only a very small boy.

As time passed and Sophia and James spent more time together their regard for each other had blossomed into something more like husband and wife. There was only one part of a marriage lacking and James slowly began to realise that he wanted that part of the relationship too.

More than two years had passed since George's death and he considered that a suitable period of time for others to judge his proposal as not being somewhat forward. But not being a man of the church he was not sure what to do next. Fortunately, Samuel had come to his aid one day while they were crossing the stream to check on the sheep by asking bluntly, "Are you going to make an honest woman of my sister, James? It is about time, you know."

Words had never come easily to James and he mumbled a response from which Samuel only discerned the word, 'church'.

"Don't worry about that, my friend," Samuel had replied clapping James on the shoulder, "We can talk to the minister together. Let's go and see him this afternoon."

Reverend Nicol was surprised to see James Mackenzie in church that afternoon with Samuel Morling. "Good afternoon, Samuel, and welcome Mr Mackenzie. We are pleased to see you here." Again James found it hard to work out the words in his head and make them come out of his mouth, so it was Samuel who had explained James' dilemma.

"I hear rumour that it will soon become a more complicated process to marry in this land as laws are being brought in to ensure that both parties are of the church and the union is acceptable to the community," said Reverend Nicol.

He noted that James looked concerned at such bureaucracy. "But at this time, we have no need of that. We just need to set a date, turn up at the altar with two witnesses and myself to say the appropriate words, and the deed is done. Though I rather think Sophia will want a bit more religion in the service than you would like, James," said Reverend Nicol, with a twinkle in his eye. He liked James and he was pleased to hear that Sophia would have someone to share her life with again, and Freddie would have a father figure.

As a proposal still needed to be made to Sophia, a date had been pencilled in for the following Friday, subject to her agreement. It would be a small affair befitting a second marriage. Samuel and Carrie, Nancy and Edmund, Betsy and Edgar Franks and the Reverend Nicol performing the service with his wife in attendance too. But first the most important guest needed to be invited.

Sophia would look back on that evening many times over the next few years. She had been busy all day bottling the last of the fruit harvest. It was a messy job at the best of times and she felt like Freddie had been under her feet all day because of the misty rain which had soaked everything outside since daybreak. She had sent him packing after their lunch for some fresh air, but, on his return, his muddy footprints and dripping clothes just made her more irritable. As the shadows lengthened the sun shone at last from behind grey clouds, so she was able to send him out once more to play with Roy and the other dogs while she prepared supper. She wondered where James and Samuel had got to and hoped the supper would not burn on the stove if they were late.

James arrived back alone from the village with a handful of white flowers he had picked on the riverbank near his little cottage. He did not tell Sophia that he had come from the church, nor that he had paused in the churchyard to seek blessing from George's grave for his mission tonight.

Though Sophia, like any woman, was happy to receive the flowers, she was faintly irritated with the gift. All her pots had been used for the day's preserving and barely a surface was clear for want of apple peelings, which needed to go to the pigs before dark. She sought out a cracked pottery jug and went to fill it with water. Coming back inside she found James standing silently in front of her holding something in his hands. Over the months they had found it easy to talk of many things but it seemed he had lost his tongue tonight.

"What is the matter, James?" she asked.

"My dear, I have a question to ask you." He opened his hands to show a small plain gold ring to her.

"This was my mother's ring and I want you to have it. I want you to be my wife," he said hesitantly, "if you will have me, that is?" he added sheepishly.

There was a moment when everything stood still. In that moment Sophia thought of George and Freddie. She thought of the strength of James and his care for her since George's death. She thought of the love that had grown in her for this gentle giant of a man, and she thought of the possibilities that life may throw at her if she shared it with this man.

"I will have you, James, I would very much like to be your wife," she whispered. Once again he took her in his arms, but not before he slipped the ring over her finger to see if it fitted. It did indeed fit perfectly, but she would not wear it until the ceremony next week.

Nancy, of course, had been delighted. She had expected it to happen soon enough and she had great respect for James leaving an appropriate time for Sophia to grieve for George and "not look as though she was jumping into bed too quickly," as Nancy had put it to Edmund in her usual down-to-earth manner.

James had, for the benefit of his new wife, tolerated the religious words which surrounded the legal phrases of the marriage ceremony. Anything that pleased Sophia made him happy too, so he was content to let Reverend Nicol speak whatever words he wanted to speak, just as long as Sophia said, "I will." She looked radiant in her Sunday best dress with new ribbons tied in her hair. These had been a gift from Betsy Franks, who dabbed at the corner of an eye with a small lace handkerchief as James was invited to kiss his new bride. Of course it was impossible to keep such an event secret in a small community and Mr and Mrs Mackenzie were greeted by a throng of neighbours and friends as they emerged from the church into the sunshine of the early February day. Most people were pleased to see Sophia married again. They knew how hard it could be to run a home and farm without a man and, being practical folk, they felt it was time for her to marry again so that she could bear more children. Freddie needed a brother or sister soon.

Sophia's friend, Nancy and sister-in-law, Carrie, had prepared a small feast to celebrate the wedding. All the food had been brought on platters to Sophia's house where they were able to eat at a long wooden table under the trees. After eating and drinking, the girls remained at the table while the men wandered across the stream to lean on a gate and talk once more of their plans for the future.

They returned to find the girls laughing and chattering as they tidied the table away and washed the pots and pans. Nancy was pregnant again and she told the other girls she thought it could be twins again as she seemed to be growing a huge belly. "And you will be next, Sophia," Nancy had said. Sophia looked slightly embarrassed, especially as Betsy Franks was there too, looking wistfully into the distance, perhaps wishing that she was the one who was bearing a child at last.

The party broke up early to allow James and Sophia some time alone and, once it was dark, they had moved inside to sit at the small table and talk about the day. Long into the night they talked and planned their future together. Once Freddie had fallen asleep Sophia moved closer to James and it was not long before she led him to the bed she had once shared with George.

"Are you ready for this?" asked James. "We can wait, you know, there's no need to rush?"

"I want to, my dear, I have wanted to do this for a long while now," she replied as she pulled his strong body towards her and he took her gently and laid her down to start the pleasant task of consummating his marriage.

Life continued for Sophia and James and their friends and neighbours as summer came to an end. Though Sophia's name had changed, nothing much else had needed to be altered. James' cottage was rented out to the young man who had joined the community to assist Reverend Nicol as curate for a while. It was basic, to say the least, but it allowed the earnest young man to study his bible without distraction. It reminded him of his time at the seminary. James had asked Samuel and Carrie if they wanted to take the house rather than pay rent to the Franks. But Samuel had plans to move into farming and wanted something bigger for them both and the children they hoped would come along quite soon.

James and Edmund had some big ideas to develop their farms. They had heard stories of the land beyond their homes, over the hills and onto the plains beyond. The river that trickled down past their houses for most of the year had formed a narrow gorge through the hills as it fought its way to the sea. The native people had walked that way many times and spoke of the fruitful lands beyond, but driving sheep and bullock carts through the narrow pass would not be easy. Leaving the girls to look after their children and their stock, James and Edmund had set off to find the easiest route and to find a place beyond where homes could be set up.

They had returned triumphantly, full of their plans and excited by this new venture. The journey, they had decided, would be easier by cart by climbing up the river bed. So this set a time constraint for them all. The river was at its driest at the end of the summer, but it would be best not to leave it too late, as they had learned that heavy showers could bring a sudden build up in water levels. James reckoned the beginning of March would be perfect.

The men had spent a considerable amount of time pacing out the boundaries of the land they needed to claim. It required a map be drawn. James was not a man of letters, so it was Edmund who had taken paper and pen and had drawn two copies of a rudimentary map of the route they needed to take over the pass and the two square areas either side of the stream they found flowing downhill and onto the flat plain beyond. They had found plenty of stones lying around and had built cairns at each corner. They had felt very much like pioneers in a new land. The other side of the hill did indeed seem promising. They had been observed from the hill by Atewhai and Hunu, who had spent the summer in a small hut under a tree looking out across the basin towards the mountains, which remained covered in snow all summer.

Once they returned with all the news, they had decided not to share their ideas with the rest of the community for now, although Samuel and Carrie had already been consulted. They had agreed to take over the farm for the season and were happy to be moving into the house for a while. Samuel had picked the perfect spot beside the stream to set up his forge. There was less work for a blacksmith in the winter as people tended not to travel so much or have need of repairs, so he and Carrie could easily manage the farm too. Sophia was particularly keen to move on now. So much reminded her of George and, now that she had the company of James, she wanted to escape those memories. Freddie had all but forgotten his father and was happy to accept James as an able replacement. Not that she wanted to forget her first love, rather that she felt it was now time to move on.

Nancy had a natural desire for new adventures and a sunny disposition that assumed that anything new was going to be better, so she was happy to join the adventure too. She rather liked the idea of her boys growing up in a wide and open place where they could roam as freely as the sheep. And she was anxious to make the move sooner rather than later as another baby, or maybe babies again, were due to arrive quite soon now.

So towards the end of February final plans were made over supper. Reluctantly, Nancy had been persuaded to stay behind until after the birth. Edmund, of course, would stay with her so it was just James, Sophia and Freddie who would set off to begin the journey. It would be a temporary move so that, if it all went wrong, they could return to their homes without loss at the end of the winter. It would mean sleeping under canvas again and travelling in a cart, but they had done that before and were not concerned by it. All that remained for the four young pioneers to do was to acquire some extra stock.

Meanwhile, Taiko and Seventeen had been travelling for two days towards Marytown with their flock of about a thousand sheep. The native shepherd boys were finding it hard to keep their flock together. They had no skill in controlling the dogs so the task of rounding them up into a group that would move forward as one was a slow one. Mr Sidebottom would not be pleased at their lack of progress.

Thomas and Simon Baylis had put together a plan to make money with the arrival of the huge mob of sheep while plotting revenge upon James Mackenzie. They were very pleased with themselves. They had done business with the native folk before and generally found them to be gullible and easily misled. The trade usually ended in profit for the Baylis brothers, not always to the benefit of the other party. But it was not just for the profit of this deal that they had come to call on the shepherds that day.

So when Thomas and Simon rode up to Taiko and Seventeen's camp that morning the shepherds were more than happy to accept their offer. The brothers said they were asking on behalf of one of the farmers from Marytown who was keen to buy more sheep to take over the hills and onto the fertile plains beyond. He would take all they had at a good price.

Thomas and Simon explained that they did not have enough money to pay for the deal at this stage but their friend, who was travelling back from exploring the land beyond the hills, would pay his dues as soon as he returned. In the meantime, the brothers were happy to pay them a small retainer which they could keep as their own, perhaps without the need to tell their boss about it. Taiko and Seventeen discussed the deal between themselves.

"It is a good price for the master and we get something too," reasoned Taiko, "and it would save us driving these creatures any further up the river."

"Yes, I agree," said Seventeen, "we would be stupid to do anything else. We can camp here for a few days and wait for the boss to turn up. By then this buyer will have brought us the money, no doubt."

So the Baylis boys handed over their meagre payment and put their dogs to work to drive the sheep across the river and onto a piece of land that bordered James and Sophia's residence. The two Maori men settled down in the comfort of their tent where they slept soundly without interruption from the noisy creatures moving around them all night long.

The next day James was surprised to hear the sound of sheep. Not that it was an unusual noise to him, but this was the sound of many sheep. He could see dust rising downstream from where he had been wandering in order to find any stock that had avoided the shearer. Friday stopped to sniff the air as well. She was all set to round them up, however many there were she could cope, although her paws were tired from the long journey from which she and her master had recently returned.

James and Friday were just about to head home when Simon Baylis appeared. Friday gave a low growl. She didn't like those two men at all. "What does he want?" said James to Friday. "We don't see much of the Baylis brothers these days, do we girl, thank goodness?"

"Good afternoon to you, James," said Simon. "I am glad I came upon you today."

James thought to himself that Simon had probably not just come upon him today as neither of the brothers did anything without a reason. But at least it was Simon who stood there. He would have been tempted to land another blow with his fists if Thomas had been the one in front of him.

Simon went on to tell James about the sheep they had purchased from the two shepherds. He explained that the native shepherds had struggled to herd the sheep upstream and had been happy to sell the entire flock to the Baylis brothers, though they had driven a hard bargain as the sheep were in good condition. However, neither Thomas nor Simon had enough land on which to keep the sheep and were hoping to sell them, in part, or as a whole, to local folk. Was James interested in purchasing any, perhaps?

Indeed James was interested in buying the lot. It would answer their prayers to acquire a new flock for their journey. But he was not prepared to settle on a price without seeing the condition of the stock. Perhaps Simon would ensure he could view them without his brother being present, as Simon was surely aware of their grievance with each other?

He followed Simon downhill leaving him time to go ahead and warn Thomas to leave their camp. Thomas was happy to retreat, he had no desire to face his antagonist at this stage and it suited his plans well for Simon to seal the deal while he put the next stage into action.

And so the deal was indeed done at a price which suited them both. The sheep were in good condition after a summer on lush green pasture and they soon became the property of James and Edmund while Simon held a bulging pouch of coins, which amounted to a bonus for them both for the deed yet to be done. Everyone was happy.

Meanwhile, Mr Sidebottom was checking up on his shepherds and the flock in their care. He was somewhat confused by the lack of sheep surrounding the camp of his two young employees. He was not at all pleased to find the boys sleeping in their tent while the sun was high in the sky.

"Wake up, you two idiots. Where are the sheep?" he said as he kicked the blankets off the two boys.

"No problem, boss, we've driven a good deal for the lot. You should be pleased with us, we need a pay rise, sir," said Taiko as he scrambled to his feet.

"I'll be the judge of that," replied their boss tersely. "Tell me what you have done."

So they explained that they had sold the whole mob to a rich man from up the river. He would be coming to pay any time now and the price was as good as anything they could have set by selling them in small lots.

"But you have no sheep and no money as yet," hissed Mr Sidebottom, "and you call that a good deal?"

He reached for his horsewhip with the intention of beating his two young employees for their foolishness. But before he could make contact with any skin not covered by clothing, he heard the sound of a rider approaching. It was Thomas Baylis. The two shepherds relaxed a little as they fully expected the visitor to have brought the money.

Thomas pulled his horse to a stop and dismounted swiftly. He had a face like thunder and with annoyance he spat, "That scoundrel James Mackenzie has taken the sheep. He drove them on up hill at night while we slept. He has no intention to pay, I am sure. Will you come with me to track him down and claim the sheep back?"

Mr Sidebottom listened with annoyance to this outburst. He could not believe that his employees had been so gullible. And what part had this man played in the deal? He had not taken to the Baylis boys on their first meeting, and he certainly didn't trust Thomas now. But what could he do but send the three of them off to track this freebooter, James Mackenzie down? Surely they could travel faster than a man with a thousand sheep. He would go himself, but he knew there was a good roast in the oven back at home and he was too old to sleep rough these days. "Let them make amends by getting the sheep back," he thought to himself. At that he mounted his horse and set off back towards his plate of roast lamb.

"Come boys, I will ride on ahead and seek more help to track this rogue down," said Thomas as he mounted his horse. He knew that the Maori people preferred to walk than to get on the back of a horse, so he guessed they would take their time to join the search.

"Follow me as soon as you can," he shouted, as he galloped away.

Taiko and Seventeen looked at each other. Surely it was not that urgent. It would be easy to find a thousand sheep. They set about breaking camp, but not before they had eaten and drunk a late breakfast. Sometime later that afternoon they set out with the intention of reaching the place they called Marytown where they knew they could find a good feed and a bed for the night with Taiko's Aunty Atewhai.

Thomas and Simon were pleased with themselves. They could just leave events to take their course now. Revenge felt sweet indeed.

Not only had they painted their arch enemy as a sheep rustler and freebooter, but they were in profit on the deal. The small amount they had paid to the shepherds was but a tiny part of the money Simon had taken from James in payment for the sheep. And nobody would be any the wiser of their involvement in James' demise. Once he was removed from the scene in chains Thomas could make another move towards Sophia.

In the end James and Sophia, with Freddie and the dogs, started the journey almost immediately. That same evening James told them all about the sheep he had bought, and though everyone was suspicious of any deal done with the Baylis brothers, they could see no issues in this case. James thought the sheep were in good condition considering the price he had paid. But they were suffering from being crowded into a small space at the moment with little to eat, so James was keen to start as soon as he could. Sophia and Nancy had been busy for days packing the cart with all that they may require so it would not take much effort to get ready. They agreed to get going at first light. James had been into the village to let Samuel know he would need to start his farming duties the next day. And Nancy and Edmund would be out and about early so that they could make their farewells as the sheep were driven ahead of the cart past their riverside home.

The Wideawake Hat

Chapter Eight

Journeys

4th-5th March 1855

It was hard going. Once Sophia and James had said their farewells to the Lawtons they headed up the dry bed of the river with the cart rocking from side to side as they negotiated dips in the stony ground. Many times James had to halt the horse and jump down with a small shovel to dig the stones out from around one of the wheels. Sophia then took the reins and pushed the horse on as fast as she could.

Their journey was a stop and start affair, but the sheep made much better progress. They could see them streaming ahead constrained by the banks of the river and kept moving by Friday and Roy. The dogs needed no instructions apart from the odd whistle or click of his fingers from James.

James and Edmund had done a good job of clearing a route for the cart. Sophia could see where the men had rolled big stones to the banks to clear a pathway uphill. In places, where a waterfall had cut out a ledge too deep for the cart to climb over it, the men had flattened the ground out with spades. If necessary, they had lain tree trunks across the track to form several shallow steps for the cartwheels to cross more easily.

By the time they stopped for a cold lunch the sheep had almost reached the summit of the pass. James knew what lay beyond, but he wanted it to be a special moment for Sophia, so he suggested stopping at a flat area beside the stream where it was easy to pull the cart out. Sophia could see signs of a cooking fire, perhaps it was a place where Atewhai had stayed with her husband, Hunu. Or perhaps James and Edmund had boiled some water here one day to brew their tea. Freddie was keen to stretch his legs after a morning sitting still on the wooden bench seat next to his mother. So while Sophia unwrapped a fresh loaf from the cloth she had wrapped it in and found some slices from her latest cured ham, Freddie and James went on uphill to help the dogs push the flock over the top of the pass.

Sophia watched her tall husband and small son with love and pride in her heart. They were so happy in each other's company. Freddie chattering about all sorts of things while James answered with a single word. But Freddie seemed happy with that arrangement. James took big strides, but it didn't seem to worry Freddie that he had to skip along beside his adopted father, just to keep up. She felt her belly and wondered for a moment whether a new half-brother or sister stirred inside her. Soon, she hoped.

As the sheep streamed over the hill the sound of four thousand feet and a thousand sheeps' tongues fell silent. Sophia marvelled at the difference and, for the first time that day, she heard birds singing and insects whirring. She looked up to see the outline of her family standing like silhouettes against the afternoon sun. It was a picture she would cherish during the following months.

James turned to raise an arm encouraging her to join them. Ever practical, Sophia threw the cloth over the food to stop those insects or birds taking their lunch before they had a chance to eat it themselves and then hurried uphill. What breath she had left after the climb was taken away entirely by the view that met her. They had told her and Nancy that the place they were going to was paradise, but nothing could have prepared her for its beauty. A vast, flat plain lay before them dotted with tussock grasses and small bushes. The stream they had followed uphill took a turn behind them and wandered gently to their left before disappearing from their view. But they could see and hear water to their right as at least one other stream began its journey down the other side and across this huge basin.

Somewhere not too far away to the right she could see a plume of blue smoke rising. "What's that, James," she asked, "I thought we were alone in this place?"

"I think it may be your friend Atewhai," replied James, "they have a camp of sorts over there and you may be pleased of the company, perhaps."

As James had suspected, Sophia certainly was happy that her good friend Atewhai was nearby. Freddie too would love to see her. Since the accident they had held a special bond with each other.

The sheep had spread out as they went downhill onto this plain, moving through the bushes and tussock grasses with ease. Trees punctuated the hillside and some of the flock had taken refuge in their shade. The poor animals lay breathing heavily after their strenuous journey, steam rising from their fleeces in clouds.

But what made this view even more wonderful was the backdrop of mountains on the far side of the plain. Sophia could see immediately why James and Edmund had referred to it as a basin. It did indeed feel as though they were standing on the edge of one of her flat pie tins. But someone had sprinkled flour on those mountains beyond as they were topped with a white coating, even though it was barely the end of summer. She wondered what they would look like covered in winter snow and looked forward to seeing how this place changed throughout the seasons. James was thrilled that Sophia had caught his enthusiasm for this place. He could see it in her eyes as he put his arm around her shoulders. Life would be perfect here, he just knew it. No words needed to pass between them as they stood together surveying their new land.

James and Sophia turned back reluctantly to their temporary camp, calling for Freddie to follow them. They were happy to let the sheep wander where they wished for now. The dogs needed a rest. In fact,

Roy and Friday greeted them by shaking the water from their thick coats all over them. They had found a pool of ice cold water and had been standing in it up to their bellies with their tongues hanging out so far they could take a good long drink at the same time. Now, with a thorough shake from their noses to the tip of their tails, they were dry and could lay down under a tree to sleep while their master and mistress ate their lunch. They knew they would get a portion of this meal, even if it was only a crust of bread thrown in their direction.

After their simple meal Sophia began to pack things away, but James was looking up at the gathering clouds. He was growing a little anxious about the weather and was not sure whether they should stay at this site for the night or push on over the hill with the horse and cart, risking getting a soaking before they reached the flat area he hoped would be part of their new home. If they stayed here there was a chance that the sheep would spread themselves out across the plains and it would be a hard job for the dogs to bring them all together again.

"Let's push on," he said to Sophia, "there's rain in those clouds and I would like to keep everything dry tonight if I can."

And so they made their entry into the basin, pushing the horse over the hill and then reigning him back hard to stop them all tipping downhill in a heap. The dogs had been sent on to gather the sheep together again while Sophia and James took a diagonal path towards the stream they had seen earlier. James was familiar with this route and deftly drove the horse along until they reached a flat area of land sheltered by trees behind them, but with an open view across the plains beyond. He knew already that it would be the place where they would build a new home, and he could see that Sophia was already working out where the best shelter would be, where to build a fire for now and how to set up a temporary shelter before the impending rain set in.

Leaving her to her domestic tasks James called out to Friday to bring the sheep across towards them. A natural dip provided an enclosed area where the sheep could stay for the night at least. The grass would provide adequate feed and a fork in the stream formed boundaries on two sides meaning that the sheep were unlikely to wander far overnight, though he would leave the dogs on duty for a while, just in case.

The rain came as they finished their supper, which Sophia had cooked over a fire built from twigs and branches she had found along the edge of the stream. Slowly at first, the rain was just a mist, but soon it had soaked them all and was in danger of putting the fire out. There was nothing for it but to retire under the shelter of the canvas cover which Sophia had set up between the cart and the overhanging branches of a tree. Freddie seemed a little subdued, but Sophia assumed he was overly tired after their long day. He shivered a little as she wrapped him in a coarse blanket and hummed a lullaby to him. He was asleep in moments and she lay him down on the mattress they had carried in their cart for them all to sleep on.

She too was ready for sleep but James was concerned for his flock, so he stayed fully clothed while Sophia snuggled under the covers next to Freddie. Her dreams were full of plans for a new house, a new start and perhaps a new child. Friday and Roy had been called home at last and had both managed to sneak under the canvas cover. They were fast asleep, paws and noses twitching in their dreams.

All seemed well outside despite the rain falling incessantly now. He could hear the sounds of sheep moving around in the dark, but one would expect a certain amount of disturbance from such a large mob. James was reluctant to shed his boots and coat lest he should need to call the dogs to order and head out into the night. But he rested his tired body against the wheel of the cart, tipped his hat forward over his nose and snoozed. One hand idly stroked Friday, who nestled against her master in pure contentment.

Two other people had been travelling hard that day too.

Taiko and Seventeen had spent the previous night at the hut which Taiko knew belonged to his Aunty Atewhai. They had arrived full of hope for a good warm supper and a bed for the night. But no smoke came from the fire and the hut lay empty of anything you could call a soft bed. Taiko knew that his aunt and uncle travelled for the summer onto the far plains, but had thought they may be home for the winter by now. So it had been a cold and uncomfortable night for them both. By daybreak they were hungry and not in the least bit refreshed by their sleep on a cold floor without covers except for their cloaks.

Reluctant to engage with any of the locals in case they were part of the conspiracy to steal the sheep, the boys considered their options. Had the sheep been nearby they would have heard and smelt them, no doubt. And Thomas Baylis had told them that this James Mackenzie fellow was taking them over the hill and onto the plains beyond.

"We must head upstream, Seventeen," said Taiko, "and we had better get going before the boss catches up. He is not going to be happy if we are empty-handed. We need to get the sheep back and catch this man who has stolen them. Then the boss will be pleased with us both again."

They passed two houses as they headed uphill. In both places they could see pioneer people going about their business of running a farm, but they were not seen by these folk as they moved quietly through the bushes on the other side of the stream. They managed to pick a few berries along the way, but it barely stopped their bellies from rumbling and to add to their misery it looked like rain. But they carried on climbing, occasionally finding signs of travellers on the same track. Here a wheel track, there a footprint in the soft ground.

The rain had started to fall in a fine mist which soaked through their clothes in no time. They reached a flat area beside the stream where the remains of a fire could be seen, although the rain had turned the ashes wet and cold. Just a short distance beyond this point they reached the summit and stood side by side surveying the plains beyond. It was hard to see too far ahead as the rain was now falling steadily and the clouds had come down low. Darkness would come very soon, but in the twilight beneath the layer of mist they could make out the white shapes of many sheep and they realised they had reached their goal. To their right they could see a cart where a shelter had been set up, a horse grazing next to the tree that held its tether and steam rising from a fire which had not survived the incessant rain. Now all they had to do was turn those sheep back the way they had come and seek out this freebooter Mackenzie from his camp. Mr Sidebottom would be pleased with them both.

Roy gave the alarm first as he sat upright and gave a low, fierce growl. James was immediately awake to the sound of sheep being disturbed. Leaving his new family to sleep he called the two dogs to come with him, lit a lantern with a flint and set out to see what was disturbing his flock. He suspected the Baylis boys were up to no good, perhaps, or maybe a herd of wild pigs. He chuckled to himself as he thought, "well, not much difference between those two, eh?"

There was no doubt the sheep were in turmoil, and he could see an odd flash of a lantern between the bushes as he ran down to the edge of the natural enclosure which had kept his sheep safe until now. Roy gave another deep growl as the shape of a person came out from behind a tree and, although James could not see who it was, it certainly didn't look like Thomas or Simon.

"Are you James Mackenzie?" said the shadowy figure in an accent that James found hard to understand.

"Aye, I am, sir," he replied tersely, "and who wants to know it?"

Taiko was not sure what James had said in his thick Scottish dialect, but he assumed correctly that this was indeed their quarry.

"You stole our sheep and our boss wants them back," accused Taiko. "And you will be hanged for it," he added, just to make it sound as serious as possible.

"No, I did not," answered James. "I bought them fair and square from Simon Baylis. If there's wrong in that, then go and talk to those Baylis brothers."

Much of this exchange was lost in translation between the Maori and Gaelic words, but none of that really mattered as Seventeen appeared suddenly, knocking James to the ground. Roy and Friday were not having any of this nonsense and leapt at the man who had assaulted their master, bearing their teeth and growling as fiercely as they could. Taiko raised his staff to them both and they slunk back into the shadows to avoid any further blows, but it was enough to distract the shepherds while James got to his feet and ran off in the direction of his camp. He didn't quite understand why these men wanted to take him prisoner, but he instinctively knew he needed to get Sophia and Freddie to a safe place.

Sophia woke suddenly when James shook her by the shoulder. She knew immediately that something was wrong.

"Get Freddie and go to Atewhai," James said, "and don't waste any time. There's two men wanting the sheep and they think I stole them."

"They can't get far with the sheep tonight, surely," she replied, not quite fully awake, her mind still woolly with sleep.

"But they seem to want me too," said James. "They are after blood, I think. I suspect the Baylis boys are mixed up in it, and I don't want you involved in any more fights with those rogues."

"You've got time to grab a few of your things and maybe take our pouch with the money and valuables in, just in case," he ordered, as he grabbed a sack for Sophia to bundle a few clothes into, along with the precious leather pouch.

"But then you must get going to Atewhai's hut and I'll sort these fellows out. They are slow men with slow brains it seems. I'll be back for you by daylight, my dear, but we must move quickly now. Can you manage to carry everything in the dark? I dare not light a lantern. Just keep to the path and take the dogs. If there's a problem they will let me know," he said and he gave the signal to Friday and Roy to say "away." Being obedient animals they did exactly what they had been told, although it seemed to them a strange thing to do in the dark.

Before she realised what was happening he had slipped away into the shadows so there was nothing left for her to do but to hoist the sack over her shoulder, pick the sleeping Freddie up from his bed and follow the dogs towards the tiny flickering light that she could see from Atewhai's dwindling fire. Although it was dark and the mist seemed to be closing in around her, she managed to keep to the narrow path along the ridge and it seemed to her only a few minutes before she reached the hut to find Atewhai standing at the entrance as if she was waiting for someone.

"You have come," said Atewhai, "and you will both be safe here for the night." Sophia wondered how Atewhai had known of their surprise visit. But then many things this native woman did were a mystery to her and it usually turned out fine somehow. She was indeed an angel, and one that her son had grown to love. Freddie had hardly opened his eyes throughout their walk, but now he stirred in her arms as she laid him down on the soft bed that was shared by Atewhai and Hunu. His young face looked flushed and his forehead was hot to the touch, but she was too distracted by the events of the evening to notice. Roy and Friday remained on guard duty at the door. They knew they had charge of their mistress and young master. Their grown up master would call if he needed them.

Meanwhile, James was trying to draw the men away from the camp to give Sophia a chance to get away. The ground was treacherous after the rain and he had to tread carefully to avoid slipping downhill. He hadn't dared to light a lantern and was now finding it hard to see a clear path ahead. The thick bushes seemed keen to slow him down by catching him in their thorny branches and it wasn't long before he heard the sound of the two younger men approaching from behind. With the advantage of a lantern they could move more quickly and soon set upon James and brought him once more to the ground. Despite much struggling against his foes, James was quickly pinned down face first, his nose in the wet ground, with his hands tied behind his back. The Maori men pulled him to his feet and started to push him back towards the camp, but not before a good check around to see if the dogs were likely to attack again. Taiko was still feeling the pain of a vicious bite on his hand, and he expected to find the skin broken when he had time to check.

Rain still fell steadily and the two men realised it would be foolhardy to travel further tonight. Instead they would share James' camp and perhaps there would be food. It would be their first proper meal of the day and they were ready for it.

It came as a surprise to them both to see more than one set of footprints in the soft ground around the camp. It was obvious that James had not been alone but an even bigger surprise was that it appeared that his companions were a woman and child. A hairbrush lay by the bed and a small wooden horse had been knocked to the floor as if someone had been in a rush to leave. The shepherds were concerned that there may be other people about. They had no idea as to whether this Mackenzie chap was working alone and they assumed it would take more than one person and a couple of dogs to control such a mob. But perhaps this woman was all the help he had. They were nervous and on edge at every noise they heard.

James was not in the mood for cooperating and refused to give them any more details, so they just had to assume that his only companion, and perhaps her child, had taken off into the night. They would look for her in the morning, though she would have a cold and wet night under a tree somewhere nearby, no doubt.

James sat plotting his escape in the corner of the shelter where he had been thrown, his hands still tied behind his back. The two men raided Sophia's stores and put together a meal, which they devoured hungrily. He half expected the Baylis boys to turn up too, but kept an eye open for an opportunity to make a bid for freedom. Once, he managed to get to his feet, but Taiko knocked him down again. The boys were very tired and wanted to sleep so they tied James' feet together as well and removed his boots, placing them well out of reach. Despite agreeing that they would take it in turns to guard their prisoner they both found it impossible to stay awake for long after their good supper. What a strange scene they painted under that canvas. Two young Maori men asleep at one end and the brooding Scotsman wide awake and ready to run at the other.

James realised that the rain had stopped, though the drips still fell steadily from the edges of the canvas cover. With his hands and feet tied firmly with rope he saw no chance to make his escape and now it would be doubly difficult without boots. But a sound he recognised made him sit bolt upright. It was Friday. He whispered a word to keep her quiet, but she was used to working in silence so as not to disturb the sheep. Leaning backwards from under the shelter he offered his tied hands to her. "Bite, Friday, bite," he whispered.

She was a clever dog but she hadn't heard that command before. But why could her master not put his hands out to pat her? Perhaps the rope was like her collar? She didn't much like her collar and if she could have bitten at it she would have removed it by now. So maybe that is what she should do with her master's rope collar thing that went round his hands.

She began to chew through the thick rope. "Quietly," said James, although he knew she would work in silence.

James pulled his hands apart and felt the threads of the rope offering less resistance as Friday chewed and chewed. In a rush the rope came apart and his hands were free at last. He reached down quickly to pat Friday whispering a quiet, "Good girl." She was pleased with herself but kept her tail still so as not to make a noise by beating it against something.

He quickly untied the ropes that bound his feet, but the boots were a bigger problem. One of the men had fallen across them in his sleep and there was no chance of him picking them up without disturbing them both. So he had no choice but to escape without them, silently thanking Sophia for providing him with good, thick woollen socks to wear.

But luck was against him at the very last minute. As he grabbed his hat and ducked out under the canvas shelter he was just too late to see the water bucket which he sent flying with his bare foot. It spilled its contents before coming to rest with a metallic clunk against the pots and pans which had been neatly arranged by his wife that afternoon on a low shelf.

Though by this time it should have been daylight, the low cloud had turned into thick fog, so it was easy to roll out of view into the bushes before either of the two men had come to their senses. Friday was not quite so fortunate. She had wasted precious seconds in turning to face her master's captors for one last deep growl, but turning away to follow James she found herself trapped by Taiko's firm hand holding onto her collar. Try as she might she could not follow him and neither could she turn to take another chunk out of the man's hand. She was soon sharing a firm tether with the horse where she stretched the rope which held her as far as she could, even standing on her back legs to get away from the tree, but it was no use. And the rope was kept short so it was impossible for her to turn and chew it as she had done to aid her master's escape.

James gave a series of low whistles from his hiding place, expecting Friday to follow him. After a considerable time, that he knew he should not waste in waiting, he turned reluctantly away and set off to find a safe place where he could consider what to do next. Friday had taken off before and she usually found her way back to him, so he was not too concerned.

"If we can't have the man, we will at least have his horse and the dog," said Taiko to Seventeen. "We will not find him in this fog anyway, so we may as well wait for it to clear before we start to drive the sheep back to their proper home."

"Maybe we can get that dog to help us," replied Seventeen. "She's a good worker and loyal, so we can sell her for a good price once we get the sheep back home."

The two shepherds decided they could do no more until the cloud lifted and settled back into the comfort of their borrowed camp. They found oatcakes which made a good breakfast and dozed a little longer, not wishing to leave this warm haven for the damp and cold outside.

Friday gave the first warning of someone approaching and the boys were instantly on the alert for an attack from James, or his accomplices. So John Sidebottom, arriving on horseback, was greeted by the two boys with sticks raised above their heads.

"What in the Lord's name is going on here?" exclaimed the boss.

The two men put their sticks down and started to explain what had happened. The man, they told their boss, was very tall and strong and it seemed he had accomplices who may still be hiding nearby. They showed him several sets of footprints in the soft ground around them. He had escaped, but they had hold of his dog and his horse and his boots. And after all, they had rescued the sheep.

"Hmm," replied Mr Sidebottom, "that's all very well, but we need to put this outlaw before the magistrate. Too many sheep have been taken recently and I daresay it is all down to this freebooting criminal."

John Sidebottom was happy to accept the hospitality afforded by their captured camp while he considered what to do next. It had been a long hard ride for him yesterday, and an early start in the cold mist this morning. So a fire was lit in the ashes left by Sophia and a kettle boiled for a mug of strong tea. The last of the oatcakes were shared between them.

"Right boys, here's what we will do," he said, as he wiped the crumbs from his waistcoat. "Let's get these sheep back to where they belong first. The three of us can cope and perhaps that crafty dog will give us a hand, if we beat her hard enough."

Taiko felt his hand gingerly. It throbbed painfully from the bite Friday had delivered him earlier.

"Once we've got the mob home, Taiko, you can come with me to Lyttelton to meet the magistrate and see what can be done to catch this criminal. You are the best horseman of the two of you. And we can take that dog with us. I am sure she will recognise her master once he is caught and that will prove the crime. That will see him put in chains."

James, hiding in the bushes nearby, had seen the arrival of a horseman at the camp that he and Sophia had built only yesterday. It seemed an age ago and how different their dreams had become in only that one day. Hoping to find out more about these men who thought he had done wrong, he crept within earshot of their shelter. For a big man he could move swiftly and silently for he was used to moving amongst his flock without setting the sheep on the run.

In that way he heard the words of Mr Sidebottom. They suspected him of rustling sheep and not just these sheep it seemed. There was only one thing for him to do. He must go to Lyttelton too and protest his innocence with the magistrate. If he set out immediately he would arrive before these folk, though the journey would be long and uncomfortable, especially without boots. His thoughts ran over his options. Should he try to steal a horse, perhaps? Or try to get Friday back? And most important of all, what was he going to tell Sophia? Her dreams of a new beginning would have to be put on hold for a while. She would probably be best to go back to Marytown and wait for his return, once he had proven his lack of involvement in stealing the sheep. Damn those Baylis brothers, they had stitched him up good and proper. He supposed they had found a way to wreak revenge for Thomas' broken nose and shattered dignity.

Sophia's night had been a sleepless one. She and Atewhai had spent their time sitting in silence while Atewhai's elderly husband, Hunu slept soundly, undisturbed by the unexpected guests. And Freddie slept, but restlessly, occasionally throwing the blankets from his hot body, or shivering violently as if he was frozen cold. He had a fever, there was no doubt, and Atewhai had already started to mix a brew of leaves and roots over her re-ignited cooking fire.

Sophia's face was crossed with fear for both her men. Freddie would no doubt get worse before he was better, and though she had great faith in Atewhai's potions, she knew that a fever could be a sign of many illnesses from which there may be no recovery for a small boy. And as for James, she had no idea what he had been doing overnight and what had become of the men who seemed to be chasing him. He had told her he would come at daybreak, but the watery sun was high in the sky now and there was no sign of him.

A small movement in the bushes caught her eye. Roy had seen it too and rushed over, tail wagging, to greet James as he stepped out into the open, checking behind him for unwanted followers. He kept his body low and, catching Sophia by the hand, slipped quietly inside the hut where he greeted Atewhai and Hunu and thanked them for looking after his family overnight. While Atewhai prepared him a most welcome plate of food he told them all of the events of the night. He found it hard to tell that Friday had been captured without a tear in his eye and Sophia stretched out to take his hand in hers across the table in comfort.

Freddie lay quietly on the bed and James wondered why he was still asleep. Nothing much kept this young man inside once daybreak came. Sophia explained that he appeared fevered and that Atewhai had fed him a tea made of leaves and roots which should soothe him. She did not want to worry him unduly. He had cares enough to deal with himself just now.

Although James wanted Sophia to take Freddie back to Nancy's house, Atewhai was not so sure. The child needed rest and time to recover and, if it was a disease which could be given to others, then Nancy had the twins, and perhaps a new baby to consider too. Sophia could stay with them a while, perhaps. Once the other men had gone they would be able to rescue whatever belongings had been left and that would enable them to live comfortably for the few weeks it would take James to travel to Lyttelton and back.

He needed to start his journey as soon as possible, but there was time to make some hurried preparations. James counted out some coins from their money pouch. Enough to buy some food and a bed for the night in Lyttelton, perhaps, and some extra for a new pair of boots which he would need to buy at the first opportunity. He put the money into the deep pocket in his cloak and, as an afterthought, added his copy of the map of the area that Edmund had drawn. For some reason he felt sure it would prove useful.

Next came the question of boots. Though Sophia's knitted socks were thick and comfortable, they would be unlikely to survive a walk of ten days or so across wild terrain. James would not dare to go to the coast and take the easier track which had developed to the north. He did not want to risk being captured again before he had made time to see the magistrate. It was Hunu who solved the problem. He did not understand much of what these people said and had not learned the words as his wife had done. But he knew that a man could not walk far without something to keep his feet safe. Under the bed he found a pair of his woven sandals. The soles would be small for this big man, but by strapping them over his socks they would give some protection.

Atewhai showed James how to tie them to his feet, wrapping the long threads of flax in a criss-cross manner up to his knees. It reminded James and Sophia of the black pumps that they had seen worn by the Scottish sword dancers, held in place with ribbons in much the same way. James tried them out by taking a few steps and found them comfortable and strong. He thanked Hunu for his generosity with a hand to his shoulder.

Hunu's wife had also been busy preparing for James' journey. She had filled a woven bag with food and now handed it to James. He thanked her and slipped the bag over his shoulder, the strap being too short for it to go over his head.

And so James began the long journey to plead his innocence. He put a hand on Freddie's forehead and silently prayed for his recovery and, with a word of thanks to the Maori couple, he and Sophia went outside to say goodbye. It was a swift farewell as James did not want to be in the open for too long. He knew the men were still about as the sheep had not been moved back over the hill yet. He hoped that Friday would stand her ground if she was made to work. He knew she would only react to his commands in Gaelic, or his whistle, so he doubted she would be much use to them anyway, and was likely to slip her leash as soon as she could. He would spend the whole journey expecting her to join him with a click of his fingers behind his back.

His embrace with Sophia was as long as he dare, and then he was gone, leaving his wife standing forlorn in front of the hut. Atewhai emerged to take her in her arms and lead her back inside to tend to her son's fever. It would be many, many days before Sophia and James embraced each other again.

The Wideawake Hat

Chapter Nine

Innocence

6th March - 16th April 1855

The shoes that Hunu had given to James were proving to be most effective. On the odd occasion that a sharp stone caused a hole in the woven fibres of the sole, James could easily repair it. He gathered a supply of the strappy harakeke leaves and carried them in his woven bag and it was but a simple job to weave a new one in place while he took a rest by a stream or under the shade of a tree. He began to realise how the Maori people had travelled so easily across the rough terrain, and he found himself with a growing respect for their design skills and the way they took what they needed from the environment to make their lives more comfortable.

For the first day of his journey James had travelled slowly, more intent on not being discovered than in making progress. He stopped often and, from the shelter of a bush or tree, he issued a low whistle. Each time he did so, he fully expected Friday to make an appearance, tongue hanging out, head down, racing to catch up with her master. But each time he waited he was disappointed. If he heard a noise it usually turned out to be a bird, or perhaps a lone sheep. He missed Friday and he missed Sophia. But at least he knew that Sophia was free and no doubt being well cared for by Atewhai. His last view of Friday was ever in his mind, straining at the leash which held her captive. Under his gruff exterior James was a sensitive soul, and he could not think of Friday without shedding a tear. "I should have rescued her," he often thought to himself with a shake of his head.

But he had a job to do and a deadline to meet. Time enough to deal with Friday later and there was always the possibility that she had escaped already and was sitting in the sunshine at the door of Atewhai's hut with Roy beside her, or chasing a stick that Freddie had thrown for her. Thinking of Freddie made James wonder if the boy was feeling any better.

His route cut across wild country, but it was the kind of terrain he was used to, though he had to admit it would have been easier with a stout pair of leather boots. Atewhai had pushed so much food into his bag that the flap on top would not fold over, but he still felt the need to ration himself. He was not at all sure where he would get further sustenance as the journey continued. As darkness fell on the first day he found a sheltered spot under an overhanging rock. First he fashioned a mattress out of bracken that he gathered from around his camp, and then he curled up with his cloak around him as a blanket. He was thankful he had remained fully clothed last night so that he now wore his cloak. It was nowhere nearly as comfortable as the plump mattress on which he slept with Sophia, but he was cosy and dry and, most importantly, safe, even though he would have loved to feel his wife's warmth beside him.

He laid the contents of his bag out in front of him on the ground and divided it into four shares. That gave him adequate rations for the next four days. Anything he found along the route in the way of supplements, berries perhaps, would be counted as a bonus for the day. He wanted to avoid lighting a fire which could bring attention to him and leave a trail behind him, so it was cold fare washed down with water collected in his cupped hands from a nearby stream or pool. Since his marriage to Sophia he had eaten well. Perhaps for the first time in his life he had regular meals designed to feed a working man. And he had gained weight with all that Sophia had prepared for him. He reckoned he could spare a few pounds of reserves as he travelled. He savoured every mouthful of tonight's feast of a corner of dry bread, a tiny chunk of cold mutton and a small green fruit that he didn't recognise but it tasted sweet and succulent as he bit into it.

He had walked as far as he could before night fell, and he was ready for sleep immediately his supper had been taken. The fog had lifted in the late afternoon and the night was clear. The Milky Way stretched overhead like an arch and he could see exactly why the Maori people considered it to be a fat eel swimming across the sky.

He was familiar with the layout of the night sky and could identify south by following the Southern Cross through its long axis. In this way he could plot an approximate direction for tomorrow's walk. He reckoned if he kept roughly north east he would meet the coast some way below the port of Lyttelton. He had never travelled that far north in New Zealand, but he was sure that he could seek directions discreetly as he got nearer to his goal.

And so the days continued for James. Walking from daybreak to sunset and resting in the most sheltered spot he could find overnight. After four days the land became flatter and he started to see smoke from the buildings which formed small settlements. For the first time since he said his goodbyes to Sophia, he was forced to speak an occasional greeting to a shepherd in the fields, or two young women leaning on a fence watching their husbands drive a plough through the fertile soil. But he kept his hat low over his face and chose to give a simple greeting and move on. He had no wish to engage in conversation, nor to give details of his reasons for passing by. Those who saw him wondered only why a man like James was wearing woven sandals and carrying a flaxen bag.

One advantage of walking through a more populated area was the discovery of windfall apples. His bag was empty now, so he felt no guilt in picking up the best of the harvest from the ground on which it had fallen. He felt sure the owners of this land would not begrudge him the fruit which would likely be worm-eaten soon anyway.

Though the apples were ripe and juicy they did not constitute an ample diet for a man expending much energy in his travels. But on the sixth day of his journey James awoke to see a bigger settlement in front of him. It took him an hour or so to reach the small town, and he was glad to see a main street containing several stores and a tavern. He calculated he was more than half way, so perhaps he could afford to restock his supplies at the general stores with a loaf and a piece of cheese to see him through the remaining days. Further down the street he found a store selling equipment for the local farming folk. At the back of the store, behind the tools and buckets and leather saddles and bridles, hung checked cotton shirts and brown corduroy trousers and heavy waxed waterproof coats on hangers. On the floor beneath stood a neat line of boots in various sizes including a pair of stout leather boots which fitted him perfectly. He counted his coins out carefully and found he could just about afford them and still have enough for a mug of ale now and the rest to pay for a bed for a night or two in Lyttelton. The young girl behind the counter wondered why this well-dressed stranger had no good boots to his name and quietly slipped a new pair of woollen socks into his hands too. James thanked her for her generosity and went outside to sit on the step where he peeled his woven sandals and worn out socks from his tired feet. It was a pleasure indeed to wriggle the new socks over his toes and step into the firm leather boots.

The beer tasted good. As good as any drink he had ever tasted. And the chair he had taken in a quiet corner of the small tavern was as comfortable as any seat he had ever had the pleasure of using. But he could not rest for long. It was vital that he reached Lyttelton before his accusers, and he had no way of knowing how much of their journey they had completed so far. He downed the last drops of beer in his mug and took his leave with a hand raised in thanks to the man behind the bar. The proprietor of the tavern wondered what had brought the tall stranger to his small town, and where he was headed.

It was going to be a close run race for James. John Sidebottom, and his companion Taiko were well on their way to Lyttelton too.

In John Sidebottom's opinion the return of the sheep had been an absolute shambles. Taiko had found the horse hard to handle as it was a spirited beast more used to the shafts of a cart than a man in the saddle. Taiko had spent much of the first hour or so on his bottom in the mud and had now resorted to walking alongside and leading the horse. Seventeen was left to deal with the dog. They didn't dare let the animal loose for fear of her running after her master, but any command they issued was entirely ignored by her. In fact, every command was interpreted as the 'sit' command, it seemed. Seventeen had spent most of the morning walking backwards while dragging the poor dog through the wet ground. It was not a good way to make fast progress home.

The direct route to their farm did not require passing through Marytown, which in many ways was fortunate, as they would have been the laughing stock of any who saw their efforts. Sidebottom's horse was the sole worker for most of the day, as the foreman drove him hard, catching runners from the pack or tucking in stragglers. At the end of the first day they were still heading down hill with a considerable distance to cover once the ground flattened out. So a camp of sorts was made in the open and a roster drawn up for guard duties. There was still the possibility of another attack on the sheep, or perhaps an opportunity for the freebooter to reclaim his dog, so each person would be awake for four hours at a time, while the others tried to catch some sleep under the stars.

They had not been travelling for long the following morning when Mr Sidebottom saw two horsemen approaching. It was the Baylis brothers coming to see what they could do to help. Though he didn't trust the boys as far as they could be thrown, John Sidebottom had no real choice but to accept their offer, even though they would no doubt ask for payment for their services later. The brothers and their pack of dogs quickly and efficiently tightened things up and the mob of sheep started to move at a better pace. By the time the sun began to set behind them they were within reach of home and, though the last few miles were covered with the light of lanterns, they did indeed reach their home pastures by the end of the second day.

That night all the men slept in comfortable beds having eaten of a warm supper provided for them by Mrs Sidebottom. But before retiring to bed the conversation had inevitably turned to James Mackenzie.

"Why did you not chase him down and give him a good dose with your fists?" asked Thomas.

"We prefer to do things by the law here, Mr Baylis," replied John Sidebottom, thinking to himself that he really didn't like the way these two men behaved.

"We will seek out the authorities in Lyttelton and the law will decide on his guilt and punishment," he continued.

"Oh, he's guilty, believe me," said Thomas, "and guilty of many another crime too. Just look at all those sheep you have lost in tens and twenties over the year. He will be at the root of that, there is no doubt. He hoodwinked us good and proper into dealing with you with not a thought of paying good money for those sheep."

"Hmm, well we will see about that once the facts are put before a magistrate. And now I am ready for my bed," said John Sidebottom as he got slowly to his feet and headed to the comfort of his wife, "Good night to you all, and be ready for the next part of the journey tomorrow, Taiko. And make sure that dog is tied up properly, we need her as evidence."

Much to their annoyance the Baylis brothers were still in their beds when Mr Sidebottom, Taiko and Friday set out the next morning. Poor Friday had to run to keep up with the horse that Taiko rode. Her collar had been attached to a chain, which in turn was fixed to the saddle, so wherever the horse went, so did Friday at a horse's pace. And the chain was hard to chew on. She had tried and it had only resulted in a very sore gum and a broken tooth.

By the time the two brothers had risen their only companion was Seventeen. They could get no sense from him. Mr Sidebottom had been very firm. He had told Seventeen not to allow the boys to follow him. He did not trust them to tell the full truth and even a thief like Mackenzie deserved a fair crack at justice. Nevertheless, Thomas and Simon decided to add their weight to the evidence against James and packed their saddlebags with supplies for the journey north. They had, of course, visited Lyttelton only recently and were happy to spend some time there in the taverns and boarding houses awaiting the trial of their enemy, James Mackenzie. Their revenge had not quite gone to plan, but there was still a chance they could ensure a guilty sentence was forthcoming.

The route north along the coast was a well worn track these days but nevertheless it was by no means a smooth road. Though Mr Sidebottom drove his horse hard and expected Taiko to keep up, their speed was limited by the terrain, and in places by the sheer amount of traffic in both directions. Two horseman were expected to give way to carts and carriages as they passed and in many places it was impossible to pass slower moving traffic unless it pulled over for them. At the various river crossings a queue formed while small groups traversed the gravel banks and deep pools of water from one bank or the other. John Sidebottom wondered if he would do better alone, or perhaps he should have taken the inland route, leaving the shepherds to take the flock home. But they would probably still be trying to round the sheep up, let alone drive them back to the farm.

They spent the first night on the banks of the Rangitata River awaiting their chance to cross early in the morning before a queue had formed. The next night was a more comfortable one in a boarding house in the small settlement of Ashburton. And so the journey proceeded slowly. Too slowly for Mr Sidebottom, but too fast for Taiko, who was not used to such long periods of time in the saddle. And he had the sores on his thighs to prove it. Poor Friday was exhausted at the speed of her enforced run. Her only shred of comfort came from a good feed at the end of the day. John Sidebottom was not a cruel man, and he knew the benefit of a good working dog. In this case he needed Friday to be able to identify her master and if that meant providing a good meal each night, then that is what he would do. In so far as she was provided with food each day, she was willing to trust this man, but that didn't mean for one moment that she intended to work for him, that was for sure. Only one man could use the right words and she was certain she would be reunited with him soon.

Despite the difference in their route, they all arrived in Lyttelton at opposite ends of the same day. The last part of the journey took both sets of travellers over the pass from Sumner to Lyttelton along a rough track crowded with foot traffic and carts carrying supplies in and out of the port. James, unused to such a crowd, was at first inclined to walk alone, but it occurred to him that his presence would be less noticed if he mingled. A small group of farm workers were making slow progress with a few miserable looking bullocks so he walked alongside them, looking very much the part. By mid-morning he had arrived in the bustling port and set about finding a quiet place to stay overnight. He planned to visit the magistrate as soon as he could. But first he needed to remove those boots to tend to his blistered feet where the new leather had yet to soften.

Mr Sidebottom and his Maori shepherd followed a similar path after lunch had been taken in Sumner. They had no need to disguise their reasons for travelling and they had no idea that the person who had caused them to take the journey had beaten them to it by a few hours. Taiko was nervous of so many people and unused to the crowds on the road and in the busy town. Even the buildings seemed tall and frightening. So his boss arranged accommodation for them both in a boarding house on the quayside and left Taiko to rest his sore and blistered bottom for the afternoon. Taking Friday with him to explain the reason for her being there, he set out for the sheriff's office.

At that very same moment the Baylis brothers rode into town.

Sergeant Seager was having a quiet afternoon for a change. Those brought into the jail to sober up after last night's revelry had all gone to their homes again and the constables had swilled their vomit from the prison floor with buckets of water and a stiff brush. The business of crime in the region of Canterbury was a bit slow at this time of year, or at least the reporting of it to Lyttelton. Who would want to travel far in the shorter hours of daylight? He knew that many a misdemeanour would go un-reported until spring, by which time the gathering of evidence would be impossible, no doubt. In the meantime, he was not averse to an afternoon at his desk with his boots resting on the table top, a mug of strong tea within his reach.

Suddenly there was a commotion at the front desk.

"You can't bring that dog in here, sir," he heard the constable say to a visitor.

"Oh yes, I can," said Mr Sidebottom. "She's evidence of a crime I wish to report and she will be vital in the capture of the perpetrator. Let me in to see your superior officer, if you will."

At which he pushed past the constable and into the office of Sergeant Seager who, as he quickly put his feet to the floor, knocked his mug of tea over spilling its contents across the papers on his desk.

"Bother, my man, what is it that demands my services so urgently?" he asked. "And why have you brought me a dog as evidence? What crime has she perpetrated?"

As he spoke the sergeant took a large handkerchief from his pocket and mopped at the liquid which was now spilling over the edge of the desk and soaking into his reports to the superintendent.

"It is not the dog who has committed the crime, but she will lead us to her owner who has stolen sheep from us all," replied Mr Sidebottom.

"Then please be seated and tell me all the details," said the sergeant, as he reached for a dry piece of paper and his pen.

And so John Sidebottom explained his view of the facts of James' crimes and his wish that the sergeant and his men should join him in the search for the freebooter. It would, he said, be easy to identify the man. He loved his dog and the dog would recognise him, of that there was no doubt. That way they would know he was guilty of the crimes.

Agreement was reached that there were indeed crimes to be investigated and it certainly did seem that this chap was guilty of them. The sergeant thought it would take a day to organise a search party made up of three or four constables and their hounds, but they would then accompany Mr Sidebottom back to the south, where they would search this man out. Justice would be done once he was returned to Lyttelton to be tried by a judge at the courthouse.

With a shake of hands and an agreement to meet the following day Mr Sidebottom took his leave, dragging poor Friday by the short chain which she was now used to wearing, but certainly didn't like. In the open air she gave herself a shake and pricked her ears up. On the way to this building she had found a lot to sniff at in the gutters and had managed to grab a mouthful of decaying food before this man had pulled her closer. Maybe there would be more food on the way back.

But all thoughts of food were suddenly forgotten as a more familiar smell hit her nose. That smell was her master's special aroma of warmth and love and kindness. Poor Friday could not resist the temptation to prick her ears up, wag her tail frantically and altogether stand to attention as her master came down the road towards her!

James was on his way to the sheriff's office to explain his innocence in a crime he wasn't even sure he understood. He walked with his head down and the brim of his hat low over his eyes. He felt sure he would be better off not being recognised until this affair had all been sorted out. And that shouldn't take long as he was an innocent party in the entire thing. In fact, he thought he should explain the part played by the Baylis brothers in all this, perhaps he should even tell them about Thomas' attack on Sophia.

All of a sudden he was stopped in his tracks. There in front of him was a dog just like Friday. "Oh how I miss my two girls," he thought to himself, "and now I'm imagining them."

But then there was no doubt of it. Friday had seen him and was making it obvious to everyone around that she knew and loved this man.

"What is it, dog?" asked John Sidebottom. "Come here, you beast, and walk properly."

But there was no moving Friday from her mission to get to her master. So much so that she dragged John Sidebottom along the street for several yards leaving two skid marks in the dirt from his boots, her tail wagging madly. All at once Mr Sidebottom understood that her owner had come to town too, and here he was approaching them.

"Stop that man!" he shouted, "He's a thief!" and he pointed to James who stood indecisively in front of him. How he yearned to stretch out and take Friday in his arms, but common sense told him to make a run for it. Whispering in Gaelic "Good dog, Friday, Stay," to his dog, he turned and walked quickly away towards the next corner hoping he had enough of a lead to get away. But he hadn't counted on the Baylis brothers.

Thomas and Simon had spotted James leaving his boarding house and had been following him through the streets hoping for a chance to catch him out. They saw Mr Sidebottom leaving the sheriff's office and, not wishing to be recognised themselves at this stage, they both turned into a side street and then leaned against a post to watch events unfold.

They were in luck. They heard John Sidebottom shout and saw James turn and make his way quickly towards them. He had turned into the street before he saw and recognised the two men. Stuck between them and the gathering crowd behind him, James could not escape. He put up a good fight, but Thomas wrestled him to the ground and Simon called for help.

"This way," he shouted, "we've got him good and proper."

It was not long before James was truly captured when two constables arrived to take him firmly by the shoulders. In that short space of time James had managed to inflict a couple of damaging blows to both brothers. Thomas would sport yet another black eye given to him by James, and Simon would suffer several days of discomfort in his groin, forcing a period of enforced abstinence with the ladies and a severe dent in his pride in that direction.

What sadness there was in James' face as he was marched past Mr Sidebottom who still held Friday on a close chain. Her tail was now between her legs and her ears pressed back against her head. Though she wasn't sure what she had done wrong, she knew it was all her fault.

From his cell James could only hear a little of the conversation in Sergeant Seager's office. He heard the Baylis brothers demanding a reward for their part in catching the criminal. He also heard them identifying him as a long-term sheep rustler. He heard Mr Sidebottom and the sergeant agreeing that the dog had saved them a whole lot of bother by doing the job of finding Mackenzie without all the complications of a long journey. And he heard that he was to be tried the following morning at 10 o'clock.

The constable who brought his supper was a kind man who loved animals. After opening the door of his cell and putting the tray down which held a bowl of soup, a wooden spoon and some bread, he could see that James was upset. His impression was not of the hardened criminal that the Baylis brothers had told them about, it was of a sensitive man who was missing something badly. There were signs that tears had been rolling down his cheeks making tracks in his dusty face.

"I'll make sure the dog is well treated, you can be sure of that," said the constable. James hoped that Friday was indeed being given a meal and some shelter, but he took comfort from this man's kind words and slept fitfully on a bed of straw covered by a thin, coarse blanket.

Prisoner Mackenzie was led into court by two constables at precisely 10 o'cock the following morning, being the first and most important case of the day. Theft was a crime that required a stiff sentence. The rest of the day's cases were of drunk and disorderly behaviour, apart from a young woman who had stolen two fishes from a basket on the quayside to feed her family. Hardly the same as the stealing of thousands of sheep.

The courtroom was crowded with spectators. It was not often that a criminal was captured in full view in the street and those who had witnessed yesterday's events were keen to see the outcome of the case. To start with the proceedings were mundane with the checking of names and the basic facts of the case read out by Sergeant Seager from a sheet of slightly stained paper covered with his neat writing.

The noisy crowd were convinced to a man of his guilt, there being no evidence offered to the contrary. And this was reinforced by the evidence of Thomas and Simon Baylis, who stated under oath that they knew this freebooter and could state categorically that he had been involved in the stealing of sheep from various farms in the area to the south over several years. In fact, Thomas made it clear that he knew that Mackenzie had left Australia under a cloud after being accused of similar crimes. Simon was happy to confirm that important piece of evidence too.

James was having trouble understanding what was said in the noisy room. He was not used to the fine language spoken in court and, standing with his head on one side, he looked a sorry sight. If asked a question he appeared slow to respond and the words came out of his mouth in his mother tongue as his mind seemed unable to translate them into English in front of all these people.

The final witness for the prosecution was a Mr Sidebottom who, when summoned, appeared in the courtroom leading a dog on a chain. His entrance brought a cheer from the audience followed by so much noise that the judge had to call for order.

There was a change in James' demeanour with the arrival of the dog. He reached over the wooden bar around the prisoner's dock in an attempt to feel Friday's touch once more, but the constables beside him pulled him back. He could not hide his tears. Friday was pleased to see her master again so soon, but overcome by all the people in this hot and crowded room. Try as she might she couldn't reach James. Her front paws scratched at the wooden panels of the dock, but she was pulled sharply away by Mr Sidebottom. It was obvious to everyone in the room that the man and the dog knew each other.

This was the most damning evidence, which proved beyond doubt that Mackenzie was a guilty man.

"Remove the dog," said the judge firmly.

"Leave her to me, she was mine," James pleaded. "I would do anything if you let her stay with me. Come here to me, wee lassie."

But it was not to be. Friday was removed while James sank back into the stand looking like a broken man.

"You tell us, James Mackenzie that you will do anything if you can keep the dog," said the judge in pronouncing his sentence. "Well, indeed you do not have the right to make that offer because we know that you are guilty. Your dog has proven that to be the case."

Lifting his gavel and tapping it firmly on the wooden mount, the judge declared, "You will return to custody forthwith pending your sentence to be decided by the Supreme Court sitting in April."

As James left the court with his head bowed down all he could hear were the shouts and cheers of the crowd. Out of the general noise he heard Thomas say triumphantly to his brother Simon, "We've got our revenge, brother, at last. We've got our revenge."

Leaving the courtroom Thomas had taken Mr Sidebottom on one side and asked if he could take the dog. Thomas thought it would be the final indignity for James' dog to come to them, and he knew her to be an effective animal. She would need a firm hand to get her to work without her old master, but she would get used to the stick, no doubt.

If truth be told, John Sidebottom had taken a liking to the little dog. Even though these two men had helped him in his cause in court he still didn't trust them entirely. He thought they had said more than they needed in evidence in a bid to ensure James' guilt, and he was beginning to feel uncomfortable about the whole affair.

"She is coming home with me," he said. "We always have need of a good dog and she will learn our ways from the rest of the mob."

"And good luck with that, Sidebottom." replied Thomas. "She'll not work without some discipline and will need to feel that stick of yours before she will move sheep for anyone else but that blackguard."

As Thomas and Simon celebrated their victory over James Mackenzie with copious quantities of ale, John Sidebottom and Taiko were packing their bags to make the journey home. Friday had served her purpose as evidence, so they were both happy to treat her a little more gently now, though she would need to stay on her chain until they were well clear of Lyttelton, lest she take off in search of Mackenzie.

Their journey back was a more gentle ride, much more to Taiko's liking. By the time they reached Ashburton again they felt confident in reverting to a rope for Friday and, knowing only that she was now being fed and given the occasion tickle under the chin, she chose not to chew it through as she had once done for her beloved James. It was a good six days later that they greeted Seventeen and the other farmhands and told them all the news. Friday was allocated a kennel with the other dogs where she spent much of her time tied up, but was otherwise content with her new life for now. She would await her chance to escape, just like her master.

At the April sitting of the Supreme Court in Lyttelton on the 15th of that month James found himself once more in the dock. This time there were no crowds, partly due no doubt to the deteriorating weather outside. Snow was forecast and the clouds hung low and menacing over the port town. And James' accusers had all begun their journeys home which meant that the magistrate spoke only to James and Sergeant Seager when he pronounced a term of five years imprisonment to be spent in hard labour.

"This strong man can join a road gang," he thought himself, though it occurred to him that nobody would be working outside for a while if this snow fell thickly. "We are in need of good men to improve that dreadful track between here and Sumner. Let him break rocks for a few years to pay for his crimes."

Chapter Ten

Births and deaths

March - April 1855

Atewhai wrung out a cloth she had soaked in warm water to bathe the sweat from Freddie's young body while Sophia gently drew his shirt over his head. Atewhai saw the look of horror on her friend's face before she saw the deep red rash which had appeared across his back and chest. As they bathed Freddie's tender skin he flinched with the pain of it all, but gained some relief from the heat that seemed to be burning his little body up.

Freddie's fever had not yet reached its peak but it was becoming obvious to Sophia that his symptoms were those of a disease that all the pioneers dreaded. It showed every sign of being Scarlet Fever. He complained in a rasping croak that his throat hurt a lot, and he was racked by bouts of a dry cough, which worried both women in its intensity. Despite the beads of sweat on his face, he shivered so violently that he was in danger of falling from the bed. Sophia had heard about an outbreak of Scarlet Fever in Hawksbury a few months earlier and, though she knew that Freddie was young and fit and could fight disease better than most, she was really concerned for his life. Secretly, she was also concerned for Atewhai and Hunu. The native people who lived in and around Hawksbury had seemed more vulnerable to disease than the pioneers, and she had heard that they had a tendency to fall ill and die quickly, almost before a diagnosis could be made. Hunu was an old, frail man and she didn't want to put him at risk, so she fashioned a mask for him from a handkerchief and Atewhai tied it around his head to cover his mouth and nose whenever he was inside the hut.

The hours slipped by on that first day and through the night with Sophia thinking only of her son. It felt like her head had no room in it to worry about whether James had escaped the shepherds, or to think about how far he had got on his journey to Lyttelton. Neither woman felt like eating, but Atewhai put a pot over the fire at some point in the day and left Hunu to stir it occasionally while she went back to her nursing duties. It was better for Hunu to be out of the hut anyway so that he could breathe fresh air. There were times when Freddie slept, but Sophia could not leave him even then in case his rasping breathing stopped completely. In one of these quieter moments Atewhai forced a bowl of soup into her hands and made her swallow a few reluctant spoonfuls.

After the rain and fog of the previous day the sun had come out from behind the low cloud in the late afternoon and dried everything out. Hunu was happy to be able to get outside and leave the women to their young patient. His eyesight was poor, but he was surprised that he couldn't see any sheep on the hillside. Perhaps James had returned already from his journey and had taken the sheep further down onto the flat plain. He picked the wooden spoon up to give the pot a stir, as he had been instructed, and thought to himself that he must tell Atewhai about the sheep later.

It was not until dawn had broken on that second morning that the fever finally reached its peak and Freddie whispered hoarsely, "Mama, Mama."

Mama had been snoozing with a blanket around her shoulders, but was awake in seconds. However it was not the fevered, delirious young boy who greeted her, but a tired, pale one who was trying to sit up in his bed.

"Stay still, my sweet, you will be tired," said Sophia, as she gently pushed her son back onto his pillow. Almost immediately he was asleep again, but a sleep without the constant movement of the fever, a gentle healing sleep.

Atewhai had prepared a drink to calm Freddie's fever and a balm for his itchy skin. Both medications came from the same kumara plant, which Atewhai produced by boiling the tuber from beneath the ground and the stems and leaves from above. The liquor could be sipped to reduce fever and the mashed remains spread on the skin to soothe it. Using the same kowhai bark that had helped to mend his broken arm, Atewhai made a tea which she encouraged Freddie to drink to relieve his painful throat, even though he found it very hard to swallow.

As each hour passed he seemed a little brighter. Perhaps the worst was over.

On the first day that dawned with clear skies and sunshine Atewhai encouraged Sophia to take some time outside for her own wellbeing. She gladly accepted Atewhai's offer to sit at Freddie's bedside while she went outside to take in gulps of fresh, clear air. It was as if the rest of the world around her had been closed off to her since James left and it all came back to her in a rush. His hurried embrace, his last wave as he disappeared into the bushes to avoid being seen by his pursuers. Suddenly, the cares and worries for her son and husband took over her whole body, and she was racked with huge, heaving sobs as tears ran down her cheeks. First George, now Freddie and James. Was she to lose all her men? Was she to be alone in this isolated valley with their dreams of building a new life and home out of the question for now? Loneliness had fallen like a heavy cloak over her shoulders when George was killed. As the years had passed and her love for James had grown, the cloak had lifted and her spirits soared. She could hardly bear the thought of it creeping over her soul once more.

It was Atewhai and Hunu who brought her comfort for now. They both sensed that what Sophia needed was to be kept busy with domestic chores. So she and Atewhai changed the blankets upon which Freddie had been laid, washed them and laid them to dry across the bushes in the sunshine. Hunu was happy to sit with Freddie, although not so happy to be wearing his mask again. The women set about tidying their camp after all the rain and laid a new fire before turning towards Sophia's camp to see what could be salvaged. Roy came with them and spent much time sniffing around looking for Friday. There was a smell of her, but no other sign, and he could smell James as well. He liked that smell.

There was not a sign of a single sheep to be seen and the horse had gone too. Food had been taken and the covers on much of the food had been carelessly left so that the birds had been at the oats, flour, biscuits and bread. Some of it could be salvaged, as could the bedding and cooking utensils, and the canvas shelter would be useful too. The cart remained but the women could do nothing to move it without a horse, so it stayed where it stood for now. They could carry things across the valley as they were needed and the rest could be packed safely into the cart. The canvas shelter, the mattress and some of their clothing were carried between them back to Atewhai's hut. Sophia held the pile of folded blankets close to her face for a moment. Could she smell James in them, perhaps?

Once the shelter had been set up to increase the living space, and the mattress had been made into a comfortable bed for Sophia, they had time to think about the events of the last day or so. Sophia was not at all sure she understood what had set these things in motion. James had said he was being chased for stealing the sheep, but she trusted him to have paid properly for them. She could only presume that it was the Baylis brothers at the root of the confusion, but couldn't work out how the two shepherds had been the ones in pursuit of James. And why did he need to go all the way to Lyttelton to prove he had paid for the sheep? He had said he was going to see the magistrate, but surely he could have sorted it all out with Thomas Baylis. She shivered at the thought of that name and knew in her heart that he had found a way to get his revenge for the day that James had saved her from his unwanted advances.

"Never mind," she thought to herself. "James will sort it all out and be home in a week or so with Friday and the sheep."

She wanted to go back down to Nancy's house to see if Edmund could help them to move the cart and to find out if they knew any more about the Baylis brothers' involvement, but she knew she could not. If Freddie did indeed have Scarlet Fever, and it certainly seemed to be so, she had to stay away for several weeks. She could not risk the spread of the disease to the twins and especially to Nancy, who was due to give birth any day now. But she missed her friends so much. Even though Atewhai was a great comfort to her, it was not the same as sharing her dreams with Nancy and her other neighbours back down the valley.

Freddie's health improved each day with the mixtures that Atewhai made him drink and the salves which she applied to his tender skin. But how he itched! In places he had scratched his skin raw and even in his sleep his fingers stretched out for the bits he could reach to scratch some more. Sophia cut his finger nails as short as she could and made some cotton mittens to tie over his hands at night. He hated wearing them as much as Hunu hated his mask, but the women were strict with them both and they were right to be so. After a week, Freddie was sitting up in bed and eating small mouthfuls of food. But he tired quickly and slept for much of the day and then was restless at night. And in that week there was no sign of illness in the three adults. As the days passed Sophia grew to hope that they had all escaped the infectious fever. When Hunu sneezed the two women exchanged worried glances, but he claimed it was just the fibres from the inside of his mask that tickled his nose.

The day that Freddie got out of bed for the first time was a real step forward. His legs were wobbly and his muscles wasted to nothing. He stood unsteadily by the bed leaning heavily on the stick that Hunu had made for him. He was so proud of his staff with the top carved into a man's face with his tongue sticking out. Freddie liked to put his tongue out to make his face look the same as the one on his stick, until Sophia told him off for being so rude. The women laughed to each other as the two men, young and old, wobbled their way across the camp, young Freddie trying hard to match the steps of the older man.

Freddie had liked Atewhai since she had helped to mend his broken arm, and now he came to love Hunu just as much. Sometimes he didn't understand the words that Hunu used and sometimes Hunu didn't hear what Freddie was saying but, with some pointing and waving and pictures drawn with their fingers in the air, they managed somehow to communicate.

Hunu and Atewhai were never blessed with children, but they enjoyed the real pleasure that is given to childless couples by the occasional visits of borrowed children. Taiko and his brother were too grown up to visit these days, so Hunu was more than happy to take on Freddie as an adopted grandson at this late stage in his life. Freddie had no family nearby to teach him things that would normally be learned from a grandparent. Hunu filled that role quite happily. As Freddie's strength returned he started to explore his new home and it was Freddie that found the waterfall where fish streaked across a clear pool of deep water and it was Freddie who learned to mimic the glorious sound of the black bird with the funny white beard who sang from the tallest tree each morning. Although the days of early winter were short, Freddie filled them full of activity and slept well in his bed under the canvas shelter next to his mother. From there he could reach out a small hand and touch the warm fur of Roy's back. Roy liked that. He loved his young master.

One cold morning under heavy grey clouds Hunu and Freddie, with Roy at their heels, set off to look for some late berries to add to their supper. Sophia went about her housework for the day her mind racing with the decision she had reached overnight. She needed to go back to Nancy and Edmund, and she thought that Freddie was no longer infectious and now strong enough to make that journey. They would need to walk, but they should be able to get there in a day, if they were ready to go at first light. Not only was she keen to tell

Edmund about the loss of his portion of the flock, but she so wanted to see how Nancy's pregnancy was proceeding. She had lost track of time to some extent, but surely it would be any day now. Perhaps Nancy already had a new baby, or two. It was funny how they had all assumed that Nancy would be having twins again. Even Nancy was prepared for it this time, and she and Sophia had spent a lot of time preparing two of everything, just in case.

Two things happened that day to prevent Sophia's plan being put into action.

The first was a familiar feeling in her stomach which led her swiftly to the bushes where she very quickly lost her breakfast. "Surely not," she thought to herself. "Surely I can't be expecting James' baby." As in her first pregnancy on board ship, she felt much better once she had been sick and was filled with joy to think she had another baby in her belly. But how she wished she could share the good news with her husband. Every day she had expected James to come striding down the hill with Friday at his heels, but today she willed it with all her heart.

With these thoughts running around in her head she had failed to notice that snow had suddenly started to fall around her. In no time at all huge flakes of snow settled on every surface. Sophia shook her head to remove the drifts which had quickly accumulated in her hair. She was pleased to see Hunu and Freddie hurrying back to the shelter of the hut, stopping occasionally for Freddie to pick up handfuls of the fascinating white flakes. He had never seen so much snow in his short life and was very excited by it.

In a very short time the ground had been covered by a thick white carpet, deep enough to make it clear to Sophia that nobody would be travelling anywhere for several days.

Back down the valley Nancy and Edmund were watching the snow fall and wondering when they would get to see Sophia again. They had so much to tell her and so much to find out from her about recent events. Despite all that Nancy had been through herself in the last few weeks she felt sad for her friend and wanted so much to be with her once more.

Of course, they had not been aware that she was alone until two days before the snow came.

They had seen James, Sophia and Freddie set out on their journey that March morning with the sheep being driven efficiently onwards by the dogs. How they had wanted to join them that day and start their dream together. But Nancy's pregnancy had not been as easy as her first, and she was certainly not well enough to travel and not fit enough to give birth in a temporary home. But they were not concerned that day. James and Sophia were happy to set things up and see out the winter while Nancy and Edmund added to their family. Time enough for them to join them in the spring.

The first few days after Sophia and James left were filled with activity which kept Nancy's mind busy, but her swollen body tired out. Samuel and Carrie had moved into Sophia's house and Nancy was happy to help them to settle in. She liked Carrie who, though younger than her and Sophia, was a resourceful girl. It was obvious to all that Carrie was absolutely in love with Samuel and would have followed him twice around the globe if that was what he had wanted. But she was young and had not learned a lot from her mother about running a home, so Nancy was only too pleased to pass on some of her knowledge about things like cooking and storage and cleaning and laundering. Carrie was a fast learner and mopped up all the hints and tips that Nancy gave her. Their friendship was not on equal terms, like that of Nancy and Sophia. Nancy was more like a mother to Carrie, or perhaps a teacher, but friends they certainly had become. In much the same way, Samuel was learning how to run a farm from Edmund, who in turn, was happy to hear some ideas from Samuel. He was particularly keen to follow up the idea of metal roofing sheets to replace their thatched roof which required so much attention and maintenance each year. Once the winter was over they had agreed to take the cart to buy some sheets of the new material. Samuel thought they should find some in the growing community of Oamaru on the coast. It would be a shorter journey than to Hawksbury and a place where much building work was being done, so supplies would be more readily available.

Completely unaware of the events unfolding further up the valley, the four young people settled into the day-to-day routine of their respective farms. Nancy found she could do less and less each day. Carrie was happy to look after the boys each afternoon while Nancy rested, and she welcomed the quiet times where she could rest while darning a sock, or flicking idly through one of Betsy Franks' magazines. But she often found her eyes closing and her chin dropping forward these days. And the day came when she gave into her growing tiredness and lay down on her bed. It was getting dark when Carrie brought the boys home and, as she approached the house, she was surprised to see no lantern lit in the window. Ben and Ed ran ahead expecting supper to be on the table. They were hungry after an afternoon of activity, but found the table bare and the fireplace cold.

It was not until Carrie put a hand to Nancy's shoulder that she woke with a start.

"Just you stay there," ordered Carrie. "I'll light the fire and get some supper under way."

It was not like Nancy at all to agree to this request, but her body seemed unwilling to move, so she was happy to lay back and listen to the sounds of the supper being prepared. The food smelled good and she thought to herself that she had taught Carrie well. But she certainly didn't feel hungry herself. In fact, she felt quite sick.

Edmund arrived home to be greeted by Carrie at the door looking anxious.

"I think her time is coming very soon," she said to her neighbour. Edmund took stock of the situation and realised it was going to be a long night.

"Right, Carrie, can you take the boys back with you for the night and ask Samuel to fetch some help from the village, please?" asked Edmund.

He was glad that Carrie had taken the boys away before Nancy's labour began. Whereas her first labour had been a straightforward affair, except perhaps for the unexpected arrival of the second twin, it was obvious from the start that this time it would not be so easy. Edmund did what he could to ease her pain, but he could do nothing to help when she doubled up in pain as contractions came nearer together each time. He had no idea how long he was alone with his wife, but he greeted Clara Nicol with relief when she and the vicar arrived holding a lantern and bringing a cold blast of air into the room. Job Nicol led Edmund out into the yard where they sat down together on two upturned logs with blankets thrown over their shoulders to keep the cold night at bay and to await developments indoors. Although Reverend Nicol preached regularly about the demon drink, he was not averse to the need for a drop in certain circumstances, so he produced a small silver hip flask from his pocket. He held it out to Edmund who accepted the offer gratefully.

Inside the cabin Clara was getting very worried about Nancy's health and the condition of her unborn child. The labour was exhausting and progress seemed unusually slow. Clara Nicol had gained much experience in childbirth over the last few years, and she knew the danger signs. Nancy was too tired to push and the child seemed reluctant to help things along from inside. She had once seen a mother manipulating the baby into the right position to be born, and she thought she may need to attempt that now. It concerned her greatly that she felt only a very faint beat of the heart as she held Nancy's stomach and massaged her baby gently but firmly, and she tried hard not to pass her concerns onto Nancy.

With the next contraction Clara encouraged Nancy to push as hard as she could and, all of a rush, the head appeared. The problem was immediately obvious to Clara. This was a big baby with wide shoulders. No wonder it was a hard job for Nancy. And perhaps Nancy's enormous size in pregnancy had just been because of a big baby. Not twins after all.

With much encouragement from her midwife, the shoulders and then the rest of the baby appeared and it was only a moment or two after the birth that a hearty cry could be heard from the healthy baby girl. Though Nancy was in no fit state to understand everything that Clara told her, she was pleased to have a girl to match her boys.

But then the familiar feeling of a further contraction hit Nancy and she knew at once that there would be another birth. This time it seemed a much quicker affair and Nancy was soon lying back in relief imagining her two new daughters gurgling together, just like the boys had done after their arrival.

From Clara's viewpoint it was not relief but dread which hit her. The birth had indeed been swift but rather than the pink, healthy glow of the first birth, here lay a tiny body with skin of an ominous blue in colour. The cord had been around the child in such a way that it had starved her of life entirely but, just in case, Clara removed the baby girl towards the warm fire, wrapping the tiny body in a cloth and rubbing and rubbing to see if life could be restored. No sound came from the child, no tiny lift of the chest, no tiny fingers moving. There was no doubt that this child was stillborn.

It took a while to tidy things up and Clara broke the sad news to Nancy before she called the men inside. With tears in her eyes, she asked to see her second daughter and briefly held her tiny cold body before handing her back to Clara. She had another daughter to tend to, and, hard as it may be to bear the death of a child, she knew she needed any energy she had left to tend to the living baby.

Reverend Nicol took the tiny child's body and quietly spoke the prayers that go with a death. He and Clara whispered together in the corner of the room and agreed to take the body home with them. Edgar Franks would be asked to construct a tiny coffin and Samuel would dig a tiny grave outside the church door. A burial could wait until Nancy was fit enough to attend.

After checking that Nancy was comfortable, and wishing the couple well with their new daughter, the Nicols took their leave. Job carried the tiny tragic parcel with sadness in his heart. Clara had suffered both the sadness and joy of childbirth that night and, as they knelt side by side at their bed to pray, they asked God to bless both the living and the dead.

For the sake of her family, Nancy dragged herself back to normality as soon as she felt physically able, despite her feelings of grief for a life lost mixed with the joy of a life gained. The boys were too young to understand about the death of one baby, but were happy to enjoy the arrival of a new sister. Nancy had chosen two pairs of girls names in case she had twins again. She kept one of those pairs aside for the tiny body of her lost daughter and awarded the other to the healthy girl who sucked at her breast and cried loudly beside her. Adelaide Rosina, names chosen to honour Nancy and Edmund's own mothers, were thereby granted to this hearty child. She had grown fat in the womb, presumably taking the goodness that was not required by her dead sibling, and she hungrily accepted every drop of her mother's milk. Young Adey Rose would grow to be a chubby child, none the worse for the loss she had suffered at birth.

On a cold and wet morning with the clouds lowering around them, a small group gathered in the churchyard to put the tiny wooden coffin into the ground. Her small headstone would later hold the words, "Edith May Lawton, died at birth, April 1855."

The small group consisting of Nancy and Edmund, taking it in turns to hold the surviving twin, Samuel and Carrie, Edgar Franks and Clara and Job Nicol were reluctant to leave the tiny grave. As they walked slowly and sadly to the church gate they were met by Betsy Franks holding the hands of Ben and Ed. The boys sensed the sombre mood and were unusually quiet, resisting the urge to climb a tree, or race each other up the path as would be their normal way, unless issued with a stern warning from the Reverend Nicol, who considered it a serious misdemeanour to run in church grounds.

As Edmund turned to thank the vicar for his words at the graveside, the sound of horses approaching caused them all to turn towards the stream. Two horsemen were driving their mounts through the shallow water and as they got nearer the mourners realised who these two men were.

"Why do these two turn up at the worst moments?" said Edmund, between gritted teeth. "I have no desire to talk to Thomas and Simon Baylis today even though they seem so pleased with themselves."

But it was too late to ignore them as the brothers were already jumping from their horses and coming across to join the group.

"What brings you all to church on a weekday?" asked Thomas.

"We are here to bury a child, Thomas, so please show some respect," replied Job Nicol. He had no time for these boys, particularly since he had heard some of the details of Thomas' attack on Sophia.

The brothers had the decency to remove their hats at least, but this news was not going to stop them passing on their own information to whoever wanted to listen to it.

"Would one of you be so good as to pass a message to Sophia, please? She is not so keen to see me in person these days," said Thomas with a wink in Edgar Franks' direction. With great difficulty, Edgar resisted the temptation to punch this man in the stomach.

"Perhaps you could tell her that her husband is in Lyttelton jail and will be there for a very long time," continued the older brother. "Maybe it will teach him that sheep stealing is a crime. That is, if he survives five years of hard work breaking rocks."

James' friends looked truly shocked, the colour draining from Nancy's face as she knew how she would feel if it had been Edmund accused of such a thing. And Edmund was thinking to himself that, if they were referring to the sheep James had taken up the valley, they had made a joint purchase, so maybe he was guilty in some way too. But then they had bought them from Simon Baylis in good faith, so there must be more to this tale than Thomas was telling them.

"What do you mean, Thomas?" asked Edmund. "How do you know this to be true?"

Thomas and Simon had already decided it would be best to keep the details brief so as to avoid any awkward questions about their involvement. The less they knew the better, but it well suited the brothers' need for revenge to make sure Sophia knew about her husband's imprisonment.

"We heard it from Mr Sidebottom who owned the sheep he stole. About a thousand head, we heard," said Simon.

Before he could stop himself Edmund said, "But James bought those sheep from you, Simon, or at least that's what he told us." A small seed of doubt had been sown in his mind as it had been James who had actually done the deal on his behalf.

"Well, we don't know what he told you, but those sheep belonged to Sidebottom and that's where they are now grazing back on their green coastal pastures," replied Thomas. "Please make sure that Sophia hears the news, and tell her I am happy to give her comfort in her loneliness any time."

Aware that he had crossed a line, albeit deliberately, he swiftly mounted his horse and, followed by Simon, galloped away across the river again before any of the men could take their fists to him.

Nancy and Edmund, leaving the boys to play outside and putting young Adey Rose to sleep on Carrie's bed, had joined Samuel and Carrie at the table in their borrowed house to talk through the revelation of James' imprisonment. They just couldn't believe what had happened and knew that the only way to find out more was to get up to see Sophia in the valley. But then, perhaps she had gone to Lyttelton too. There was nothing for it but for Edmund and Samuel to take the trip as soon as they could, leaving their wives to look after the children for a day or two. And if nobody was there, well then, somebody would need to make the journey north to find Sophia and to see what could be done to explain the truth and plead for James' release.

But, in the end, the worst snowstorm ever seen by the people who had made their lives in the community put a stop to their plans for some considerable time.

Chapter Eleven

Friday's tale

April 1855

Friday was not a happy dog these days. Even though she had a warm bed and shelter from the wind and rain and food was delivered each day, it was not provided with any love or affection. She was not hungry or cold, but she missed the kind hand that patted her head and the words that went with it of, "Good dog," or "Well done," in the language she understood from her master. Like a foreigner in a land where others spoke a strange language, she couldn't understand the commands she was given and so looked foolish and slow when trying to do the job she had been bred to do so well. As a result of this, she found herself more often than not left behind in her kennel, tied with a chain so as to stop her escape, while the other dogs went about their working day without her.

She had no intention of escaping until it suited her, but they didn't know that of course. She knew that they would follow her if she simply ran off from the fields, or even worse, they would raise the stick that gave out fire and she would lie bleeding to death like the wild pig she had once seen dispatched in that way. She was a clever dog with a rare gift of reasoning. It was not the usual way of dogs to think of the consequences of their actions. Enough to run or jump or eat or play with only that action in mind until the next thing came along, but Friday had the ability to say to herself, "If I do this, then that will happen." That is why James could use her on her own to move large flocks of sheep instead of needing a whole team of dogs. Friday could anticipate the movement of a single errant sheep, work out how to get ahead of it in no time and encourage it back to join the others. She was indeed a special dog.

So she was prepared to bide her time putting up with the other dogs ignoring her and the rough intolerance of the young shepherds, who had quickly abandoned any attempts at making her work for them. If it hadn't been for Mr Sidebottom she would probably have been shot. A working dog is just the same as a plough or a cart. If it isn't good enough to perform the task required, then it is surplus to requirements and is to be discarded. But there was a corner of John Sidebottom's heart that felt respect for this dog and for her master. He had spent many hours considering the events surrounding his journey up the valley and the long ride to Lyttelton, and he had reached the conclusion that perhaps he had presumed too much from the Baylis brothers' reports of what had happened. Though he could do little to save James Mackenzie from his fate, perhaps he could earn redemption by at least caring for his faithful dog. The dreadful picture of the broken man standing in the dock as his dog desperately tried to reach him across the courtroom was one which John Sidebottom would have preferred to forget.

Friday tolerated the odd good word from the boss, but it was not enough to keep her in this flat, green, unfamiliar land. She yearned for the hills and the touch of her family. To play with Roy and her puppies again and to see Freddie and his friends. To sleep in comfort next to her master's gentle hand and to hear, "Dihaoine, Trobhad," once more. Oh how she would love to be called to her master's side.

Taiko and Seventeen were both feeling the effects of the night before. They had been persuaded by a recently arrived Australian shepherd to drink far too much ale, a drink with which they were not naturally familiar, but they liked the taste without realising the effects of an excess of it. It humoured the rough foreign shepherds to encourage the native folk to get drunk. These hardened pioneers were used to downing mugful after mugful of the strong brown ale without any ill effects, but it took barely one drink before the native men began to act strangely, slurring their words and staggering around the room. Both Taiko and Seventeen had very sore heads now and were reluctant to leave the comfort of their beds. Leaving Taiko asleep, Seventeen had gone on ahead to avoid the boss being woken by the noise of the dogs barking for their breakfast.

It was their usual routine to let all the dogs out of their runs into the fenced paddock to allow them to do their toilet against fences or bushes while the men put bowls of food in each pen. Today they had the spare scraps of meat from a sheep who had died of old age. Working dogs generally ate well as it was important for them to be kept fit and able to tackle the long, hard day ahead of them. It took Seventeen a while to mix each dish with a few hard biscuits and to hand them out single-handedly, especially as the smell of the raw meat made him retch more than once. When all the dogs had eaten their food he called them for work and led them out into the fields beyond. A storm looked like it was on its way and Seventeen's task for the day was to drive the sheep back towards the home fields for safety. Just one thing had slipped his woolly mind. The chain that kept Friday in her kennel each day had not been re-attached to her collar.

Friday stayed as still as she could and hoped that the shepherd had forgotten her completely. Quiet fell in the paddock as the other dogs went about their daily tasks in the fields beyond. They seemed to be heading into the hills today and that suited her fine. She bided her time in case the other shepherd came near. But Taiko was still snoring loudly trying to sleep off the awful pain in his head.

When it became clear that she was alone and the rest of the farm was quiet and still, Friday realised the time had come at last. It was in her nature to run fast and keep low, moving in a slight curve, and this she did in the general direction of the wide river. She knew with an innate sense of direction that somewhere along that river, as it went uphill and grew narrower, was her home. Working collies make their outrun in a long curve and, all of a sudden, they will turn and face the way they have run, head low, tongue hanging out, sides heaving, every bone in their body awaiting the next command. Friday did exactly that, but she hoped with all her heart there would be no command or her brief escape would be over. She looked back, fixing her gaze on the farm buildings. There was not a sign of movement.

After a few moments of absolute concentration Friday turned, took two big leaps down the steep river bank and started to run upstream over round pebbles, across grassy mounds and through streams of crystal clear water. She ran at a fast but measured pace conserving her energy for the long journey ahead and picking her route carefully. Never looking back and rarely taking a straight course, she covered the ground swiftly and efficiently. She had a full belly from her breakfast and only needed occasionally to slake her thirst in a pool of icy cold water.

When the wintery sun was at its highest point she took a rest in a sheltered spot under the river bank where the water had washed the soil away to form a kind of canopy. Friday turned round and round until she had trampled a small indentation in the soft gravel into which she curled her tired body. She was still concerned at being tracked by the shepherds. She was not aware that Taiko, once he had raised his head from his bed, had presumed that Seventeen had taken Friday to work for the day, so the alarm was yet to be raised.

She slept in the winter's sun, but fitfully and lightly, in case of disturbance. Once a duck-like bird shuffled its webbed feet past her, digging its beak around in the dead leaves that had accumulated at the water's edge. Friday was so still that the bird was unaware that it would perhaps have become a dog's supper if she had been at all hungry. For perhaps an hour she rested and then stood up with a stretch. Front legs first, she stretched and arched her back, then her back legs, her tail in the air. It felt like she was putting her bones back in the right places and warming up her body for the next leg of her journey.

Her afternoon continued at the same steady running pace. The river began to narrow and sometimes she had to take to the bank to avoid the water where it covered the whole riverbed. Was she far enough away from the farm now for it to be safe? It worried her to be in full view, but as the sun sunk towards the hills and the light diminished, she felt herself relax a little. She suddenly realised she was hungry and longed for a feed before night fell but, not having had to seek out food for herself before, she didn't know what she could eat or how she was going to find something. A fish darted past her as she stood at the water's edge and she tried to jump on top of it to catch it with her paws. The fish was gone in a flash and all that remained were four very wet and cold feet. Earlier she had seen birds which might make a tasty supper, but it seemed they had now found safe roosting spots for the night. She tried digging at the base of a plant to see if the roots could make a meal, but the bitter taste of her first mouthful made her shake her head, spit the nasty fibres out and lick her lips.

So it was that she spent her first uncomfortable night of freedom under a tree with cold, wet feet and an empty belly. It was a long and sleepless night, the only sound to be heard was the occasional rumbling noise in her tummy.

One could hardly call it a sunrise the next morning. Heavy grey clouds hid the sun as it climbed above the horizon as Friday looked back the way she had come. But in the gloomy light of day Friday set off once more, her bones aching and her increasing hunger making every step hard. Her desire to get away from the place where she had been kept and to return to people she knew was all that kept her going. Today she ran along the river bank where the grass was easier on her paws than the stony river bed. With her head down and focussing only on the route ahead, she barely noticed the snowflakes starting to fall around her. Slowly at first, each flake that landed on her back melting before the next one hit, but soon her long black fur was matted with a white coat of snow. She stopped to give herself a shake and realised that she could hardly see the path ahead. As time went by the snow lay deeper and deeper and, were it not for the path of the river beside her, she wouldn't have been able to find her way. Her long, low running motion turned by necessity into a kind of jumping run, each time her front feet landed she sunk into the snow and had to push her back legs upwards to make the next leap. It was exhausting work, the only benefit of which was that it kept her warm with all the effort.

Friday had no sense of time passing, just a need to reach familiar territory. The snow obscured every landmark and, though she stopped often to lift her nose in the air and seek out a familiar smell, all she could smell was snow. The cold and hunger could be born, but the exhausting journey was hitting her hard. It was late in the afternoon when Friday reached a point where a stream joined the main river. She stood for a moment on the bank looking into the swirling currents beneath her. She was not brave enough to leap into the water, but to turn upstream would mean a steep climb, dangerously slippery from all the snow. She scampered along the bank, this way and that, trying to decide what to do next, but in the end she realised there was nothing for it but to give in to her exhaustion. A tree with overhanging branches stood nearby, the branches dense enough to have stopped the accumulation of snow against the trunk. Friday used her tired paws to scratch the surface of the earth beneath the tree into a makeshift bed and lay down to sleep or die, whichever came first.

It may have been moments, or perhaps hours later that Friday heard a familiar sound. It caused her to sit up straight and put her head on one side trying to work out where the sound had some from. It was the sound of a sheep in distress. She had heard that noise on many occasions when being sent out to find a lost sheep, perhaps one who had fallen into a valley, or found herself stuck in the undergrowth with her fleece tied up in the spikes of a bush. Forgetting her own exhaustion at once she set off up the steep valley in the direction of this sound. It was hard going in the near dark and on the slippery rocks with deep snowdrifts between them. But Friday had little need to see where she was going as she used her nose to give her directions this time, a nose trained to home in on that special sheep-like odour.

The plaintive sound grew louder as she got nearer to the beast and suddenly, in the last moments of daylight, there she was, stuck between two huge rocks close to the water's edge. She had obviously slipped backwards down the icy bank and had no way of using her cloven feet to push herself back again. Her eyes rolled in fear, which became sheer terror when she saw the dog and she started to back away. But that is what saved her in the end. She slipped further towards the stream, her back legs under water, but now on firm enough ground to push herself sideways onto the safety of a snow covered shingle bank. As Friday knew only too well, sheep are not the cleverest of beasts, so despite her change in fortune, the sheep's instinct was merely to stand still, not quite sure where to go next, her sides heaving with fear and exhaustion.

Instinct of a different kind had overcome Friday's exhaustion and she knew she must try to help this sheep to safety. It was easy for her to slip forwards and slide down the same route the sheep had taken backwards, ending up on the same bank. Now they faced each other, both too tired to do anything but stand and look into each other's eyes. For a few moments that is all they could do, but then Friday started looking for a way to encourage the sheep back up onto the bank. Only then could she drive her back to join her flock. Friday knew with certainty that there would be a flock somewhere, there always was in her experience. Each time she tried to find a path, the sheep turned to watch her with suspicion, but there was no way to be found. Snow still fell and was now beginning to cover the marks they had both left on their way down the bank. Friday was beginning to give up hope as the snow continued and the temperature fell further. They had both had a dip in the river and neither of them would dry properly overnight.

The poor sheep began to stagger on her unsteady feet. Friday knew that she was likely to fall to the ground and it would then be impossible to raise her. But her legs were very tired too, perhaps they should both just lay down for a rest. Yet, what was that sound? A whistle, a familiar whistle too. Moments later a face she recognised appeared above her. It was Blue, his tongue hanging out and his tail waving madly. Blue barked furiously when he realised he had found the sheep, though he was somewhat confused to find Friday there as well.

Edmund and Samuel heard Blue's bark and wondered what he had found. By the middle of the afternoon it had become obvious to them both that the snow was going to form drifts, so they had set out to see if they could bring the sheep closer to Samuel's home for safety. They had walked for an hour or so and had gathered a good mob together. Both men were just thinking it may be time to get home for supper when they heard Blue's urgent bark coming from some distance ahead of them. Thinking he had found a sheep stuck in a bush, perhaps, they whistled for him to come back and show them the way, but to no avail.

It took them a while to walk through the gathering snow drifts with only the barking to guide them, but there was Blue, tail wagging madly, standing to attention at the top of a steep bank. A sheep gave a plaintive bleat below them, accompanied by the whining of a dog. From where Friday was standing she could see two faces appear above Blue's head and, recognising these men, all thoughts of exhaustion were forgotten.

"Good Lord, its Friday!" exclaimed Edmund, as he held the lantern high. "Where in God's name have you come from?"

The men took stock of the situation and quickly sent Blue down the bank. Edmund followed as best he could, although it was a steep and slippery journey for them both. Using Blue to encourage the sheep to put her two front hooves on the bank, he manhandled the beast up the bank where she stood for a moment and then happily trotted off to join the rest of the mob as if nothing had been wrong at all. Edmund scooped Friday into his arms thinking, "Goodness, she's a bit skinny," and handed her up to Samuel's waiting hands. Once they were all safely back on the bank above the river, muddy and wet but otherwise unscathed, the dogs circled each other with tails wagging while Samuel and Edmund patted Friday gently and wondered what had happened to her since James' arrest. Heading home it soon became obvious that Friday was very tired indeed as she fell further and further behind the main party. So, in the end, Carrie and Nancy were reunited with Friday in Samuel's arms where she had travelled for the last part of the journey. She managed a tiny wag of the tail, but could hardly raise her head to greet some more familiar faces.

The following morning Friday woke for the first time in a very long while to a feeling of utter contentment. She had a nice full tummy and a soft, warm bed inside a house, and some of her friends were nearby too. In fact, wasn't that her babies, Ruby and Blue, she could see playing in the yard? She stretched her back and her tired legs, stood gingerly to test out her aching joints and sore paws, and trotted out to find a place to relieve herself in the grass. Ruby and Blue came over to greet their mother, and then there were some more familiar faces. Little Ed and Ben ran towards her grabbing her in their arms and rubbing her tummy when she rolled over on her back in sheer pleasure. Just as she would have done to check that every sheep in her flock was gathered together, she did a count of the people and dogs around her. Roy, Ruby and Blue. Edmund and Nancy, Samuel and Carrie, the twins. Several names were missing from that list. Where was Sophia and where was Freddie? And most important of all, where was her master?

So her journey was not yet done. She would rest and eat and enjoy the company for a while, but then she must leave once more to find the rest of her family.

AMANDA GIORGIS

THE WIDEAWAKE HAT

Chapter Twelve

Prisoner Mackenzie

April 1855 - January 1856

In the same way that Friday was prepared to tolerate her captivity until an opportunity arose for escape, prisoner Mackenzie was biding his time in Lyttelton jail.

On the day of the committal James had left the court with tears in his eyes, not for the sentence bestowed upon him, but for the separation from his two loves in life, Sophia and Friday. So his slow walk in chains from the courthouse to the jail, accompanied by the booing and jeering of the many onlookers, and his return to the prison cell, where he had spent the previous days since his capture, were all a bit of a blur. Fortunately, nobody seemed to be worried about him for now. The chains had been removed and he had taken himself to a corner of the small cell, curled up in a ball in the straw covering the floor and cried himself into a fitful sleep, punctuated by dreams of seeing Sophia and Friday running towards him across the valley he loved so much.

He awoke to a touch on his shoulder, instantly alert and expecting the worst. But he was greeted by the kindly face of the duty constable, who indicated a tray containing a plate of bread and cold ham and a jug of flat ale.

"Eat your supper, man," said the jailer. "It'll be the best you get for a while. In an hour they will take you to the main cells where you may have to fight harder for your food. And shed no more tears, perhaps. Keep those you have left behind to yourself, as there will be little sympathy amongst the other prisoners."

James sat up and gratefully accepted the food and the kind words. The constable leaned against the door and watched as James ate his cold supper and sipped at his jug of ale.

"Are you crying for your dog, or is there someone else who will miss your company tonight?" asked the constable.

Having heard tales of wives being blamed for their husband's crimes, or, even worse, forced into jail with their husbands, James had made the decision to keep silent about his married status, so his reply was, to some extent, short on the truth.

"Aye, I will miss the dog, she's a good gal, and a faithful friend," he replied.

Constable Paine was having trouble understanding the thick accent of his latest prisoner, but he could see the anguish in this man's face. As a child, he had grown up with the family dog as a playmate and he would have done anything for it, so he could feel something of the same emotion. He had seen lots of prisoners grieve for wives and children, but never a dog. But then, this chap was a strange fellow, there was no doubt.

Once James had finished his meal down to the last crumb of bread and the final drop of ale, Constable Paine picked the tray up and handed James a neatly folded pile of clothes.

"Change your old clothes for this prison uniform, please," he said, "and you can keep those sturdy boots and your hat. You'll need both on the road gang, no doubt."

Alone again, James peeled off his ragged clothing, gave himself a most inadequate wash from the water bucket placed in one corner of the room, dried himself with his old discarded shirt and re-dressed slowly with the coarse corduroy trousers and check shirt with broad arrows sewn roughly across it. Someone, who certainly did not have Sophia's touch with a needle and thread, had crudely stitched the numbers 1248 unevenly across the left breast. There were good thick socks, for which he was grateful as his old ones were showing signs of his long journey, and a waistcoat made of cloth which contained the only pocket he had, there being nowhere, he presumed, to hide a weapon or a means of escape. All the items fitted loosely on his frame having been made for a much bigger man, it seemed. He would need to find a way to keep those trousers from falling down round his ankles. For the first time since his trial he chuckled to himself at the image of a prisoner with his trousers falling down. The two prison guards who came to collect him were surprised to find a man laughing to himself about something and suspected he was perhaps due for the mental asylum rather than the work gangs.

He was given time to re-lace his boots and place his soft-brimmed hat on his head before being marched roughly out of the building and into the courtyard in the centre of the main jail. The guards failed to see James place a small, much-folded piece of paper into his waistcoat pocket. It was a tiny pencil drawing of Sophia, sketched by Nancy, which he had carried with him since their marriage. Over the time he was in jail it would be carefully and secretively unfolded from that pocket every morning so that James could retain the image of his wife and carry it through each long and tiring day.

The prisoners were kept in cells designed for two men, but housing four or more at present. Lyttelton jail had only recently been completed, but demand for space had grown with the decision to house lunatics on the same site. So James found himself taking up the last available mattress on the floor of a dark, square cell with a small window above head height giving the only light. In the corner hung a hessian curtain behind which was the lavatory bucket, shared by them all and emptied at dawn. By the smell of it, it was almost full.

James was not a man to be sociable and he had no intention of making friends with his fellow inmates. The man who had already taken to his bed turned and nodded in his direction but James gave the merest return. The other two men, rough looking characters, were sitting facing each other on a mattress playing with some dice. They took no notice of the newcomer.

He silently thanked the constable for allowing him time to wash and use the toilet bucket before he left his cell as he knew he could last the night, well fed and watered, without the need to relieve himself. With a quiet goodnight to his family he fell asleep wondering what shape his life would take for the next five long years. That is, if he chose to stay that long.

Promptly, as the clock struck six, a bell began to ring in the courtyard. The four inmates of cell fourteen stirred slowly, stretching to ease the aches brought on by sleeping on a thin mattress. James, unsure what would happen next, put his boots on and stood up straight awaiting events. The young man next to him put on his boots too, but James noticed they were old and broken with soles barely attached to the uppers. It was, it seemed, this young man's job to empty the bucket, a task which he did swiftly and effectively without spilling any of the awful contents. He had obviously done that for many mornings before.

The jailer unlocked each cell in turn and James, the man with the bucket and the two other inmates stood awaiting their turn, counting the jangle of keys as they approached number fourteen. The man with the bucket went first and shuffled across the courtyard where a swarm of flies indicated a midden had been dug. All the other inmates mingled in the courtyard until a whistle was blown bringing everyone to attention. Having washed his bucket and returned it to the open cell, the man stood himself next to James.

"Follow me," he said. "I'll show you what to do. I'm John, John Douglass."

James was happy to accept some assistance, but was not prepared to make friends of anyone until he knew the lay of the land. "James," he simply replied, "James Mackenzie."

And so the routine of prison life began for James. Morning roll call, a breakfast of cold food laid out on a table for the prisoners to help themselves, work groups allocated for the day. That work took them usually outside of the prison walls for labour on road building or construction in the growing town of Lyttelton. Those incapable of hard work were allocated duties of sewing uniforms or cooking for the prison and for the local workhouse, some were given jobs to make furniture to fit out the new prison so that men could sleep in proper beds rather than on the floor.

If work was allocated outside the prison there was no provision for lunch. Fortunately, the locals would generally give a loaf or a pie to the jailer who, if he was of a kindly nature, would share it between his prisoners. Sometimes he would eat the lot himself.

By nightfall, all the prisoners would be back in their cells where a supper of hot food, perhaps a thick soup, or a meat casserole, would be given to each cell with a wooden spoon and small bowl per prisoner. There would often be fights between prisoners over the shared supper and many would go hungry rather than cause a stir with their fellow inmates.

Then the long nights would begin. James found this the hardest part of the day. He could cope with the rough and ready discipline and the heavy work he was given. He was younger and fitter than most of the men and soon earned a reputation as a good worker. He was happy to wait his turn while the two other men in his cell took the best of the supper. He and John Douglass took what was left and shared it between them. Sometimes it was not much at all. But those long nights were enough to send a man mad. He suspected John had succumbed to that affliction already. He heard him mumbling to himself, or sobbing as quietly as he could, in the bed next to James. He seemed to shuffle when he walked, though that may have been in part due to his ailing boots. He wore the demeanour of a mad man and James wondered if he was feigning it in order to be moved to the lunatic wing where inmates were left, in the main, to their own devices. James wondered if he would go the same way. Was he beginning to go mad himself?

It seemed to the other inmates that Mackenzie was an odd sort of person. He was strong and worked hard, there was no doubt of that. Most of the prisoners had spent their lives in public houses or gaming rooms where they had grown fat and lazy. They secretly admired James' ability to swing a hammer high and carry a full load of stone in his arms. But he was an odd sort of character. When he spoke, which he did as little as possible, his words were thick with a Scottish accent and, it was said by his cellmates, he muttered in his sleep about a dog and a woman called Sophia. Or was the dog called Sophia? It was hard to tell.

At morning roll call he would stand, a solitary figure with a faraway look, clicking his fingers behind his back as if calling that dog to heel. His only friend, it seemed, was John Douglass, albeit a case of tolerating rather than liking the fellow. He seemed to accept him rather like an annoying fly, occasionally flapping a hand to dismiss him, but generally allowing him to shuffle alongside in his strange gait. They made an odd pair.

Towards the end of April a concession was made to the weather with the morning bell being rung at 6:30am. There seemed little point in getting the men up and about in darkness. And at the end of the day, it being dark by 5pm, supper came an hour earlier and the curfew bell rang earlier too. This made the long nights even worse for a lonely man.

On one such morning the men found the courtyard covered in a growing layer of snow. Large flakes continued to fall, clinging to their clothes and sticking to their hair. An air of expectation hung in the courtyard while the jailers talked in a group about the day's work groups. It seemed unlikely that road work would be possible, so perhaps some of the prisoners could be diverted to more useful tasks today.

James and John joined a small group of prisoners whose task for the day was to clear the pavements in the town and, if there was time, deliver firewood to any needy local families. It made a nice change for them both, although it was cold and wet work. By lunchtime they had made good progress along the town's main streets, although it seemed they may need to revisit the task tomorrow as the snow still fell. James, John and a couple of other men were sent to manhandle a cart through the streets looking for the needy who may be short of firewood in this cold weather. They called on a large family down by the port where the father had been out of work since a bad fall on the dockside. His children, so many that James lost count, were in rags, shivering by a tiny fire made from scraps of paper and one last log. The wife was so grateful for his gift that she pressed a biscuit into each man's hand. The man, leaning on a stick, hobbled to the door to see them off.

At the door he stopped saying, "I can go no further as I have no boots."

In a moment John had removed his grubby boots and handed them to the man. He wore good thick socks and knew he would be fine walking back to the prison where, no doubt, he could ask for new boots. James was not so sure this would happen, but he was pleased to see the look on the man's face.

"Thank you so much, it will help me look for work again," said the man. "I owe you a favour if you ever need one."

It seemed to James that John walked better without the encumbrance of his broken boots, and he wondered how long they would be of assistance to the crippled man. But by the time they had returned to the jail John was shivering with the cold of his wet socks. His request to the jailer for new boots was met, as James had suspected, with derision. Someone tossed him an extra pair of socks, so at least his feet stayed dry overnight and James reached up to the big window sill to lay the wet ones out to dry a little.

To the outsider looking in, James was a model prisoner. It was an image that James was keen to back up. But underneath he was ready to escape whenever an opportunity arose. He didn't know when a chance would appear, but he knew he would take it when it did. Little did he realise that Friday had thought exactly the same way and had already made her way back home.

The snow kept them all in their cells for the next two weeks. Even prisoners were entitled to stay relatively warm, and the cold wind and drop in temperatures after the initial snowfall made any kind of outside work impossible. But shutting men up all day and night was proving an issue for discipline with many fights breaking out and even the jailers becoming more short-tempered than usual. A small fire had been started in one cell causing the guards to run with buckets of water to put it out before it spread through the bed straw.

James and John's fellow prisoners became more irritable as the days passed by. They tired of playing dice and took to taunting John at every opportunity. James would have preferred to stay quietly in a corner, but felt the need to defend John from the verbal assaults. This only led to an increase in the abuse. In fact, it became a game to the two men. Sometimes they played the game as a pair and sometimes they seemed to be set against each other in an ongoing feud.

It was a dangerous game, in the end. One quiet afternoon James and John were both snoozing when one of their cellmates crept across the room and grabbed John's spare socks.

Before anyone could intervene the man had stretched one of the socks out and placed it around the neck of the other man, twisting it tighter and tighter. With bulging eyes, the poor man choked and gargled and tried to paw at the sock which was beginning to take his life away entirely.

James shouted as loud as he could to alert a jailer. "Come quick, he's killing him," he called, rattling the bars on the small window in the cell door.

It took a moment or two for the guard to understand James' accent, but he realised something was amiss and came running, blowing his whistle as he ran. He fumbled with the keys and eventually managed to open the door at the same time that another guard arrived. Both men took hold of a prisoner each. It was going to be a fight to subdue them.

James' mind worked quickly. The door was open and the keys still in the lock. Had he got time to take the keys and make his escape? Would he be seen? Would other guards be coming too?

It was a risk worth taking, but he needed to be quick about it. No time to grab his precious boots, but he knew a man who would be happy to wear them. As quietly as he possibly could, and secretly blessing his stockinged feet, he grabbed his hat, slid across to the door and, gently working the keys out of the keyhole, slipped out of the cell. He had learned the layout of the place over the last few weeks, so he had no difficulty in walking swiftly towards the door which he knew would take him straight outside. As long as he could work out which key to use before anyone else saw him.

It took him a couple of attempts, but he guessed correctly that the biggest key would fit the biggest door. Luck was on his side this time as the streets were quiet while everyone huddled round their home fires. With no boots his feet were cold and wet in no time, but at least he left no real footprints. He had thought about this escape for a long time and had worked out a plan to get himself home as quickly as possible. But he needed to rid himself of his prison clothes first.

He was heading for the port to find a coastal ship heading south when he realised that he would pass the house he had visited at the start of the snowfall. Perhaps he could call in that favour after all.

He knocked on the door. It was opened, just a crack, by one of the many children in this house. The grubby child called his mother, who immediately recognised the man who had delivered the means to keep her family warm.

"Come in, quickly," she waved her hand, "and keep the place warm. I guess you are on the run, then?"

James was taken by surprise at her blunt question. "I guess I am," he replied.

James quickly explained his request, realising that he was asking a lot of a family with so little themselves. In no time at all he was changing his shirt for a ragged one belonging to the husband. It was tight, but it would do. An old jacket was also found, but James was not keen to take something so valuable from the family.

"I doubt he will wear it until he is laid out in it," said the woman with a shy laugh. "Take it, with our thanks for the boots. Now go. Find a ship to take you home to your loved ones."

James wondered how she knew about his family, unaware of the distant look in his eyes that betrayed his lost love. Only a woman's intuition would see it.

Stopping himself from breaking into a run, James walked with as much confidence as he could muster towards the dock. There were two or three ships in dock, but he had no idea when they would leave, or where they would be going. The light was beginning to fade on this short winter's day and he knew he would draw attention to himself if he started to ask questions at this late hour. This was confirmed by the ringing of the prison bell. His escape had been discovered.

He had been at work around the docks for a few days before the snowstorm, helping to build a huge stone retaining wall to hold back the steep hillside. He had scouted out a few possible hiding places while the guard wasn't watching his men too closely. There was a wooden shack behind the harbourmaster's house where his old dog slept. The dog had seemed docile enough and James had slipped him a crust to help their friendship along a little. He slipped unnoticed beside the house, dodged the light of the single lantern which was lit at the front, and approached the kennel. The dog recognised him and gave a deep but welcoming bark which elicited a shout of "Be quiet, dog" from the house. It was warm inside the shack and the dog seemed more than happy to have a companion for the night. James settled down to the most comfortable night he had enjoyed for many months. In his dreams the old wolfhound became a collie called Friday with whom he had shared many a night, and he slept soundly knowing it was unlikely that he would be pursued on a cold night. It would be a different story in the morning, no doubt.

Sheriff Simeon was not pleased with his incompetent staff. To be honest, he was extremely angry. Nobody had escaped from Lyttelton Jail on his watch, and he was not at all happy that Prisoner 1248 Mackenzie had become the first.

By daylight the following morning he had teams of men out searching the town. He wished he had more dogs to track the man, though it would have been a hard job in the cold weather for a dog to keep to a scent, but perhaps they would find a lead soon enough. It was unlikely the prisoner would have got far overnight without his boots. He picked his pen up and started to write, his anger increasing as he pressed hard on the paper. The nib gave way and splattered the page with ink. Screwing the sheet up into a ball, he began again.

"£50 Pounds Reward
Sheriff's Office, Lyttelton,
May 11th, 1855.

Whereas the Prisoner, JAMES MACKENZIE, sentenced to a term of imprisonment, at the last session of the Supreme Court, for sheep stealing, did, on the 10th instant succeed in effecting his escape and is still at large, the above reward will be paid to any person or persons, who may succeed in apprehending him and handing him over to the proper authorities.

Description of MACKENZIE:- Height, about 5 feet 11 inches; hair, light; eyes, small and grey; nose, large and aquiline; face, long and thin; body spare and muscular

At the time of effecting his escape he had on a brown wide-awake hat; cloth waistcoat, check shirt, marked with a broad arrow, and numbered, corderoy trousers, a pair of worsted socks, no boots or shoes. Speaks English imperfectly, feigning generally that he only understands Gaelic. Has a peculiar habit of putting his hands behind him, and snapping his fingers.

Charles Simeon
Sheriff"

The description had needed to be garnered from his jailers and fellow inmates as he had never met the man. But it seemed unlikely that a man of his features and habits would go unnoticed for long. He summoned a constable who was to take the paper, with all swiftness, to the printer for ten copies to be made. It would then be the constable's responsibility to ask for one copy to be placed in today's newspaper and then to pin the remaining posters at points around the town which seemed suitable.

By late morning small crowds could be seen gathering around the posters. Fifty pounds was a big reward. This man must be a real rogue. A few people began to stand with their hands behind their backs, clicking their fingers. "Take me in," some wise guy said, "and claim the reward!"

The man with the flapping boots and the heavy limp was one of the people standing in a small group at the docks. His wife had told him about the man calling last night while he was at work, and he had been glad to have returned the favour given to his family. But fifty pounds was a lot of money. More than he could ever dream of earning at the dockside, even if he was a fit and able man. It would feed and clothe his family for a good while. He spent the rest of the day in a dilemma. One which he chose not to share with his wife. He paced the streets, thinking that perhaps he could find the man single-handedly. After all, only he knew what he was now wearing. The old prison clothes, apart from the shirt which he had carried around with him all day, still lay at home where his wife intended to pick the arrows and numbers away and turn them into something new for the children. She was an excellent seamstress.

He passed the door of the sheriff's office more than once that day. In the end he felt he had no choice. He entered the front office and waited his turn to speak to the constable. There were several men there already, who claimed to have seen Mackenzie in a pub, or shopping for supplies. The constable, a wise man of many year's service, knew a lie when he heard one and sent each person on his way with a warning that deception to claim a reward was a crime in itself.

So it came as a shock to the constable when a prison shirt bearing the number 1248 was placed on his desk. The bearer of the shirt, a crippled man with broken boots, explained what had happened and the story of the firewood and boots was corroborated by John Douglass, who was summoned under guard from his cell to give evidence. His wife had been wrong in supporting an escapee, but the man hoped the constable could understand her desire to help someone who had helped them. John Douglass had the grace to squirm in his newly acquired boots.

The only thing that could be added was that his wife had presumed he was heading for the docks to find a ship to take him back home, wherever home may be.

The sheriff and the constable checked the broadsheet, which indicated ship movements from the port, and they were pleased to see that no ship had left today and that only one was due to sail tomorrow. A small coastal lugger heading for the newly created port of Oamaru where it would pick up a haul of the white stone so much favoured by the builders of fine architecture. Mackenzie's crimes had been committed somewhere down south, so surely he would head home that way.

In the end, James' recapture was a rather tame event. Constable Paine, who knew Mackenzie's face, was stationed discreetly on the dockside and, when he spotted the escapee about to step onto the gangplank, he quietly took him by the shoulder and marched him back to jail. James' attempt at escape had been thwarted this time, but he knew there would be other chances. He knew he would not wait five years to get back to Sophia.

In the ramshackle house down by the port the man and his wife sat facing each other at the table, fifty gold coins piled up in front of them both. They felt like Judas betraying Jesus Christ, but what was a man to do if offered a chance to feed and clothe his family?

James spent the next five days in solitary confinement, which was no hardship to a solitary man. For part of each day he was supervised in his task of re-applying number 1248 to a new shirt, a hard task for a man with hands more used to manual labour than the dextrous requirements of a needle and thread. If Sophia was there beside him the job would have been done in no time at all. How he wished that were the case.

After his escape a new routine was established in James' life. His two cellmates had been removed to separate cells, where they could brood over the injustice of it all, so his only roommate was John Douglass. A pair of boots had been found for John at last, so he was able to return the borrowed footwear to his cellmate. Without others present they became good friends and talked quietly each long night. It calmed John to have a soulmate at last and he walked more normally, there being no further talk of a move to the lunatic wing. And James found a certain contentment in his company. They shared their life stories with each other and, by doing so, they felt a bond which was strong. In all the time that he had been captive James had kept silent about his wife and adopted family. Only John got to know about Sophia and Freddie.

John's story was a sad one. He had taken a ship from England, not caring one bit where it was headed, to escape a cruel life at the hands of his brutal father. He still bore the scars across his back of the belt which had been used many times for the smallest of misdemeanours. He was barely sixteen when he saw the chance to escape and, stealing a few coins from the jar on the mantelpiece, he had paid for a steerage berth on the first ship out of the port of London. It took him to Lyttelton. With no experience, John had found it impossible to get work. He had drifted from place to place across the plains where, more often than not, he had stolen food from a farmhouse kitchen or the back door of an alehouse. In the town of Ashburton he had been offered his first paid job to hold a horse for a man while he entered the post office. Little did he know that the man had planned a robbery of cash destined to pay a local farm's staff. The man came out of the post office clutching a bag and, throwing a coin to John, he had set out down the road minus his horse.

Despite John's earnest protestations of innocence he was seen as an accomplice to the crime and sent, like James, to do hard labour for two years. Where James saw his period in jail as a mere interlude in his life, John saw it as a life sentence and could see no further than his current situation. He was not a stupid man, and he had a way with horses that James knew would give him work if he was pointed in the right direction.

John was due for release at the end of the year, having been of good behaviour throughout his sentence. Where he had faced his future with despondency before meeting James he now knew he could make something of himself. James had given him the confidence he needed to grasp any opportunity he could find once he had his freedom. He wished that James could be free at the same time, but it was unlikely that an escapee would be released early, of course.

The short winter days were replaced by the longer, hotter days of spring. This was a mixed blessing for the prisoners, who enjoyed the sunshine, but endured the flies and mosquitoes which seemed to swarm around their cells by day and night. It meant longer working days in hot and dry conditions, but their bodies turned brown and healthy in their outdoor jobs. John and James worked side-by-side on the road leading into the city of Christchurch, breaking rocks and rolling them to the steep sides of the road which was being hewn into the hillside. Progress was slow, but steadily each day they had to walk a little further over the newly laid surface to start their work. In general their jailers were not cruel men and became friends rather than captors as time went by. Passers by would find John and James leaning against a large rock next to their guard sharing their lunch as if they were all colleagues together, or hear James asking Constable Paine how his wife was getting on with her latest pregnancy in this hot weather. Life for them all was not bad, considering their state of incarceration.

One morning in early September Constable Paine seemed on edge and spent more time than usual ensuring his uniform was up to muster. He told the two men he would be taking them back early as a new magistrate was due to arrive that afternoon, and he was to be part of the honour guard to meet him. So while John and James spent an uncomfortably hot afternoon in their cell, the new magistrate, Henry Tancred, a man of substance and education and owner of a substantial parcel of land near Ashburton, was welcomed to his new post with all the pomp and ceremony befitting his status. Little did the prisoners know that today was to be a turning point in many of their lives.

Tancred was a man of much intelligence who had been in New Zealand for a full five years and felt he understood the peculiar ways of the native Maori and the newfound pioneers. Above all else he was a man of impeccable fairness, and he had promised himself that he would deal justly with those who came before him in his new role. It concerned him greatly that this prison, built for three hundred men, now held nearly double that number, and he felt certain that there were men here who did not deserve their imprisonment. It became his first task to begin a review of the current prison population, man by man.

It was a very large pile of paperwork which faced him. Each sheet a description of a man and his misdemeanours. James Mackenzie's sheet was near the bottom of the pile, but John Douglass' name reached Tancred's desk after only a few days. As it happened Henry

Tancred knew the story of his crime, and he knew his so-called collaborator to be a real rogue, who had used this same ploy once before. It took but a stroke of the pen to set John Douglass free, there being no basis to the evidence given against him.

Though happy for John, James found himself alone and despondent in a cell on his own. His goodbye with John had been poignant, with both of them thinking that perhaps they may never meet again, but he hoped that John had gained the confidence to find work, perhaps with the horses he loved. He did not realise that part of magistrate Tancred's philosophy was not just to release prisoners whom he perceived to be innocent, but to rehabilitate them as much as he could. In John's case this meant finding him work as an ostler at a public house where he had a bed for the night, all the food he required and the work he loved with horses.

Constable Paine noticed the change in James and was sad for him. In many ways he was not surprised when he came back from relieving himself behind the bushes to find James gone. There had always been that wild look in his eyes, like a caged bird yearning for freedom to spread their wings and sing their songs. He took his time in blowing his whistle, silently hoping it had given the man time to get away. But it was not to be. This time the dogs tracked him down in a couple of hours and he gave himself up willingly without injury from the hounds. Even in capture he had a way with dogs. They sat calmly by while they awaited their handlers. Something the men had never seen before.

A second attempt at escape meant the rest of his sentence in chains, so James was led to a solitary cell where his ankles were circled by strong metal clasps, a short chain between them and a huge, heavy iron ball, which had to be dragged along behind the prisoner at all times except when he was at work. Even then the chains remained making movement slow and painful.

It was the final straw for James, who raged against his chains in a manner which inclined his captors to book him a place with the lunatics. Only one good thing came out of it all. The sheet containing his name was pulled out from the bottom of the large pile of notes and placed on Henry Tancred's desk. What had caused this man to make his escape twice? The magistrate was keen to learn more about this James Mackenzie fellow.

Henry read and re-read the notes. It made no sense to him. The evidence seemed to hinge on this dog recognising his master. But how did that prove the crime? Surely it meant only that the dog belonged to the man. And what part had these two brothers taken, or the two Maori shepherds? It seemed to Henry Tancred that there was a big hole in this story somewhere. As he turned the page a small, neatly written sheet fell to the floor and it was this that finally decided him on James' fate. It was the written report of Constable Nevis from Hawksbury noting the details given to him by four men from a small community called Marytown, including the local vicar, which had arrived in the office only a few days before, given the date scribbled on the top, although the interview had occurred some three months previous. He wondered why this man had not dealt with the matter sooner. He picked up his pen and began to write a letter to John Sidebottom.

Sidebottom was not at all surprised to receive the letter by horseman just a few days later at the very beginning of January 1856. He had, for some time, been considering taking the journey to Lyttelton himself to discuss the matter with the new magistrate, whom he knew to be a fair man. He knew now that he and the shepherds had been duped by those Baylis brothers and it was indeed them who had stolen the sheep in the first place, setting Mackenzie up to be punished for a crime he had not committed. Even though the sheep had been returned, no doubt the brothers had made a packet of money out of the deal while James Mackenzie rotted in jail. He quickly wrote a note to be returned by the same horseman which informed the magistrate that he would be pleased to make the journey to Lyttelton, but he had a task to complete beforehand so Mr Tancred could expect him to arrive in a week or so.

He then made hasty arrangements to travel, not north, but west, where he wanted first to speak to James' family and neighbours. Once that had been done, he made haste to Lyttelton. It was indeed eight days later that he arrived in the magistrate's office and in due course his apology for jumping to conclusions was given honestly and frankly and accepted completely by Henry Tancred.

So two documents were signed by the magistrate in short order. The first being a pardon with compensation for Prisoner Mackenzie with immediate effect. The second being an order for the arrest of both Thomas and Simon Baylis at the first opportunity with all available resources being given to the search for these criminals. The charges included theft, deception and perjury in the trial of James Mackenzie.

James found himself having the chains removed next morning and he walked unfettered, though rather awkwardly, to the magistrate's office. It was hard for him to understand all the reasons for his sudden release, and even more difficult to see why he was due some compensation for the time lost in jail, but he gratefully accepted a small bag of coins along with a sack containing the items taken from him on the day of his capture. He was particularly pleased to have his belt back and to see a rolled up piece of paper still in place too. But it was Tancred's last words that stayed in his mind as he breathed the air of freedom once again.

"I make it a condition of your release that you leave the country at the first opportunity," said Henry Tancred. "There's enough money in that pouch to take you to Australia and to start afresh."

James had no intention of making a fresh start, but he did have a plan. A plan which he had drawn up with John Douglass in the months they had spent together, little thinking that it would be put into action so soon. Constable Paine had told James where John was working so he headed straight to the public house where he found John in the stables grooming one of the fine stagecoach horses with a flat brush. Their meeting was a happy one and, once his duties were done, John joined James in the bar where he was discreetly counting the coins in his pouch. It was a generous amount and would be more than enough to put their plans in place.

The following day John quit his job stating that he had received enough money from home to buy a lot of land where he intended to farm sheep and breed horses. He then made his way to the land registry office clutching the map that James had given him the night before. Here he paid his fees to register a large plot of land above the Waitaki valley. The registrar expressed his surprise that someone would want to lay claim to land that had not yet been surveyed and could well be barren or impassable, but John assured him that it was good, fertile land which could support his family and make him a fortune along the way. In fact, his fellow pioneer, Edmund Lawton, had a similarly sized plot next door, but had been unable to travel due to his wife's pregnancy. Perhaps the registrar could pencil it on the map on his behalf. So the deal was done to lay claim to the first two holdings on the plains beyond the valley where sheep could roam and families could thrive. John almost wished he was going there himself.

At the same time James was booking a berth in steerage on a ship to Moreton Bay, which was due to leave port the next day. His was an easy task, completed in no time at all, especially as he was paying in cash, so he was waiting for John in the bar with two glasses of ale in front of him. There were a few coins left in the bag and John added a handful of money he had saved from the tips given to him by the more wealthy patrons of the public house. They shared it equally between them. In total it would be enough to get John started in a stables in Australia and enough to help James build a home for his family and re-stock his lost sheep. As they left the table they took each other's identity with them and went their separate ways with a final affectionate embrace. John's new life was about to begin in the hills above Brisbane and James set out for home with a spring in his step.

The Wideawake Hat

Chapter Thirteen

The thaw

May - October 1855

Everyone in the small community of Marytown and the surrounding hills and valleys woke to the sound of water dripping. Sophia and Freddie, up on the plains with Atewhai and Hunu heard the drip, drip, drip of melting snow from the thatched roof of their hut. Roy shook his head violently as a persistent drip fell steadily on top of his head from the canvas roof of his shelter. Down the valley Nancy was awake early to feed Adey Rose and her sucking seemed to be in time to the dripping from the roof. Edmund heard it too and jumped out of bed to stick his head out of the sacking which covered the window. He immediately returned with a very wet head indeed.

In no time at all the snow began to melt in earnest. A watery sun produced enough warmth to see it off and it began to run in rivulets across the yard and towards the river. Sliding noises and crashes punctuated the morning as snow slid in huge chunks from every surface, and icicles, which had been hanging for days, fell like sharp needles to the ground, where they shattered into a million pieces. Edmund insisted that the boys stay clear of the house lest they get a sharp tap on the head from one of these icy missiles.

It wasn't long before the yard became a quagmire, but nobody minded the mud at all. Spirits soared as the inertia that had overtaken them all over the past days, keeping them trapped in their homes with boredom and short tempers, turned into a feeling of anticipation. Now they could get up the valley to see Sophia. Now they could get to Hawksbury to talk to the constable and plead for James' innocence. Now they could sort everything out.

There was a similar feeling further up the valley where Atewhai and Hunu watched with anticipation as the water dripped from every tree and bush around them. They knew that Sophia was like a caged animal. They had watched her pacing to and fro for many days now and they shared her frustration and confusion about her husband's absence. They couldn't understand why James had been gone so long and they worried that some ill-fate had taken him from them. Sophia had not told them yet about her pregnancy but Atewhai did not need to be told. She knew these things instinctively. It was sad to see a woman without her husband and a child without a father. But they had stopped Sophia from rushing straight down the valley this morning.

"The path will still be slippery," said Atewhai, "and the river may rise with all this melt water."

Reluctantly, Sophia had agreed to wait another day. She spent it in preparing for the journey. Back down the valley, Edmund and Samuel were making preparations too, in order for them to begin their journey at first light. They headed uphill, travelling light but with a heavy load on their minds. Would Sophia be there, or had she gone with James? How would she have fared in the cold weather? So many questions to be answered.

And Sophia was getting ready to make her own journey downstream. She was prepared to travel alone, but Atewhai insisted that she should accompany her. Freddie and Hunu could look after each other for a day or two, and, if it was felt necessary, one of the men could travel up the valley to fetch Freddie later on.

Amongst all the preparations nobody noticed the dogs. Roy was behaving very strangely. He would keep rushing to the summit of the pass, standing to attention and issuing a loud and insistent bark, as if trying to send a message. It was Freddie who noticed this in the end.

"What you doing, boy?" asked the five-year-old, as if the dog could give him a reply. "What can you see?"

Friday wasn't about to wait for the humans to pack their bags, nor for the level of the stream to drop. James could be up the valley, and so could Sophia and Freddie and Roy. She quietly slipped away and, using that long, gentle running pace that had given her a good chance to escape once before, she travelled fast. The path was slippery in places, but she did, after all, have four paws to give her balance, and sometimes she had to cross the bubbling water leaving her legs and underbelly cold and wet. Nothing a good shake couldn't sort out though. She made good progress. Occasionally, she would stop, look up the valley and give a good loud bark. The kind of bark that she had used many times before to let her master know where she was. Once she thought she heard a bark in reply, but maybe it was just an echo of her voice hitting the surrounding rocky outcrops.

Roy was barking again so Freddie called to his mother, "Mama, why is Roy barking?"

"What is that dog doing?" said Sophia to Atewhai. "He's behaving very strangely. Perhaps someone is coming."

The two women and Freddie joined Roy on the top of the hill looking back down the stream to see if anyone was coming. Sophia hardly dared to believe it could be James. Would she be disappointed if it was only Edmund or Samuel, or maybe it was just a wild pig that Roy had sensed in the nearby undergrowth?

Roy's barking became more and more insistent, and then he leapt off the rock on which he stood and set off down the valley. The humans could hear two lots of barking now and it wasn't long before Roy was back with Friday by his side. Both dogs were wildly excited to see each other again and much sniffing and racing around and tail wagging was going on.

"If Friday is here, James cannot be far behind," thought Sophia, looking wistfully downhill hoping to see the shadow of the man she loved working his way up the path.

Friday and Freddie were reunited with the pair of them rolling around on the wet ground and Friday was happy to have a pat from Sophia, albeit a rather distracted one. Sophia didn't even notice Freddie's muddy clothes.

"Where's your master, Friday?" she said as she gently and affectionately wiggled Friday's ears.

This puzzled Friday as she thought James would be somewhere nearby if Sophia and Freddie were here. She had seen him in that awful, busy place a long way away, but surely he would be home by now. She went for a good, sniffing search around the place for him, but there was no sign of his smell to be found anywhere at all. It was very confusing, so in the end, after drinking a whole bucket of icy cold water, she lay down with Roy under his shelter and fell into a deep sleep. She needed the energy so that, later on, she could carry on her journey to find her last and most important human.

The first day of the thaw sped by for those who were preparing for the following day's journey. Edmund and Samuel had intended to take Friday with them, but she seemed to have disappeared from her shelter leaving only Blue and Ruby behind. Neither of these two showed any inclination to leave their warm beds and join the party. So the two men set out alone carrying freshly baked oatcakes and some warm blankets in case they were needed. They had no idea what they would find, perhaps nothing at all, or at the very worst, two frozen bodies. However, they chose not to share their fears with their wives and left with a wave and a long list of things to tell Sophia when they saw her, not least of which was the news of Adey Rose's arrival.

In truth the parties met about half way up the valley. The women travelled as fast as their feet could go and, without much to carry downhill, they made good progress. Roy and Friday danced around them, rushing here and there along the path and through the cold stream. The men had to work hard uphill with their heavier loads but, with their longer strides and sticks to steady themselves, they too covered the ground fast. As they worked their way past a steep, rocky bluff before heading across a flat section to their right they heard the sound of dogs barking and were greeted by Roy and Friday coming to meet them across the flat, grassy area beyond. And behind them they saw the very welcome sight of Sophia walking alongside the old Maori woman, who Edmund recognised as Atewhai.

Their meeting place made a fine resting area and it wasn't long before a lunch had been laid out for them all to share. It was hardly a summer picnic, but, as they sat huddled in blankets around a makeshift fire, it gave them a place and time in which to start sharing their news. Atewhai was, at first, a little reluctant to take part, knowing as she did that Edmund had been the least keen to mix with the native folk. But Sophia, having given her brother a long and affectionate embrace, had introduced Samuel to her friend and the ice was broken when Atewhai had said, in her broken English, that a brother of Sophia's was most welcome into her whanau, the Maori word for family.

Sophia literally jumped for joy at the news of the baby girl, but then shed a tear for the lost twin. Edmund thanked Atewhai for taking care of Sophia and Freddie while the boy was ill and Samuel told Sophia that she was soon to be an aunt as Carrie was expecting their first child. Atewhai glanced at Sophia, who understood that no words were needed in that direction, but she happily told her brother that there would be cousins likely born close to each other, as she was pregnant with James' child.

James' name hung in the air for a few silent seconds. Nobody had dared to brave that subject until all the happy news had been exchanged. But there it was. The subject that could not be ignored.

"My dear," started Edmund, feeling that the news of James' imprisonment could wait no longer and it was better to just come out with it, no beating about the bush.

"My dear, there's no point in holding this from you. James is a prisoner in Lyttelton jail. They found him guilty of sheep stealing and I am afraid he serves five years for it."

The colour drained from Sophia's face.

"But he didn't steal the sheep. He paid Simon Baylis for them fair and square," she managed to say between sobs.

"We all suspect the Baylis brothers are at the root of this tale," said Samuel, moving closer to his sister and wrapping the warm blanket more firmly round her shoulders. "We will sort it out, and soon. We are going to explain it all to the constable in Hawksbury, but we needed to know you were safe first."

"But what am I to do?" pleaded Sophia, "I need to come with you, I need to see James. Now we have no sheep, and no money, and I have no husband. That Thomas Baylis, I can hardly bear to say his name. I wish I had taken the axe to him that day."

"As our mother would have said, dear sister, there's no point in crying over spilt milk," said Samuel tenderly. "But we can sort it out, and we will, and if we can find a way to get the law to deal with those brothers, then we will do that too."

In a way the two men were relieved to have imparted the news to Sophia, and relieved to have found her safe and well, if not in good spirits. Now the immediate dilemma was whether they should carry on up the valley, or go back home with Sophia and Atewhai.

In the end it seemed sensible to take Sophia back to Nancy where the two girls could comfort each other and be distracted by new babies. At first Atewhai said she would go home alone, but Sophia persuaded her to join them, assuring her that Freddie and Hunu would be having a great time together chattering away in a mixture of childish English and Maori words. The thought of the young boy and the old man together made them both smile for the first time for a while.

Nancy and Carrie were in the yard already, waiting to see who would be following the dogs down the valley. Roy and Friday had gone on ahead of the party and Nancy had taken Roy's arrival as a sign of good fortune for Sophia being safe too. But she was delighted to see her best friend and the old Maori woman, although somewhat confused by their appearance with Edmund and Samuel so soon after their departure.

As the winter day was drawing to a close the first task was to arrange for places to sleep. At first Atewhai said that she would sleep outside, but Carrie had taken to Atewhai straight away and would have nothing of that idea. Atewhai had been introduced to Carrie, who was always a bit shy with strangers, but in this case the friendship had been sealed when Atewhai had held her hand against Carrie's belly and quietly told her that she thought she was carrying a healthy girl. Carrie so wanted a baby girl who could grow up with Adey Rose, and now it seemed perhaps with a cousin too. So Atewhai went with Carrie and Samuel back to what had been Sophia's home. Freddie's old box bed would suit her for the night. It was a more comfortable bed than she was used to and, after a long day and a good supper, she slept soundly indeed in her temporary home, despite some trepidation of the thick walls of the house making her feel a little claustrophobic.

Nothing was going to separate Nancy and Sophia tonight. Edmund left them to the children while he settled the farm for the night. As he went about his tasks of feeding the dogs and ensuring the stock were all safely enclosed he heard laughter and joy, along with periods of silence as the two girls caught up on all the news, good and bad. By the time he returned the boys were fast asleep, Sophia was sitting contentedly with Adey Rose on her lap and Nancy was at the stove stirring a pot of something which smelled very tempting indeed. After supper, talk inevitably turned to the plan to clear James' name. It was very late indeed before the candles were blown out in the house that night.

The following day was a Sunday and, being winter-time, the one service of the day at St. Mary's church was in the afternoon, it being the easiest time for everyone to attend in daylight. Just a small number of people knew that Sophia and James had set out for new pastures further up the valley, and apart from wondering why Clara Nicol was playing the organ these days, nobody else had questioned Sophia's absence. At this time of year the flock tended to be a little less inclined to turn out every week anyway, so the congregation varied from week to week.

Of course, Reverend Nicol and his wife were aware of James' imprisonment, as were Betsy and Edgar, so these four people were pleased to see Sophia join the two families from across the stream today in church. After the service they gathered together at Betsy's store, opened especially for the group, though the closed sign stayed firmly in place in the window. Atewhai was looking after Adey Rose, but the twins had joined the family at the service and were feeling very pleased with themselves as Aunty Betsy had given them a choice of sweet jars to take down from the tempting shelves. Their cheeks now bulged with sugary pastilles of red and green and yellow. Sophia explained what had happened on the day James left for Lyttelton and how she had left Freddie with Hunu and met the others on the day after the snow melted. Reverend Job and Edgar agreed with the others that it was now obvious that James had been duped by the Baylis boys in an act of revenge and the four men put together a plan to travel to Hawksbury as soon as they could do so.

The women were giggling in the corner while they flicked through one of the latest magazines to come into the shop. It was a long time since Sophia had been able to read such a publication and she wallowed in the luxury of the latest fashions displayed in front of her in print.

"You would look lovely in this," said Betsy, pointing to a tight-waisted dress in deep mauve.

"But this will not fit me for long, I suspect," replied Sophia, holding her waist, which she could feel was not quite as slim as it should have been.

It took a moment for Betsy to realise what had been said, but then it dawned. Another baby in the village for her to look after, and James' firstborn. Now the men really must get him back and as soon as they could.

The following day, Edmund and Samuel, accompanied by Atewhai, set out to go over the pass again. This time they knew what they would find and they were happy to progress slowly to allow Atewhai to keep up with them. Conversation was scarce as neither man could understand much of what Atewhai said. She was pleased to be going back to Hunu and the familiar hut that she shared with him. But she would be sad to see Freddie leave, although she knew she would see the family again very soon. She had calculated when Sophia may be in labour and would arrange to be there to help. Something told her it would be an easier birth than last time, but she could still ease the pain and perhaps shorten the process with her potions and draughts.

Hunu was pleased to see his wife, a little suspicious of the two men and reluctant to give up his guardianship of Freddie, but once

Atewhai explained all that had happened, he gave the boy a bear-like hug, touching noses as he had taught the boy with eyes wide open in the native hongi, and released him into the care of his uncle and friend. There was no need for the men to take anything from the camp as Edmund assured Atewhai that he and Nancy, Sophia and James would all be back once the weather improved to pick up where they had left things and to start their new lives on the vast plains in front of them.

The elderly Maori couple stood together at the door of their hut and watched the two men and Freddie climb to the summit, turn to wave a final goodbye and then they were gone.

"Back to normal, toku aroha, back to normal," said Hunu.

"Ah yes, but I will miss the boy and his mother," replied Atewhai as together they turned back into the warmth of their hut.

While the men were fetching Freddie, the girls had been busy tidying and organising James' little hut next to the stream. Carrie and Samuel had lived there for a while so it was furnished simply, but adequately for Sophia and Freddie to live in until James returned. The story was to be put about by Betsy Franks that James had gone to Lyttelton to lay a claim to the land further up the valley on behalf of himself and Edmund. So while he was away, and considering her current state, Sophia and Freddie would live nearer the village. In the spring they would all move to their new land. It was a plausible reason for Sophia being there and most people accepted it without a thought. It was fortunate that the Baylis brothers were nowhere to be seen, as Sophia felt sure they would be more than happy to spread a very different story indeed around the community.

By a stroke of good fortune everyone was settled into their various homes before the snow was replaced by heavy frosts and low cloud. Trees and bushes turned white overnight and seemed to have been decorated by fingers of ice crystals. Washing that had been hung out to dry in the winter sun turned hard and brittle and there were reports that Betsy Franks' apron had crumbled into a thousand pieces as she tried to remove it from the line. It was beautiful to look at, but the fascination began to wear off after a few days of unrelenting cold, ice thick in the buckets and fog so dense Sophia could barely see Carrie and Samuel across the stream. It put paid to the men's journey for a few more days.

Then, suddenly one morning, everyone heard the sound of the wind. It had been still and quiet for days so the unexpected gust blowing through stopped everyone in their tracks. And then the rain started. Frost was washed off in seconds and it wasn't long before the buckets contained water instead of ice again. In their respective home countries the pioneer families had been used to wild weather. In Devon Edmund and Nancy would have seen fog over the moors and relentless rain which helped to turn everything green, and Sophia and George and James would have been all too aware of the harsh Scottish winters. But it did seem to Sophia that the weather here turned on and off like a tap with extreme rain, or wind, or snow, or frost, or even sun. Betsy Franks had joked one day that you could experience five seasons in a day here. As the sun began to shine through watery clouds, Sophia thought how right that was today.

It turned out to be a clearing up shower and the first sign of spring approaching. Each day seemed a little brighter and warmer and there were occasions when one could sit outside without a blanket around your shoulders. With the lengthening days the four men, Edmund, Samuel, Reverend Job and Edgar Franks, worked out that they could make the journey to Hawksbury in a day, stay the night and be back the next day having had time to speak to the constable there. The whole journey was made quicker these days by a better track and the use of the horses.

They set off one morning in early September as the dawn broke. They made good progress, with their only stop being when they reached the coast, where they took a cold lunch, which had been packed in their saddlebags by the girls. It was twilight when they arrived in the small town and they took rooms at the only public house in town where the horses could be stabled too. Job Nicol had met Constable Nevis on one occasion when he had been staying with the Reverend Atkins and his wife during the previous lent. He knew him to be a dour and sober man from the valleys of South Wales, capable and dependable, but with not a jot of humour in him. He had given the Reverend a sense that he wouldn't stand for any nonsense, and he was hopeful that he would listen to their story and take it seriously.

So, after a night in the rooms above the public house, the four men presented themselves to the recently completed police station, a building of red brick imported from Australia with an imposing facade, which offered a 'no nonsense' approach to those who entered the door.

Constable Nevis was at his desk, a pen in his hand, which he was using slowly and ponderously to write on a printed form. He held a hand up to stop the men from speaking until he had completed the sentence. With a final full stop, he put the pen back in its holder, slowly blotted the paper, folded his arms and then looked up at his visitors.

"Now, what can I do for you, gentleman?" he asked.

Reverend Nicol took the lead, as he had met the man before, and he explained in detail what he could of the story, with Edmund and Samuel adding a few words where they felt it necessary. Throughout their testimony Constable Nevis listened with his head on one side stopping them occasionally while he wrote notes in a neat hand on a fresh piece of paper. It all seemed to take a very long time indeed.

"So, you see, Constable Nevis, we know James is innocent and we just need you to let them know in Lyttelton," finished Job.

"Just!" said Constable Nevis. "It is not a case of 'just' anything. I can't just send a message to Mr Tancred, the new magistrate, without a bit more evidence than your words to back it up. And I doubt very much that, if I did just that, Mr Tancred would be disposed to simply release this man from jail. I will need first to gather the evidence of others, talk to this Mr Sidebottom and his shepherds and interview these Baylis folk. Then I will prepare a case if I feel it is justified."

"But, my man, Mackenzie's wife is with child. It is a matter of urgency that he is released," replied a rather irritated Reverend Nicol.

"The law will take its due course and if that means this woman will bring a child into the world without her husband present, well, that will not be the first time, and I doubt it will be the last as the man has contributed his sole part to the process at the start, has he not?" said Nevis with a wink of his eye. "Now, thank you for bringing this issue to my attention, and in due course I will send a message informing you of my decision as to whether to proceed with it. Good day to you, gentleman."

The four men stood their ground while Constable Nevis took up his pen and started to write again. Without looking up he waved a finger in the direction of the door, making it more than obvious that they should use it to take their exit.

There was nothing else for them to do but leave the building and start their journey home. It had been a most unsatisfactory meeting, but at least they had put their case and there was still hope that the constable would take it further. Perhaps they had been unrealistic in their hope that James would be immediately released as a result of their plea, but they couldn't shake off the feeling that it was not to be treated with any urgency at all.

Once the men from Marytown had left his office Constable Nevis blotted the page on which he had written some notes and put it to one side. He would not ignore the evidence presented to him today, but he was not about to give it any priority. He doubted that this man was entirely blameless as he knew these pioneer folk were all inclined to sail close to the wind of lawlessness up in the hills to the west. When the weather improved he could perhaps make a journey up the coast to see this Sidebottom chap, but there was no hurry. He would finish his crime statistics first, go home for a good lunch and put his feet up by the warm fire this afternoon.

So it was a miserable band of men who rode slowly back to their homes in Marytown that day. They agreed to tell the girls nothing of their fears. They would simply say that the constable had listened and written some notes and agreed to look into the case. Of course the girls would want to know how soon James would be home, but they would just have to say that the law must follow a process and that could take some time.

Sophia took the news badly and found it hard to lift her spirits. At the eighth month of her pregnancy now, she felt ugly and uncomfortable and in desperate need of being held in the bear-like embrace of her husband. She sometimes wondered if her new child would ever meet his, or her, father and whether she would ever enjoy that embrace again.

To add to her woes her closest friend Nancy announced that she and Edmund needed to head for their new home soon so that they could use the longer days and kinder weather to their advantage and get started on building a house. Nancy was the strong one of the three girls and Sophia knew she would really miss her optimism and practical dependability in the coming months. But Nancy insisted that it would not be long before James could bring his family to join them, and they could start their adventure together again. And, as Betsy Franks had said, it was another way for them to hide James' whereabouts for now because they could just say that he had gone with Nancy and Edmund to prepare things for Sophia to join him once the baby had arrived safely.

Nevertheless, it was a sad morning when Sophia and Freddie, with Samuel and Carrie watched their neighbours leave on horseback, one horse carrying huge packs across his saddle. Freddie would miss his friends too, and he shed a few tears, which he bravely hid from his mother by keeping his head down and kicking at the dust with the heels of his boots.

With that knack that she seemed to have for turning up at the moment she was most needed, Atewhai arrived back in the valley the following day where she and Hunu took up residence in their old hut on the edge of the village. Atewhai knew that Hunu was reaching the end of his life, and she needed to call his family to him before he departed. She would send a message to Taiko to gather the family together to sit and to listen to Hunu's words, which needed to be passed down to the next generation, before it was too late.

It calmed Sophia to have Atewhai nearby and, in a practical way, Freddie was happy to spend more time with his adopted grandfather, Hunu, which gave Sophia a chance to rest.

Atewhai would have two births to attend to, Sophia's and Carrie's, but nobody expected the babies to come at exactly the same time. Which, in the end, was just as well, because Clara Nicol also expected to attend the births and there was a certain amount of rivalry between the two women with their different beliefs and differing ways of dealing with the process of birth.

The girls had calculated that Sophia's child would come first, perhaps a week or so before Carrie's. This time Sophia was prepared for the feeling of restlessness which came before birth and had plenty of time to call for Atewhai and to make arrangements for Freddie to stay with his Aunty Betsy once more. The whole affair seemed much more straightforward than her first labour and Atewhai's singing provided a soporific feeling that sustained her through the initial contractions.

It was not such a calm affair in Carrie and Samuel's house. Carrie had been restless all night, which had disturbed Samuel's sleep. He had been grumpy over breakfast and had left his wife to her domestic chores with the excuse that he should be checking for new lambs. Carrie decided that she needed to sort a few things out in the house before the baby arrived. With her newfound skills as a seamstress she had made, with a little bit of help from Nancy, a pair of curtains to give them a little more privacy in bed each night. Sophia had hung a floral patterned pair there already, but Carrie much preferred the plain burgundy colour of the ones she had made. All she needed to do was stand on a chair to unhook the old ones first. It turned out to be no easy task at all to get her considerable bulk onto a chair and reach up to the rail, but all seemed to be going well so far. The first curtain was unattached and thrown to the ground with no trouble at all. However, as she reached up for the second time, she felt suddenly dizzy and light-headed. The next moment she was on the floor, landing with some good fortune on the heaped up curtain material, which prevented too much injury.

She picked herself up slowly and painfully, checking gingerly for broken bones. All seemed fine. But why was the floor wet? And why did her tummy hurt so much? A feeling of panic swept over her. Luck was with her at that moment as Betsy Franks and Freddie arrived on the doorstep. Freddie had been restless all morning so it was a good excuse to get out of the shop to come and give Carrie some help with finishing the curtains. Carrie certainly did need help, but not in the way that had been presumed.

Betsy realised immediately that the baby was on its way so she helped Carrie onto the bed, made sure she didn't mind being on her own for just a little while and ushered a scared looking Freddie out of the room. She sent him to find Samuel and bring him back home while she set off across the stream to fetch help for Carrie.

Sophia was the nearest neighbour, but Betsy knew there would be no help from her today. So on she went to the vicarage where Clara Nicol was more than happy to drop everything and help Carrie bring her first born child into the world. Betsy was excited by the prospect of two babies arriving in the village on the same day. What fun they would have growing up together! She had now come to terms with being childless herself and was able to cherish the joy of bringing new life into the world, even though it was never to be from her own belly.

News of two births in progress soon spread around the small community and people gathered at Betsy Franks' shop, or outside the church gate, waiting to hear the news. Sophia beat Carrie to it by less than an hour with Atewhai presenting her with a baby girl, wrapped in a blanket and crying loudly, some time around the middle of the afternoon. Shortly afterwards, a baby girl arrived at the house across the stream. Small, but none the worse for being early, Carrie was overcome by the emotion of holding her first child, thrilled that it was a girl and exhausted, but elated by the whole experience.

Before she had left them to set up their new lives further up the valley Nancy and her friends had spent much of their time discussing names. It had been such fun to throw their suggestions around, mix them up, shorten them to see if they worked like that too. It had become a game to try names out at different ages. A name given at birth may not be suitable for an old lady, or for a smart young gentleman, for instance. They had laughed and laughed at one of Nancy's suggestions if Sophia had a boy. Somehow Sophia would resist the urge to call her son Archibald Zachariah so that she could use both ends of the alphabet at once. But then, neither did they want to choose a common name like Mary or Ann, except perhaps in the middle where it could complement the first name perfectly. But it was when Nancy revealed the reason for her unusual middle name that the girls got their biggest laugh of all.

"Why are you called Nancy Cornfields?" Sophia had asked. "Is it because you had straw blonde hair when you were a baby?"

"Oh, if only that were true!" exclaimed Nancy. "But the truth of it is that I have a brother with the middle name of Orchard and a sister called May Copse. I rather think my parents sought some privacy from their large family in the countryside and marked the place of conception in their offsprings' names." As Sophia and Carrie realised what Nancy meant they had burst into fits of laughter. Tears rolled down the girls' cheeks as they laughed and laughed at the idea of such a thing.

When the laughter subsided Nancy asked Sophia if she knew how Friday had got her name. It was, after all, a strange name for a dog. It had never occurred to Sophia to question it, but she had to agree it was not a name you would expect a dog to have been given.

"Remind me to ask James when I see him next," said Sophia. The laughter began again, and Nancy was pleased that Sophia could joke a little about her husband's absence these days.

Carrie had not even bothered with choosing names for a boy as she was quite certain that she only needed girls' names. So it was an easy task for her to bestow the ones she had chosen upon her baby. Her own given name was just Carrie, but as a child she had wished it to be short for Caroline. Indeed, she had told her school friends that this was so. It somehow made her sound a little bit more important. So her baby would be Caroline, and always Caroline, with no shortening of the name. And Ann would fit nicely as the middle name. Caroline Ann Morling. A fine name indeed. Samuel approved, as he would have done whatever his beloved wife decided. He would love them both even if she had decided to call this beautiful baby Gertrude Maud!

Things were not so straightforward in Sophia's house. She was wishing she could consult James, though she wondered whether he would care about it as much as she did. If the child had been a boy she would, of course, have named him James and the name she had tucked away for a girl was Flora Louise. Flora was a Scottish name and she felt sure James would approve of that. But looking down at this tough little bundle the name just didn't fit. She wasn't a delicate flower to bear a delicate name. Her strong features demanded a stronger name with more distinction. What was there that still held the link to Scotland? Elizabeth perhaps, or Mary? No that wasn't right either.

And then a thought came to her, which took her right back to the dales of her native Yorkshire and the moors of the west of Scotland where she had grown up. She could see the purple and pink and white of it stretching across the scene and smell its heady scent on a hot summer's day. James even wore a tiny dried sprig of it in his lapel to remind him of home. Her daughter would be called Heather - Heather Louise Mackenzie. It suited her well. Very well indeed.

Chapter Fourteen

Downfall

January 1856

It was the third day of the new year when John Sidebottom started his journey to Marytown. He hoped that he could play a part in ensuring that the year 1856 was a better year for James Mackenzie than the previous one had been. Taiko accompanied him on the journey because he had been summoned once more by his aunt to the bedside of his elderly uncle. This suited John Sidebottom very well as it meant that Taiko could help him to guide the hundred or so sheep he had selected as recompense for James' family. Taiko had returned from Marytown a few weeks beforehand and had told his boss all about James' wife and the birth of the baby girl. His Aunty Atewhai had given him a very hard time indeed about it, apparently. She sounded like a strong character and John Sidebottom was looking forward to meeting the matriarch nearly as much as he was dreading meeting Sophia Mackenzie and explaining his unwitting involvement in her husband's imprisonment.

The letter from Tancred had been the spur that he needed to put things right. No child should enter the world without a father and no wife should be without a husband unnecessarily. It was in his power to right the wrong in which he now regretted playing a part.

He need not have been so concerned about meeting Sophia. She was by nature a forgiving soul, except perhaps where the Baylis brothers were concerned, and she admired Mr Sidebottom for having the courage to admit that he had been wrong. She was grateful for his gift and even more grateful that he was prepared to travel to Lyttelton one more time and put his apology on record.

Here at last was some real action. Nothing had been heard from Constable Nevis since the men had visited him, and she suspected he had taken no further action at all. Her spirits lifted as she realised this man could be the person to bring her husband home.

The final favour bestowed upon her by Mr Sidebottom was indeed a sweet reward. He spent a great deal of time in Betsy Franks' store telling anyone who cared to listen that James Mackenzie had been wrongly accused by the Baylis brothers of stealing some sheep and that Mr Sidebottom knew categorically that, in fact, James was innocent of the crime. Further more, Thomas and Simon were now implicated in the crime themselves and guilty of perjury in their testimony against Mackenzie in court.

Those few people who had wondered if there was more to the story of James' absence than had been told, particularly when Sophia had been with child, now understood. It was not hard for them to believe the Baylis boys had done something very much on the wrong side of the law. Many people in the community had been wronged by them in small ways, a poor deal with the sale of a horse, some rent outstanding on a room, or the purchase from them of a farm implement, which turned out to be broken and useless. Nobody really trusted them at all. It was agreed by them all that, should the brothers show their faces round about, they would be marched without ceremony to the police station in Hawksbury where the lazy Constable Nevis would be forced to take some action after all. There were a few men who thought too that perhaps the brothers may arrive in Hawksbury with the odd bruise inflicted with a boot or a bloodied nose caused by a stray elbow.

John Sidebottom visited Sophia one last time before taking his leave for the journey north. Friday watched suspiciously from the doorway wondering if that man would attach the chain to her neck once more. But she need not have worried as Mr Sidebottom had brought her a bone to chew on and she happily accepted it and put up with his gentle touch once more. She didn't understand the words of his apology to her for dragging her all the way to the trial and back, but she enjoyed his juicy gift very much indeed.

Sophia felt more hopeful than she had felt for many months and thanked Mr Sidebottom for the action he had taken. She explained to him how they had planned to move their farm to the plains beyond the pass and he promised he would come to visit them once they had settled in and was looking forward to seeing how those sheep got on there. He said that he was looking forward to meeting James again one day soon, in very different circumstances to their last meeting, so that he could apologise in person.

And so he began the journey to Lyttelton on his own, leaving Taiko at his uncle's bedside. He travelled more swiftly this time without the dog to hold him up. It was less than a week later that he met with Mr Tancred and reached the successful outcome he had hoped for.

It was fortunate that he was not aware of the conditions of James' release as this knowledge would have compromised his friendship with James in the coming years. He retired to the boarding house where he had spent the previous night, enjoyed a good meal and started his journey back home at once. He was not aware that one of the two men who sat together across the room in deep discussion was indeed James Mackenzie. The last time he had seen James in the dock, he looked dishevelled and unkempt, so little wonder he did not connect this man with the tidy, well-dressed man sharing conversation in the corner of the bar. Though perhaps it was a good thing that James was sitting with his back to the room. Both men looked happy and excited and John Sidebottom wondered what adventures they were planning.

None of these people were aware that, in fact, the true villains were also in the building. Thomas and Simon had spent much of the last few months in this establishment enjoying the company of several of the girls who frequented the place. They had arrived with money in their pockets and no plans as yet to do anything constructive with it. It was enough to set them up in business, or to buy some property, but neither brother could agree on the most profitable deal. Simon fancied buying a boarding house and employing a manager so that they could sit back and enjoy the profits without too much effort. Thomas preferred to put the money into a venture further afield, perhaps. More sheep, or maybe even gold. He had heard of a place where gold had been found in the north of New Zealand at a place called Coromandel. But Simon thought that would be hard work without the certainty of profit.

Knowing full well that they had embroidered the facts at James' trial they were keeping a low profile in Lyttelton and spent much of their time upstairs in the two adjoining rooms they had rented for the long term. But as the days went by frustration had begun to set in. Each brother resented the other one spending any of their hoard. Each brother resented the presence of a lady in the other brother's room. They both considered themselves handsome specimens of manhood and could not understand why a woman would choose one over the other.

Christmas had been a tipping point. Simon was spending too much time with a young woman called Lydia. A gaudy, red-lipped woman with an excellent figure and a disposition to enjoy lying with a man in any position he chose. Thomas had spent many a happy night with her, but his rough behaviour had become too much for her, and she had decided that Simon was better company and less likely to cause her to be hurt.

"He buys me presents," she had crooned, when Thomas had asked her why she had left him. "He treats me better than you ever did."

On Christmas Day the brothers found themselves on the balcony of Simon's front-facing room looking down on the people scurrying to church, or carrying parcels to and fro to friends and family. Lydia joined them, standing close to Simon where he nonchalantly put his long arms around her shoulders and kissed her long and hard on the lips. Wiping the crimson red lipstick from his mouth with the back of his hand, he winked lasciviously at his brother. It was the wrong move to make. Thomas had noticed a new silver locket around Lydia's neck and he guessed it had been bought as a Christmas present with cash from their shared money pouch. He saw red, and it wasn't just Lydia's gaudy lipstick on Simon's collar.

The two brothers fought like feral cats, crashing back into Simon's room where they were only brought to a standstill by Lydia throwing a jug of cold water reserved for washing over the pair of them. It was the start of a seething hatred for his brother in Thomas' heart.

Over the next weeks the brothers barely exchanged a word with each other. Lydia and Simon spent much of the time behind their bedroom door, but even Lydia grew tired of Simon's constant drinking. She was considering going back to the other brother after all.

Thomas had too much time on his hands to brood over his brother's behaviour. Slowly, over a period of days, where he did nothing but pace around his room muttering to himself, a plan formed in his head. He would leave Simon behind and take all the money. He had it in mind to seek gold in the warmer climate of the North Island of New Zealand and the pouch of money would set him up with a healthy claim. Unfortunately, Simon's half of the money was stored in his room in a locked box, just as Thomas had his locked in his room. Each brother had a key to both boxes, so all Thomas had to do was wait for Simon to fall asleep and he could open the box and leave with both parts of the money. In Thomas' irrational mind it wouldn't matter if Simon woke up anyway. After all, the money was as much his as his brother's.

Thomas waited until Mr Sidebottom had left for home. He had no wish to be seen by the man and no wish to draw attention to himself. He had seen James down in the bar and his apparent freedom just added to Thomas' growing anger with life in general. It just wasn't fair. Hadn't they had a good life so far, he and his brother? Hadn't they made something of themselves by travelling half way round the world? He suspected they would have been in trouble with the law back in England, perhaps even have received a free passage to the colonies as convicts. It was almost a shame he had ended up paying for his passage after all. Yet another injustice. Thomas was not a stupid man by any means. He realised that, if James was a free man, there was a chance that the part he and Simon had played in his imprisonment would have been exposed as a deception. And he knew only too well that perjury was a serious crime. It seemed to Thomas it was time to leave, before too many questions were asked of him.

James and the man who was sitting with him, whom Thomas thought he had seen before in the stables, both left at the same time. They looked pretty smug indeed about things and it was a sure bet that Mackenzie was heading back to the comfort of the lovely Sophia after all.

Resentment that the man he hated so much was now free and would soon be with the woman he cherished just made it all so much worse. His anger reached boiling point.

He took a swig from his hip flask and, staggering a little from the effects of too much of the strong spirit, he lurched towards the door of Simon's room. He knew that Lydia and his brother were in there, hopefully asleep after yet another bout of pleasure and passion. He remembered having Lydia himself, she had been good. But how the worm had turned. How ugly and coarse she now seemed in his eyes.

As he suspected, the pair were sprawled almost naked across the bed. Sheets and blankets were in disarray and Simon lay snoring gently with an arm across Lydia's bare breasts. He didn't feel the need to tread quietly as they were unlikely to wake in that state and it took him no time at all to open the box and remove the leather pouch inside. It was heavy enough, but would have contained much more had Simon not indulged that whore with cheap gifts.

Was it deliberate, or did it just happen by chance as he shut the door behind him? Nobody but Thomas will ever know for sure, but the candle, which burned on the windowsill, sputtered in the breeze catching the edge of the billowing curtain as it moved with the draught from the closing door. In moments, on a hot dry summer's night, the room was ablaze. Thomas was down the stairs and heading for his horse, saddled in readiness earlier that evening, before he smelled the smoke. He took no notice of it, mounted his horse and was gone, first towards Christchurch along the road built by convicts like Mackenzie and then heading north along the coast where he would find a ship to take him to Thames in the Coromandel peninsula.

Simon and Lydia had no chance to survive the fire. They had consumed a huge quantity of wine between them and were sleeping soundly. The effects of the thick smoke meant that neither awoke and they died in their sleep long before their bodies were consumed by flames. Their charred bodies were found later exactly where they had been laying.

The alarm was raised by the barman, who tried very hard to climb the stairs, but the flames were just too intense, so he resorted to freeing the horses before they panicked in their stables. There was nothing left for him to do but stand in the street shouting "Fire!" as loudly as he could. The constables from the prison along the street were joined by several seamen from a ship moored at the quayside nearby and the fire was extinguished without spreading to the adjoining buildings. The barman was able to say that he was aware of only three guests that night and that the remains presented to him on a stretcher would be one of the Baylis brothers, but he was not able to say which one. Sadly, a charred corner of the deep red dress found on the floor beside the bed was enough for him to realise his niece, Lydia, was the other victim. His sister would be heartbroken.

There was no sign of the other brother and no clue as to where he had gone. The following morning Mr Tancred took the report of the night's events from Constable Paine and considered the difficulties of pursuing whichever brother it was who had survived. It would make it very hard indeed to track the man down, but he would send a small team of men south, which he suspected was the direction taken, and a couple of men north, just in case he was heading to pastures new. Only one ship was due to leave that day and it was an easy task to check the manifest. Constable Paine was sent to do just that and the only name he recognised was that of James Mackenzie. He silently prayed that Mackenzie, of whom he had grown quite fond, would meet up with the woman he had suspected he missed so much and perhaps arrange for his beloved dog to join him over in Australia too.

Thomas fully expected to be pursued once dawn broke so he rode as far as he could in the dark. He had left the houses of Christchurch behind him by the time the sun came up. Over the next days he rode swiftly up the coast, treating his horse with the whip if she slowed and only stopping out of necessity for food, or an occasional short sleep. He turned west across the top of the island to reach the port of Nelson where, in the main, ships were coming from and going to Australia. But, after a few anxious days keeping an eye over his shoulder and very much on edge every time he saw a constable, he paid the captain of a small coastal boat for a berth on the vessel which was due to sail through the straits and up the eastern coast of the North Island.

Two or three weeks later, having lost all sense of time, he disembarked by means of a small rowing boat as the ship sheltered in the bay between the Coromandel and the northern tip of the island. He felt he could relax a little now as communication between the islands was sporadic, and he doubted anyone around here would know he was a wanted man. He found a room to rent in Thames and set about locating a good pitch where gold could be extracted from the quartz load. He spoke to no-one unless he had to and made no friends. In a town where people came and went, with a fortune or without, no-one asked any questions of him, and he liked it that way. He chose a pitch set into a hillside near the coast. Had he had the time or inclination to do so, he could have admired the lush green forest surrounding him, and relished the exotic noises of the dawn chorus each morning. It was indeed a beautiful place, ruined only in parts by the search for gold. As the other miners did, he dug into the hillside propping up his adit with wooden posts cut from the nearby trees which, with a huge effort, he cut to size with a saw made for two men to use. Over the next year or so any thought of being pursued dimmed in his mind and he settled into a solitary routine of cutting and digging, sometimes despondent, sometimes hopeful. Somewhat to his surprise he even found enough gold to live quite comfortably, spending the odd night with a girl who enjoyed his manly body and the money he threw in their direction for it. Not once did he consider the fate of his brother, not caring one tiny bit if he lived or died.

Then, one spring day, after rain had fallen day after day for a week at a time, the soft ground became sodden with water. Rivulets ran down the hillside washing muddy brown water into the sea beyond. Thomas was soaked to the skin, even inside his tunnel, as drips seemed to make their way through despite the thick roof. He had no time to escape from the sudden groaning, cracking, slithering noise of the roof collapsing behind him. A heavy wooden post tumbled on top of him knocking him to the ground and pinning his legs down. He cried out with excruciating pain in his legs whenever he tried to wriggle free, but there was no-one to hear him. In the end it was a slow death as he pawed frantically at the earth around him in the absolute darkness, using valuable air in his efforts to escape the heavy log which held him down. It took a little over a day for him to finally lose consciousness. He had been drifting in and out of delirium for a while and his final thoughts were of Sophia and what his life would have been like if she had accepted his advances.

Way down south, on the other island of New Zealand, Sophia was hanging washing out that day. After a week or so of wet weather it was her first chance to give the laundry a good blow in the fresh breeze. All of a sudden, as she stretched up to peg out one of Freddie's shirts, she shivered enough to stop her in her tracks. A memory that she had chosen to push away to the back of her mind came rushing back as clear as day. Thomas Baylis standing over her, his face so close she could smell his awful breath. She gave herself a quick shake of the shoulders and the vision was gone, but she wondered why she had recalled that awful day today, after all this time.

At exactly the same time that Thomas was making his escape on horseback, James was walking briskly in the moonlight along the road to Christchurch. Despite the darkness, he had a wish to get away from Lyttelton before daybreak, just in case anyone recognised him and wondered why he had not boarded the ship for which he had paid a passage. He heard a horse approaching from behind and ducked into the shadow of a large rock so as not to be seen. He didn't recognise Thomas flying past him in the saddle, but he did see the flickering light in the sky as a building burned in the town behind him. James hoped it was not the jail and that Constable Paine was safely at home with his wife, and he prayed that John Douglass had boarded the ship that was due to leave for Port Douglas the next day. But there was no time to linger. He had a wife, a young boy and a dog to see.

He chose to follow the route he had used on the way to Lyttelton all those months ago. His reasons for not being seen remained the same. He knew he had deceived the magistrate who had pardoned him, but he hoped that, had the man known about his wife and adopted son, his condition of leaving the country would not have been imposed. As long as he could get back to the reasonably remote community of Marytown and then spend some time up on the plains, he reckoned time would pass and memories would fade. He doubted Mr Tancred would ever visit such a place anyway, and he was thankful that the conditions had not been written down on his official pardon, so none of the other constables were aware of it. To all intents and purposes the land that he had purchased was now in the name of a John Douglass, and, if necessary, he could adopt that name as far as anything official was concerned. No-one would be any the wiser.

The half full moon gave him enough light to see his way and, as he walked quickly over the surface of the road he had worked so hard to build in the previous months, he made good progress. By the early light of dawn he had reached the plains where he hunkered down with his back against a tree and ate a breakfast of ham and bread from the provisions he carried in his leather bag. This time he would not be hungry and could afford to buy more food if it was needed. He snoozed until the sun was well above the horizon and then continued his journey.

Back in Marytown Sophia was facing something of a dilemma. Baby Heather was doing well and, though a demanding child, she had settled into a routine and was thriving. This time Sophia recovered quickly and was soon out and about in the warm summer weather. But she was restless and unsettled. At the sight of any person passing by the small cottage she would jump up to see if it was James. And she had nothing to do apart from feed herself and Freddie and Heather. She had been talking to Samuel about it the previous day.

"I think I should go to the basin again," she had said to him. "We can all sleep in Atewhai's hut and I still have most of my belongings there stored in the cart, as long as the mice haven't made a nest of them."

Samuel was concerned for her making the journey carrying the newborn baby, and worried that his wife would miss having her sister-in-law close by. But then there was the advantage that Nancy and Edmund were there already, and Carrie had Betsy and Clara and the other women of the village, who all enjoyed spending time with her and baby Caroline.

"Then perhaps you should go, sister," he replied.

Sophia's dilemma was that she wanted so much to be in their new home when James got back. A fresh start in the place they had dreamed of. But, on the other hand, Hunu's time was almost up on this earth, and she owed it to Atewhai to be there to help.

Freddie was at Hunu's side. Hunu had propped himself up in bed and was explaining to the boy what each twist and notch meant in his staff. It was the story of his family. Freddie was fascinated, but found it hard to work out who each person was that Hunu described. Their names were hard to say and it was difficult for a child of six years to comprehend the lifespan of a man, let alone several generations. But Hunu enjoyed talking to the young boy even though it tired him out. And Atewhai knew she could leave him with Taiko keeping an eye on things while she took some fresh air.

She found Sophia in the churchyard placing some white flowers on George's grave. Heather lay quietly and peacefully on a blanket beside the headstone. For a moment she stood apart from her friend watching with affection as Sophia tenderly tidied the plot and talked to George as if he was there in person. But then, as she often did, Sophia sensed the presence of her Maori friend and looked up with a smile.

"How's Hunu?" she asked.

"His time is close, my dear. Perhaps tonight, perhaps the next night," was the sad reply. "The family, of which there are few who remain, are here to say their farewells. Ara, his brother's widow and Aperahama, Taiko's brother. The young men have prepared a grave and Ara and I have woven a covering mat for his body. It is our way to leave the body in a shallow grave at first until no flesh remains and then to take the bones to a place of 'tapu', somewhere special and secret."

This process was not at all what Sophia was used to, but she marvelled at the way Atewhai spoke of death as if it was just a part of life to be planned in advance and to be carried out in a practical way. Growing up in Scotland such matters were talked about in hushed tones, or never discussed at all. She took her friend in her arms and hugged her closely.

Sophia joined Atewhai at Hunu's bedside that afternoon to bid her own farewells. It was hard to hold back the tears as Hunu lay proudly back on his bed with no fear of what was to come. He held Sophia's hand for a moment, a firm grasp despite his age, and thanked her for bringing him a grandson after all. It was a gift he cherished greatly. Then he laid a hand on Heather's head and whispered a blessing for a healthy and prosperous life. And finally his hand was on Freddie's shoulder.

"Be a good boy and it is my wish that you grow to be a strong and honest warrior who cares for the other people around you. Care for this beautiful land in which you will grow up and tread gently upon it."

It was a very long speech for the ailing man and he lay back against his pillow breathing heavily with the effort. Tears rolled down Freddie's cheeks. He didn't want to lose his grandfather, and he didn't understand all the words and wondered why Hunu needed to go somewhere else.

Freddie and Sophia spent a quiet evening together with few words exchanged between them. Freddie had been too young to understand the details of his father's death, but this time he was learning to feel real sadness. Sophia put him to bed, but sleep would not come at first. It took the gentle singing of his mother as she rocked him in her arms to make his eyes close at last. Just as Sophia was blowing the candle out in her little cottage next to the stream Hunu was taking his last breath, his wife and family all around him.

Atewhai understood that, close friends though they may be, it was not appropriate for Sophia to take part in the tangihanga. Ara and Atewhai prepared his body for the ceremony and the boys stood guard beside him while other Maori people called to pay their respects over the next few days. Some had made considerable journeys and expected to be fed and watered before they returned home. This kept the women busy. Sophia made oatcakes and a pie full of ham and potatoes. It was the best she could do to help out.

And then he was gone. Buried by his two nephews in the shallow grave that they had prepared in a quiet corner of the garden that Hunu had created next to the hut so that Atewhai could grow kumara and salad crops and the herbs she used to cure the sick and heal the wounded. It was a peaceful place befitting a man of dignity and wisdom.

So it was that Sophia's dilemma was solved. Atewhai felt the need to get away from this place for a period of quiet reflection, so she was happy to walk with Sophia to the hut at the top of the valley. She would look after Freddie, holding his hand, while Sophia carried Heather in her arms. They led a horse with saddle bags packed with all the necessities that would not already be there, taking it in turns to hold the loose rein. In truth, the horse didn't need much guidance as the path was narrow and there was little opportunity for it to wander to the left or right. It merely plodded slowly uphill with its heavy load, flicking its ears and swishing its tail to see off the flies that were prevalent in the hot summer weather. Roy and Friday made lighter work of the journey hopping over rocks and splashing through what little water there was in the stream. Friday had picked up Sophia's excitement and she was expecting something good to happen. She wasn't sure what, but she knew it was good.

Freddie had, of course, made the journey before and knew when they were close to the summit so he broke free from Atewhai's grasp and, with his precious stick in his hand, he ran ahead to see if he could find his friends, Ben and Ed on the other side. The twins heard Freddie calling their names and ran up the slope to meet him.

"We've found a tree to climb. Would you like to climb it too?" said Ben, and with a nod Freddie was scrambling up through the low branches of a tree, which grew tall and strong beside the stream. He was pleased to be back, and he looked forward to showing his friends where the fish darted through the water and the birds laid their eggs in tiny moss-lined nests.

Atewhai and Sophia settled the horse on a flat piece of ground with good grass for him to eat and access to the stream for a good drink and then unloaded the saddle bags into the hut. It seemed no time at all since the women had been here last time and Atewhai sighed wistfully as she found memories of Hunu in every corner of the hut.

And then it was time to introduce Heather to Nancy. It was a joyful meeting for all the women. Adey Rose had grown since Sophia had seen her last and she seemed more alert with her chubby hands grasping anything within reach, especially Sophia's long hair and the ribbon that held it back. She was a delightful child and Sophia looked forward to Heather and Adey Rose playing together as they grew older.

Over a mug of tea Sophia told Nancy about John Sidebottom's visit and, for the first time, tears of joy coursed down Sophia's cheeks and dripped into her mug mixing with the hot tea. Edmund arrived to the sight of three sobbing women wondering what could possibly have gone wrong but Nancy explained that he didn't need to worry. These were tears of joy for James' imminent return.

Further tears were shed with the news of Hunu's passing and it was, surprisingly, Edmund who summed it up as he put his hand gently on Atewhai's arm.

"Atewhai, your husband was a good man with a big heart. His love for Freddie, a boy from another culture to his own, was unconditional and beautiful and we will remember him as a true member of our community."

It was the kindest of compliments from a man who had been suspicious of the native folk at first, and Atewhai appreciated it more than she was able to reply in the strange English words.

Atewhai and Sophia went back to the hut to put things straight before Freddie's bedtime, but they left Nancy with a promise to return for supper. In the end Atewhai decided that she needed some time alone. She felt the need for solitude so that she could reflect on Hunu's long life and the time they had spent together. Being alone did not concern her one bit, especially in these familiar surroundings, so she didn't mind at all that Sophia left her to make her way across the valley. She was happy to tend Freddie, who slept soundly in the bed he had grown so used to over the previous months.

In a sense the supper that Sophia shared with Edmund and Nancy was the proper beginning of their new lives in the basin. It was the first time that both parties had been there together, though the absence of James hung over them all. The twins were both asleep and the two young girls lay together in one cot. It gave the adults a chance to talk about their future in this new land. Sophia found herself excited about it all for the first time in many months. She told Edmund and Nancy about the sheep that John Sidebottom had given them and that Samuel was looking after them at the moment. Edmund told Sophia what he had done so far and just before it got dark they had time to look around the building work he had been doing. The shape of the house had been laid out on the ground and Sophia could see it was a much bigger building than their first home, but as Edmund explained, it needed plenty of room for all the babies Nancy insisted she still wanted.

Edmund promised that he would accompany her the next day on a walk around her area of land where he and the boys had marked out the boundaries using the map he and James had drawn up together. She hoped with all her heart that, just as Nancy and Edmund had done, she would soon have a home on that land to share with the man she loved.

Chapter Fifteen

Reunited

January 1856

Edmund Lawton had been very busy since he and his family had made the journey up the valley. He had made a start on their new house at last, but it had taken them a while to decide on the right spot for it. To begin with, Nancy had wanted their home to look out from the highest point across the plains in front of them. But as the days went by they realised that this may not be such a good idea as it would expose them to the damaging winds which occasionally blew up from the north west. Edmund doubted that a house could even stand up in the worst of these gales where branches crashed down from trees and anything not tied down, like buckets or brooms, was set for a tumbling journey across country.

Edmund had the second copy of the map that he and James had drawn together. He and Nancy spent a lot of time pouring over it and then standing in a spot they had found on the map to see if it was suitable. It needed to be near water, of course, but not liable to flooding. It needed to be in a sheltered spot, but still have a view and some sunshine. And it needed to be built on a flat platform, but still be elevated to enable them to watch over their stock.

James and Edmund had carefully surveyed this land to give each family a piece of the hillside which formed the inner edge of the huge basin. This would be their home and would provide a more sheltered area for stock to spend their winters. The other part of each plot of land would be the plateau itself, flat as a pancake and ideal for dividing into large fields and paddocks.

There appeared to be two small streams and a bigger river across Edmund and Nancy's section of the map. One of the streams was entirely dry at this time of year so that was discounted. The main river formed the border with Sophia and James' land and, although they were friends, it didn't seem right to build so close. The last stream was not full in the summer weather, but it did have enough sparkling, clear water to fill buckets and even a few deeper pools where fish could be seen darting out of view when one approached.

In the end they decided to walk the entire length of the stream from the top of the hill to the point where it joined the bigger river looking for likely sites. The twins were running ahead waving sticks in the air and jumping in and out of the water. The sun was so warm that their bare feet dried quickly in between. They reached what could be called a waterfall, though only a trickle at the moment, tipping the water over the edge of a steep drop into a sharp-sided valley beyond. It reminded Edmund of the combes of his native Devon. Small trees grew alongside the stream as it meandered through this valley before tipping down hill at the far side on the western edge. It was a sheltered place and flat enough to make building reasonably easy. Looking down the slope beyond it there were other flat areas where shelters could be built for the stock, perhaps.

It was perfect! Big enough to contain a house and a good garden and yard, but giving the impression of being elevated as the land fell away beyond it. The worst of the north west wind would miss them, especially if the house was protected by the steep hillsides and the trees which would, no doubt, grow taller over the years. They may lose the sun a little earlier in the day than the open site they had been using as a temporary camp, but that was a small sacrifice to make for this sheltered haven.

The next day they moved their camp to this spot, setting up a canvas shelter for the boys to sleep under and a tent for Nancy, Edmund and Adey Rose. Even the dogs had a makeshift kennel. Meg, the elderly collie, and mother of Roy, who had struggled to climb to the top of the stream with them, was all too happy to rest her old bones under a canvas sheet tied between two trees. From there she could watch what everyone was doing without having to move at all.

Once everything in the camp had been sorted out Edmund had taken the boys to walk the boundaries of the place that he and James had drawn on their maps. As best as they could they gathered up small rocks and built cairns every few yards along the edges. Sometimes this was not possible where the land fell away, or a large rock stood in their way. Each time this happened they merely decided to go to the left or the right of the obstacle. In that way the straight edge that had been drawn on the map became, in reality, a more meandering boundary.

At the furthest corner, bounded by a scrape in the ground that would be full of water in other seasons, the boys found the remains of the cairn that James and Edmund had built when they mapped out the land. They put it all back together and added bigger rocks which they carried between them, or rolled along the ground. By the time they had finished, the pile was nearly as tall as the boys themselves. Then, turning at right angles, they began again across the western edge of their land. This formed a good straight line as there was little to obstruct it in the flat area.

Reaching the river the boys began again with their second cairn and, just for the sake of it, they jumped and paddled across the river to build one for James and Sophia too. There was little point in marking out the riverside as it was a shared border with their neighbours so Edmund and his sons followed the stream back to the summit where it met the track that had now formed naturally over the ridge. Following this line back to the south they got back to their first pile of rocks, so that a square had been formed, matching roughly what had been drawn on the map.

Edmund promised the boys that they could do the same thing on the other side of the river tomorrow to lay out their neighbour's plot too and, sending Ed and Ben to gather some firewood, he went in search of his wife.

He found Nancy doing a similar job on a smaller scale. She had spent the morning placing four round rocks on the flat platform of land where she thought her house might be best placed, one for each corner to start with. Every time she formed the shape she would stand where the front door could go, survey the view and try to imagine her garden before her at each season of the year. Each time she thought she had the perfect spot something would occur to her that could be a problem. The summer sun would be too strong for delicate plants. The bedrooms would get no sun at all. The wind would whistle into the house. She would not be able to see the tallest of the mountains, which was indeed a beautiful sight on this clear day, so tall that it was still covered in snow even in this heat.

But finally, just as Edmund arrived back, she had her four rocks marking the corners of her house just where she wanted them. It did seem that every time she moved those rocks the house got just a bit bigger, but better to build big now rather than run out of room later, she reasoned to herself.

Nancy had collected a pile of smaller stones and together they lay these out where doors and windows would be placed and even rooms inside. They had all been used, in their smaller home, to one large living space which they shared for day-to-day things, eating and sleeping. But now there was room for a living space and rooms for sleeping in. What a luxury that felt to Nancy! She had, with Betsy's permission, torn a page from one of the household magazines that were now available from Australia. Betsy found they were not as popular as the English magazines full of fashion ideas and things that reminded everyone of their homeland, so she was happy for Nancy to take this one. The page, which was now becoming dog-eared after much folding and unfolding, advertised a builder and showed several designs of house suitable for the colonies. Nancy had drawn a circle around the one she liked the best, a double fronted house with a large front door approached across a deep verandah. It had the symmetry she liked and the verandah would be a useful place to sit away from the sun, or under cover on a rainy day.

Edmund and Samuel had seen this drawing and were already thinking about building materials. The roof was of metal sheets and the walls of brick rather than the cob and thatch structures that they had built on their arrival. Both these items were available from Australia, but could they afford them? This was a question Edmund had asked himself many times and the answer always came down to the need to restock his farm with sheep first. His share of John Sidebottom's gift was a start, but it would not be enough to make a fortune by any means. And in many ways Edmund was reluctant to start the process of re-stocking until James returned. It was something they should do together.

Thus the decision had been made to build a smaller cob house on a flat site mid-way between the site marked out and the river, at right angles to it. It would not have a view, but it would be sheltered from the wind, and it would see them through the first year or so until the new house could be built properly. Later it could, perhaps, be turned into a shepherd's hut, or even become a barn for the animals. Having done this work once before, and helped George to build his home too, Edmund made good progress with this simple building and only had the wooden roof structure to put in place, which could be thatched very easily after that. Nancy had gathered the dry stalks of tall grass and bracken which were piled against the cob walls in readiness. They would continue to sleep under canvas until that roof was finished, but the glorious summer weather made that an easy thing to do for now.

Soon after that Sophia and Freddie and the baby had arrived with Atewhai. Nancy was so happy to have her friend nearby and excited at the prospect of James' return. Her children were happy to have their playmate back too and even the dogs seemed content to be back in each other's company. Life soon settled into a routine, but one in which every single person expected there to be a change at any moment. In everything they did there was an air of expectation, heads turning to the path over the summit at the faintest unexpected sound. Of course, Sophia was on tenterhooks. She felt like she was living in limbo, keen to start on setting up her new home, but determined not to do so until James got back. Many times a day she found herself saying, "When James is back we will do this," and, "We can do that when James gets back."

Each day passed too slowly, her only blessing being the time spent with baby Heather, who had such a different personality, even at this early age, from that of her firstborn son. Her daughter may have come into the world quietly and without trouble, but Sophia suspected she would make up for that as she grew older. There was a certain feisty determination in her already and, if she didn't get whatever it was she wanted, woe betide everyone within earshot. On one occasion Nancy had come running over to see if all was well when she heard Heather's piercing howl. But it had turned out to be merely that Sophia had removed her from the breast a little sooner than she would have liked. Nancy found Sophia dodging the little fist that was aimed at, but fortunately missed, her chest.

Sophia could tell that Atewhai was restless. They had only been staying in her hut for a few nights when Taiko arrived telling Atewhai that he had heard her calling for him. Sophia was aware of the empathy Atewhai seemed to have with her family and friends, so it came as no surprise that Taiko had just turned up when something told him to do so. Atewhai intended, so she told Taiko, to take one last journey across the plains and over the mountain passes to the coast on the other side to look for a suitable greenstone for Hunu's final resting place. The aunt and her nephew packed their woven bags, prepared their shoes and clothes for the journey and set off before dawn the next morning. Sophia was sad to see her go, but knew in her heart that she would be back at the appropriate time.

James knew nothing of these events, in fact, he was entirely unaware of his daughter's existence. He hurried on his journey home expecting only to be reunited with his wife, stepson and dog. He had been making good progress, the long days and good weather making it an easier journey than that which had taken him to Lyttelton in the first place.

Over a supper made from the last of the food in his bag, except for an apple saved for breakfast, he had calculated that he could make it back to the pass by that evening. But then again, should he go to the basin or should he go back to the village first? The question caused him a sleepless night, despite his tiredness from the journey. He lay against a rock watching with awe as the stars that formed the southern cross moved across the clear night sky. He thought only of Sophia and wondered how she had managed while he was gone, and whether she had given up any ideas of a new life over the summit of the hills. Perhaps she had forgotten about him altogether. Perhaps he should go back to the village first to find out a bit more.

The next morning, munching on his apple to break his fast, he turned from the track which would take him straight to the basin and set off across country towards Marytown. He made easy work of crossing the river downstream and entered the village from the east. All seemed very quiet in the afternoon sun and he guessed most people were keeping out of the heat. His old hut by the river looked deserted. But Betsy Franks' shop had the 'open' sign at the door so he climbed the step and entered, a bell jangling to let Betsy know she had a customer. It was dark inside after the sunshine of the day and he stood, a silhouette against the open door. Betsy emerged from the room at the back holding a young baby in her arms. James wondered if Betsy had, after all, produced a child in his absence.

"What can I do for you, sir?" asked Betsy, not recognising the man's face in the shadows.

James stepped forward. The look on Betsy's face was one of amazement and joy, all in one. Throwing her hands to her face, she nearly dropped the baby and James rushed forward to catch it.

"Oh, 'tis not mine, I'm afraid," said Betsy. "'Tis your niece, I suppose, being Samuel and Carrie's wee girl, Caroline. But come through, come and see Edgar again, and Carrie. Have you seen Sophia yet?"

James was not too sure what to say next as he already had so many things to take in. Carrie and Samuel had a baby girl. He wondered what else had happened in the community in his absence. Betsy soon had the kettle boiling on the stove and huge slabs of boiled fruitcake placed on a plate. James realised how hungry he was, and wondered how long it had been since he had last eaten Betsy's home baking. In between mouthfuls of cake he tried to answer all their questions, of which there were far too many for him to take in at one go.

And then Samuel arrived back from Oamaru where he had been to collect a cart full of metal sheets, which had arrived recently by ship from Australia. He was excited by his purchase, which he thought would make a strong and weatherproof material for roofing. But he was even more excited once he saw James at the table in Betsy's parlour.

"Have you seen Sophia yet?" asked Samuel as he took James' hand and pumped it up and down in an enthusiastic welcome.

As this was the second time he had been asked that question James felt the need to give an answer.

"I wasna' sure where she would be," he said in the accent his neighbours had missed so much. "Is she here with you?"

It had been agreed between the friends that news of his daughter should be left to be imparted by Sophia, so only part of the story was related by Samuel.

"She is up in the valley on your land with Nancy and Edmund and the children. Once we knew that you may be released she couldn't decide whether to stay or go. But we thought she would be happier with Nancy," he replied.

Then, of course, James wanted to know how they were aware of his coming, and the story of John Sidebottom's visit had to be told and then the truth of the Baylis brothers' involvement and the sheep they had been given and Hunu's death. James couldn't quite take it all in, but he was happy just to be back in the company of people he knew.

"I must go to her," he said simply, and went to rise from his stool.

"Not at this time of night," replied Betsy. "You will spend the night on our sofa and Samuel can help you take those sheep to their new home in the morning."

"Samuel," she added, "go and get the vicar and his wife. They should know that James has arrived back and, James, you can tell us all about your ordeal over supper."

Reluctantly, James realised that, even though the evenings stayed light quite late at the moment, he probably didn't have time to get there before Sophia went to bed, and that was not how he wanted their reunion to happen. One more night would make no difference after all this time, so he agreed to stay. And the idea of a good supper shared with friends and a comfortable sofa to sleep on was tempting. Very tempting indeed.

Those people who now lived on the edge of the plateau were all constantly keeping an eye open for their friend, James, to come over the summit, but it was not that sight but a sound that made each one of them stop what they were doing the following morning. Edmund was on the roof of his new house and Nancy was passing him handfuls of thatch to be pinned into place. Sophia had left her two young children to sleep in this morning and had taken a walk across the valley to see if there was anything else to be rescued from the cart.

It was the sound of sheep. Friday and Roy were the first to hear them and, with ears pricked and heads on one side, they awaited a command from Edmund.

"Away, dogs," he ordered, balancing on the roof and pointing in the direction of the track over the ridge. And they were gone in a flash, backs low and heads steady. Seconds later they were back with Blue and Ruby keeping the sheep in a tight bunch as they streamed over the top and tried to spread out as they ran and tumbled down the hillside.

Presuming that Samuel had driven the sheep up to their new home, they were not surprised to see him rise up over the hill and start to climb down their side. They both raised their hands in welcome towards him. But then there was another silhouette on the horizon which made Edmund slide hurriedly down his makeshift ladder and caused Nancy to hold both hands to her mouth in shock.

Across the valley Sophia waved to her brother too and began to make her way to meet him as he came down the hill. But then there was another man's shape on the horizon with the sun behind it causing its outline to glow around the edges. She had to shield her eyes to see who it was.

Friday came bounding towards her with a look that said, "I've found him at last. I've found my master."

And Sophia, recognising the man on the hill as her beloved James, gave the dog a quick pat on the head before breaking into a joyful run.

Samuel, meeting Nancy and Edmund, held them back to allow the husband and wife to be alone in their reunion for a few moments. James took Sophia into his arms and lifted her off the ground in a long and emotional embrace, which she hoped would never end.

All the noise of the sheep and the dogs barking had woken Freddie, who came out from under his shelter using his knuckles to wake up his eyes. He took a moment to realise who it was who was holding onto his mother and then broke into a run as well. But he stopped short, suddenly a little bit shy of this stranger. After all, he hadn't seen him for more than a year, which is a very long time to a small boy.

The grown ups both held their arms out and Freddie stepped forward to be included in the embrace.

"All my family, at last," said James with a huge sigh of relief.

Sophia remembered that this was not entirely true and smiled to herself.

"Come with me," she ordered James, leading him by the hand down the hill towards the hut where the other member of the Mackenzie family lay asleep, oblivious to her father's return.

Where everyone else had been asking James questions about his time away, Sophia knew that her husband would tell her all about it in his own good time. James loved her for that and for the way she cherished him without fuss and included him in the dreams she had made while he had been missing. Over the next few days they just enjoyed each other's company and reignited their love and respect for each other. Freddie and James took a while to get back to the relationship they had enjoyed beforehand, but it wasn't long before they were back to their old ways. Freddie showed James the stick that Hunu had made for him and explained what each curl and scroll meant. James listened with interest, especially when Freddie said he would make one for his father if he could have a sharp knife for his birthday.

"Perhaps when you are a bit bigger, my son," said James. Sophia smiled to herself to hear his words. She seemed to be doing that a lot these days.

The youngest member of the family was an absolute joy to her father. Sophia would often find him standing by her cot looking down at her with a mixture of love and amazement as she slept. James could hardly believe he had a child. It was not something he had expected to ever happen and certainly not something he expected to have happened while he was away. It made all those solitary days, when every bone ached from the hard grind of road building, worthwhile. And here she was, his beloved Heather Louise, the name such a suitable reminder of their homeland and so appropriate for a girl who he hoped would grow tough and beautiful at the same time. How clever of Sophia to have thought of that name in his absence.

For the first day or two life seemed to Sophia and James like a holiday. They did nothing but talk to each other, or walk together around their land. They just needed time to get re-acquainted and to catch up on the things that had happened to each of them over the past year. And they got to know their new home together as Sophia had hoped they would. They walked every inch of it with Freddie running ahead checking each pile of stones that had been built by his friends, Ed and Ben. Heather gurgling and chuckling to herself in Sophia's arms. Often they would stop to admire the view of the mountains or bend down to see what plant grew at their feet. It was as if they were explorers in a new land all over again. The site where James had first pitched their tent and parked the cart was still the best spot on which to build a house. In a wide valley, but sheltered from the wind and with the stream running swiftly by. Having a view across the plains, but private from others by virtue of a bend in that stream. It was the perfect spot.

It was time to give the remaining cedar trees a permanent home at last. Sophia chose the position of the three trees carefully, so that they would shelter the house but not obscure the view, however big they grew. And James dug the holes and lowered them into place. They would need watering regularly to get them started, but they would thrive here, he was certain. They both felt it was a symbol of their decision to make this place their family home and hoped that the trees would look down on the generations to come.

Meanwhile, Nancy had been planning a celebration. Samuel had stayed the night with them before returning to the village with strict instructions to pass invitations to the friends and neighbours who were aware of James' return. He was to arrange for them to bring equipment and clothing to spend at least one night on the plateau where a camp would be set up and a feast prepared.

With a certain amount of intuition Nancy kept the whole thing from James and Sophia until the last moment. But on the day she expected people to arrive, she had no choice but to tell them that a party had been arranged in their honour. James was not at all sure he felt like celebrating yet, but Sophia had caught Nancy's excitement, just as she always did.

Samuel and Carrie arrived first with a fully laden cart pulled by a hot and thirsty horse. On top of all the tents and food and clothes, tied on with ropes, four precious sheets of metal balanced. Two for Edmund and two for James. It would be enough to roof their small houses and more could be purchased if they decided to build bigger homes one day.

They were the first to pitch their tent on the flat plateau, which was to be Nancy and Edmund's home, so that Caroline could be put in the shade of the canvas for her afternoon sleep.

Next came Edgar leading a horse with panniers full of canvas on one side and food on the other. Betsy carried a basket with the most delicate of the pies and patties. It was a stiff climb for Betsy, who was not perhaps as fit as the other women and carried a little more weight, it being hard to resist trying out the goods in her shop. A seat was swiftly found for her in the shade and a cup of cool cordial arranged while Edmund got to work putting their canvas in place to make a shelter.

The last guests to arrive were the Reverend and Mrs Nicol, who had been delayed on parish matters all morning. They travelled light with gifts of food and a small bag of overnight wear. Nancy had sent their invitation with the additional offer to sleep in their newly completed house while she and her husband slept one last time under their shelter. She rather thought the boys would all prefer to sleep under the stars, so an area inside the planned out shape of the new house had been set up for them to lie, just as if they were in the bedrooms that would be created for them. There may be more talking than sleeping, but for just one night it didn't matter.

It was a wonderful sunset that night. The adults stood in a line watching as the distant clouds turned from pale pink to the deepest orange and the sun slid slowly and majestically behind the mountains. There was silence except for the sound of the babbling stream and the distant bleating of sheep. Nobody moved an inch until the last golden rays had gone from view. And then the party began.

A long table had been set up with a variety of stools and benches providing the seating. Lanterns cast their light along the table lighting up platters packed with food of every kind, sweet and savoury. After the Reverend Nicol had said grace and added a special prayer of thanks for the return of James to his family, the friends ate and drank until their plates were empty and the three boys falling asleep with their heads nodding into their bowls.

It was a very late night indeed for the children so Sophia and Nancy shooed them off to their beds. It took a while for their mothers to settle them under the starlit sky. Having checked that the babies were all asleep too, the women returned to the table.

More ale was poured and the remains of the food formed tasty treats picked up by absent-minded fingers while they caught up with all the news. James had not said much so far, though, as was his way, he loved watching Sophia and her friends enjoying themselves so much. She looked relaxed and radiant, as if a huge weight had been lifted from her shoulders.

Slowly, hesitatingly, he told them the whole story, sparing nothing but the very worst of his treatment in jail. When it came to John Douglass he told them also of the plan they had put together to give them both a fresh start. At that point he pulled two pieces of paper from his pocket and handed one to Edmund. It was a title deed in Edmund's name for the land on which they were currently sitting. Nancy came around the table and put her arms around her husband's shoulders so that she could read the papers too.

"Thank you, James," she said, looking up with a smile, "for remembering our piece of land too."

The other deed was passed around to show that it was in the name of a John Douglass. A small subterfuge and one which the friends thought would cease to be important over time. After all, who would be likely to check in this remote place?

With everything now official Nancy brought up a subject close to her heart. Just like the naming of her children, naming her home was a most important matter for her. She explained it felt like it didn't belong to you until it had a name, even though they now had the legal paperwork. She and Edmund had been discussing this for many weeks.

"Well, I've been discussing it and Edmund has been listening!" she laughed. "But we have finally reached a decision to call our new home after the valleys of Devon."

Standing up with the title deed in one hand and a cup raised to the heavens in the other, she declared loudly, as if she was the town crier, "This land belongs to Edmund and Nancy Lawton and shall from this day forward be called Combe Farm."

The formality of Nancy's words caused the friends to stand to attention as they raised their drinks in a toast to Combe Farm and the people that lived in it.

"And what will you call your home, James and Sophia?" asked Reverend Job Nicol as they all took their seats again. "Something to remind you of Scotland, perhaps?"

Sophia looked towards James. It was harder for them to decide as they had nothing much to share from their past. In fact, James had not dared, nor had the opportunity, to put any roots down anywhere until now. But Sophia had been considering a name and she thought perhaps she should share it now.

"Well, I think we have enough of Scotland in our name," she said. "But there is a place near where I grew up that holds happy memories and reminds me of my childhood. Although it is in Scotland it is the most English of names. But it suits this land and I hope it suits James too."

She looked across at James who replied, "If it suits my wife then it suits me too."

The others laughed and Nancy asked, "What is it Sophia?"

"I would like to call our home after a small fishing village on the western coast of Scotland near my childhood home. It is called Applecross," she said. "Do you like that James?"

James considered for a moment and rolled the word around in his mind. "Indeed I do, my dear. Indeed I do."

Remembering a conversation the girls had shared a while ago, before Heather was born, Sophia said, "James, while you were away we were wondering how Friday got her name. And I said I would ask you when I saw you next. I had forgotten until today, but all this talk of names reminded me of it."

James laughed out loud. "Ah, 'tis a long story, but her name is not Friday at all, in truth."

James' friends, who had relaxed into their assorted seats as the evening progressed, pulled themselves up, leaning forward in anticipation of hearing James' story.

"Tell us more, James. We are all intrigued," said Job Nicol.

"Well," replied James, "when I bought my two pups from a farmer in Australia they had no names, but I chose two phrases in my native tongue to describe their characters. One dog was a herder by nature, good at running round the sheep. I called her Cuairtean which means small circles. The other dog was a natural at taking the long run, drawing sheep back towards me. She had an eye for the distance, so I called her Fradharc, which means long sighted. Poor Cuairtean died in my arms from the bite of a poisonous snake, but Fradharc travelled here with me on the boat. Her name sounded like Friday to my fellow travellers, so Friday she became. It pleases me sometimes to call her Dihaoine, which is the Gaelic word for Friday - and now she answers to both."

It was a long speech for James and, while the girls, with varying degrees of success, tried to shape their mouths into the words James had spoken, Sophia squeezed James' hand gently. Without the need for words, they both felt, all of a sudden, how good it was to have friends around them.

A while later the party came to a reluctant halt as, one by one, the guests were overcome with tiredness. Sophia and James set off for home, leaving their friends to climb under the blankets in their various beds and tents and shelters.

They walked back across the valley, arm in arm, both thinking their own thoughts about the evening. James could hardly believe the change in his fortunes in such a short time. It seemed to him only days since he had been languishing in a solitary cell after his escape, alone day and night, and yet, here he was tonight enjoying the company of his family and good friends.

As they reached the stream marking the start of their land, without warning, James scooped Sophia up into his strong arms and began to carry her across. Sophia gave a cry of surprise, but then settled back into the comfort of her husband's warm embrace as he did his best to avoid getting wet feet himself, without them both ending up in an undignified heap in a pool of water.

"I have been waiting a very long time to carry you over the threshold of our new home," he said, as he deposited her gently to the ground on the other side. Pausing to take in the awesome beauty of the place in which they would make their home, their gaze turned skyward to see the Milky Way stretch across the sky in a wide band of infinite light directly over their heads.

"After all the ups and downs of the last few years, I wonder what the future holds for us," mused Sophia. "Do you think we can make a go of it, my dear?"

"I think we can, my love," replied James. "We have a bright future in this glorious place, a future for us and for our growing family."

All of a sudden, as if it had been perfectly arranged to coincide with this special moment, a shooting star flew across the dark sky with a streak of white light, disappearing into oblivion beyond the mountains.

"Make a wish, James, make a wish," said Sophia, dancing from one foot to another in her excitement. It seemed to her that the shooting star was the very best portent of good fortune.

"My wish is for Applecross and for the family that live here," replied James, taking Sophia in his arms once more and leading her homeward at last. "May we all prosper and thrive for many generations to come."

Friday heard her master and mistress approaching in the darkness and, barely lifting her tired head from her straw bed, she gave a welcoming bark.

"Friday agrees," laughed Sophia, as James bent down to give the dog a goodnight pat.

THE WIDEAWAKE HAT

Acknowledgements

There has always been a book inside me. It would never have escaped onto paper without the help and support of the following :-

- My husband, Terry, a reluctant model but, as ever, a huge support throughout,
- My niece, Jen who read critically and offered great advice,
- Jess, the handy dog who proved a willing, if wriggly, stand-in for Friday,
- Katie, the owner of a fine shepherd's coat,
- and, most of all, Heather, a good friend, exacting proof reader and avid admirer of our hero, James, and the wild and remote land in which he lived.

I would also like to acknowledge the information gleaned from

Toitu, Otago Settlers Museum, Dunedin

Ngā Tipu Whakaoranga database,
http://maoriplantuse.landcareresearch.co.nz

James Mackenzie's reward notice was originally published in the Lyttelton Times in 1855. Although this is out of copyright, I would like to acknowledge the National Library of New Zealand as the source of this information.

About the Author

Amanda Giorgis was born in Somerset, England and started her working life in teaching. She emigrated to New Zealand in 2008 and moved to the beautiful Mackenzie Basin.

Amanda writes while looking out onto the flat plain with snow-capped mountains beyond. It is a place where it is easy to find inspiration for stories of early pioneers, who made this unique place their home.

She shares her home with her husband, Terry and three rescued huntaway dogs, Nemo, Jess and Ted, some chickens, who are more ornamental than productive, two acres of wild garden and the dark skies of the Southern Hemisphere.

'The Wideawake Hat' is Amanda's first novel, and the first book in the Applecross Saga.

More about Amanda Giorgis can be found on Facebook at www.facebook.com/Amanda-Giorgis/ and in her blog at amandagiorgis.worpress.com

Made in the USA
Monee, IL
14 June 2023